"You're not making this easy." Lissa's gaze flitted everywhere but wouldn't alight on him.

"I'm not trying to," Carson said. "If you want to stay at a hotel, we'll stay at a hotel. I think staying here is more convenient and comfortable. Either way, the last few days are proof enough that trouble is likely to catch up wherever we go."

"And the kiss?"

She was killing him. "House or hotel, I'll kiss you whenever you ask me to." He gave in and reached for her, sweeping the heavy fall of her hair back from her eyes. "You've had a tough day on top of a series of tough days. Let's take this inside."

"Kiss me." She scooted across the bench seat, crowding his side of the cab. "Please."

* * *

Be sure to check out the next books in this miniseries:

Escape Club Heroes: Off-duty justice, full-time love

* * *

If you're on Twitter, tell us what you think of Harlequin Romantic Suspense! #harlequinromsuspense

Dear Reader,

Welcome back to the Escape Club in Philadelphia, Pennsylvania! It's a riverside hot spot for music lovers, as well as safe haven for people with problems that slip through the cracks of typical law-enforcement channels.

Carson is a paramedic who could have been an excellent doctor. Instead, he chose life on the front lines as a first responder. When an injured woman stumbles out of a cab and into his arms while he's working at the club, what else would he do but help?

Writing this story had me wondering, how is it we know who to trust in those moments when we're at our weakest? Even suffering amnesia, Melissa senses she can trust Carson. At that weak point, with no other reference, she follows the only thing she has left—her intuition.

I think we've all experienced that moment when a close friend or a licensed professional swoops in and saves us from ourselves in a crisis. Whether it's a soothing voice, a uniform or swift, competent guidance, something assures us deep inside that we can let go and accept the offered help.

Carson and Melissa have an uphill battle between her memory loss and his self-doubt, but watching them grow and believe in each other was a wonderful journey for me—as I hope it will be for you.

Live the adventure,

Regan Black

A STRANGER SHE CAN TRUST

Regan Black

HARLEQUIN® ROMANTIC SUSPENSE

Recycling programs
for this product may
not exist in your area.

ISBN-13: 978-0-373-40211-3

A Stranger She Can Trust

Copyright © 2017 by Regan Black

Printed in U.S.A.

Regan Black, a *USA TODAY* bestselling author, writes award-winning, action-packed novels featuring kick-butt heroines and the sexy heroes who fall in love with them. Raised in the Midwest and California, she and her family, along with their adopted greyhound, two arrogant cats and a quirky finch, reside in the South Carolina Lowcountry, where the rich blend of legend, romance and history fuels her imagination.

Books by Regan Black

Harlequin Romantic Suspense

Escape Club Heroes
Safe In His Sight

Harlequin Intrigue

Colby Agency: Family Secrets (with Debra Webb)
Gunning for the Groom
Heavy Artillery Husband

The Specialists: Heroes Next Door (with Debra Webb)
The Hunk Next Door
Heart of a Hero
To Honor and To Protect
Her Undercover Defender

Visit the Author Profile page at
Harlequin.com for more titles.

For my editor, Patience. Those of us who love Mondays must stick together.

And for the paramedics and first responders who make a positive difference in their communities every day.

Chapter 1

Carson Lane hesitated in the hallway, the rack of clean pint glasses growing heavy in his arms. Only a few strides separated him from the sea of humanity singing along and cheering the band blasting from the Escape Club stage. This persistent slip and slide of nerves through his gut was ridiculous. Not one person out there would notice him. The longer he stalled, the more attention he'd gain from the bartenders who needed the glassware.

His knee ached, and the muscles in his thigh burned as he struggled with the extra burden. He'd worked a full first shift today, substituting on a Philadelphia Fire Department ambulance, and though his body begged for a break, his mind wasn't ready to rest. For more than eight months, only exhaustion brought him any peace. His current choices were clear: walk into the heart of the club or walk out and keep going. He had to choose, to do *something*, or he'd drop the glasses and have a bigger mess to clean up along with the unwelcome questions about his fitness.

Pivoting, he pushed through the swinging door with his shoulder and back. The path memorized, he averted his gaze from the faces in the crowd. People were oblivious to the risks and pain that could be the end of any one of them at any given moment. Official "managed" risks and protocols hadn't kept his best friend and partner on the ambulance rig alive when they'd answered the call that would be her last.

Every day that he woke up and hauled himself out of bed, he wondered why it had been her and not him. So far, no one had ever given him a decent answer.

Unless faced with a crisis, people had a tendency to ignore the precious, fleeting nature of being alive. As a paramedic, he dealt with the frailties and miraculous resiliency of the human body through every shift. He'd loved his job, despite the occasional sad ending, right up to the shift that had changed everything with an irreversible finality.

William, the bartender working this end of the bar, made room for Carson to stock the clean glasses. "Just in time, man."

With a nod, Carson completed the task of restocking, picked up the racks of dirty glassware and headed back to the relative quiet of the kitchen. Only an hour until the last set for the band and last call for drinks. He could make it. Had to make it.

In the back of his mind, he heard the echo of his partner's voice urging him to get over his current mental roadblocks. "Mind over matter" is what she'd say about now, and shove his shoulder. "Gotta do the job." Sarah

Neely hadn't been known for her tact among the PFD emergency medical personnel, only renowned for her competence and compassion with their patients.

Carson set up the next rack of dirty glassware and pushed it into the dishwasher. He decided she just wouldn't understand how much of him had died along with her all those months ago. 254 days ago to be exact, and the terror and memories remained raw and painful. Perpetually caught at the edge of that nightmare, he scrubbed his hands on his apron, confused when his palms didn't leave bloody trails on the white fabric.

"Carson!"

He wheeled around to find Grant Sullivan, owner of the Escape Club, leaning into the kitchen doorway. "Sir?"

"I need a word." He tipped his head toward his office. "Come on back."

"Sure thing." Carson untied the apron and left it on a hook by the kitchen door, then followed Grant down the hall. The man's stocky build and easygoing outlook belied his quickness and boundless energy. At his boss's gesture, he eased into one of the two chairs facing the desk. The office was quiet, only the dull throb of the band's bass carrying through the floors.

"How did things go today?" Grant's brown eyes were bright with anticipation. "On your PFD shift, I mean."

"Smooth and normal shift," Carson replied, hoping his relief at the easy question wasn't too obvious.

Grant nodded, his thick salt-and-pepper eyebrows dipping low with his frown. "And the knee is holding up?"

"Yes." Carson forced a smile. "Feeling stronger every day." It was a small fib. The bullet had passed through his thigh, just above his knee, causing all kinds of damage to muscles and connective tissue along the way. He'd resumed walking three weeks after the surgery, but the pain had leveled out around week eight. Contrary to the physical therapy consensus, the motions never got easier. *Mind over matter*, he thought, as Sarah's face flashed through his mind.

"I got a call from Evelyn today. She says she'd like to get you back on the schedule full-time."

"She said as much to me," Carson admitted, more than a little surprised his PFD supervisor had spoken with Grant. As a former cop, Grant's connections with first responders in the city went deep, but it still seemed like a stretch.

"So, why do you keep hanging around here?"

Carson fidgeted in his chair, well aware Grant understood the complexities of recovering from bullet wounds. The blow to his confidence in his skills and his faith in the human condition were more significant obstacles than the aggravating pain lingering in his knee.

Grant had lived through the pressures and challenges of life in public service. Forced to take early retirement because of an on-duty shooting, he'd survived the upheaval of a recovery and a significant career change from cop to club owner. His compassion for others in similar circumstances had prompted him to open the Escape Club. His determination to assist those who helped the community was the reason more than half his employees at any given time were like Carson, men and women waiting with varying degrees of patience for reinstatement to their positions.

Except Carson wasn't sure he could go back to the job. Going back full-time meant a steady partner, a professional commitment and a mutual trust he wasn't ready to tackle. The idea of forging that connection with someone new terrified him.

He and Sarah had been an effective team. They'd learned to read each other, often without saying a word. Yet when she'd needed him most, bleeding out in his arms, he'd let her down. He still had nightmares of her valiant effort get out those last words. Words he'd never been able to decipher, though his frequent nightmares gave him too many second chances to do just that.

He scrubbed at the stubble on his jaw. What if it happened again and another call ended in gunshot wounds? Would he be able to live with himself if he failed another partner?

"Carson?" Grant prompted.

"I stay because I like the music here," he replied.

Grant gave a bark of laughter, drumming his fingers on the desk. "Come on. You can give me a better reason than that."

"Are you tossing me out?" Carson swallowed the lump in his throat. He would deal with it if he had to, but he hoped he hadn't worn out his welcome. Money wasn't an issue thanks to his substitute shifts as a paramedic and his occasional work with a construction crew, but shifts here filled a great many empty hours in his daily routine.

"Not tossing you anywhere. I like having you here." Grant's brown eyes turned serious as he leaned forward. "You've spoken with the department chaplain about the incident and your recovery, right?"

"Several times," Carson said. Hell, several times last *month*. Although the counseling sessions helped, they didn't keep the dread at bay for long. Nothing did. Not physical therapy, not a successful shift as a substitute on the rig. Not a beer with friends, not holiday dinners with family, not a house that was too damned big. In short, he was floundering. If the people around him were worried, he knew they had good reason. Hell, he'd told others the same thing he heard too often lately: get back in the saddle and lean on friends as needed. Too bad he couldn't go back and retract those platitudes now that he understood just how useless they were.

He'd been an excellent paramedic in no small part because of Sarah. While he could still do the job well—his substitute shifts proved that—he refused to go back full-time and put someone new at risk. What if—

"Counseling is only one piece of it." Grant's voice cut into his downward-spiraling thoughts. The chair creaked as he rocked back. "What does help, son?"

Carson bristled against the concerned tone that veered dangerously close to pity. He didn't need help generating pity. Although he wanted to resist and deny, to push back and claim one final time that he was fine, he couldn't muster the right words. "Would you believe I'm considering some different career options?"

"That's fair and reasonable." Grant nodded. "There's no judgment here," he said after a few more beats of silence. "Is it true? Whatever you say stays right here, between us."

Carson knew that. He also understood the stress he was about to put on that promise. "When you were shot, did you hate the shooter?"

Grant went absolutely still, quite a feat for the man who was always moving, tapping fingers or a foot in time with whatever beat the bands on stage were playing. "Yes."

"Given the chance, would you…would you have done something stupid?"

"I'm not on the force anymore, but I do *not* want to hear your definition of *stupid*," Grant replied. "I will admit my hate and frustrations eased when I found a new outlet and purpose."

"Even after the shooter was acquitted?" Carson queried.

"That was a hard day," Grant admitted. "Alcohol might have been involved in shaking off the news."

"He ended your career and irrevocably changed your life. How the hell do you get over that?" Carson realized too late he was shouting, and his hands were balled up into tight fists on Grant's desk. He stretched his fingers wide and raised his hands, palms out in surrender as he sat back into the chair. "Sorry."

"No need for apologies." Grant tapped out a quick syncopation on the desktop. "Neither you nor I was charged with negligence or any kind of errors in our unfortunate incidents."

Carson rolled his shoulders against the prickle of self-loathing sliding down his spine. Being cleared by an official report couldn't bring Sarah back to life. If he hadn't made a mistake somewhere during that call, Sarah and he would still be on the job together. Until he identified his mistake, he shouldn't be trusted as a full-time partner.

"What do you do when you're not here or subbing on a rig?" Grant asked.

"The police call me in as a sketch artist occasionally. I still help out a friend in the PFD who flips houses on the side." On the days when his friend had work that didn't aggravate Carson's knee injury too much.

"What do you do for yourself?"

Carson shook his head. There was nothing else. What life did he deserve after letting Sarah die? Every time that night replayed through his mind, he searched for an alternate ending. If he'd taken a different route to the call, if he'd handled the victim differently, would she still be here? Maybe, technically speaking, they'd done everything right and yet Sarah had been killed when two other men stormed the ambulance and robbed it. He had to be sure he wouldn't repeat the mistakes that got her killed.

"I keep waking up," Carson said at last. "Keep hauling myself out of bed." It was a lousy answer, but he was pretty sure Grant, having been through something similar, could see right through his excuses. "Someone said it would get easier."

"Time heals all wounds?" Grant let loose a bark of laughter. "Yeah, that *someone* is full of crap if they didn't finish that theoretical statement."

"What do you mean?"

"It gets easier only when you start letting go." Grant sat forward again. "You let go only when you start living again. I'm not you, son, and our experiences are different, but shifting the focus from the past, being in the present and finding something to look forward to, carried me through the worst of it."

Carson didn't think that accounted for the fear and doubt that plagued him in those rare moments when he managed to shake off the worst of the guilt. "You're suggesting I find a hobby or something?"

"I'm suggesting you look for something outside my kitchen and your friends in the first responder circles,"

Grant said. "And I want to hear how much you enjoy that something."

By the tone, Carson heard the words as an order rather than a suggestion. "Got it." He pushed to his feet and left the office, returning to the kitchen to finish up the last responsibilities for his shift. As he went through the motions of closing and cleaning, he forced his mind to think about alternatives for tomorrow instead of dwelling in the past. Other than his family, he didn't have close friends who weren't connected to the police or fire departments. Where was he supposed to start searching for a new hobby?

With the trash can loaded, he wheeled it through the back door to the big garbage bins out back. He paused on the way back inside, breathing in the cool spring air rolling off the Delaware River and sighing it out again in an attempt to let go of the past. Up and down the pier, businesses were bustling with customers cutting loose and making the most of Friday night. From this shore and on the far bank of New Jersey, lights sparkled and danced in the reflection of the water. Boats cruised slowly, leaving ghostly trails behind them. From Carson's vantage point, the traffic on the bridge was little more than a murmur of white noise.

Sarah had died on a hot and humid summer night. He'd survived winter and the holidays without her, made it through Valentine's Day and St. Patrick's Day, too. Didn't people connect hope and fresh starts with springtime? Maybe in this new season he could make Grant's order work and break the cycle of grief plaguing him.

Glancing up, he searched out the brighter stars in the sky, trying to recall the constellations his dad had taught him. Maybe he should pull out the telescope and set it up. It would be one positive way to pass the dark, lonely hours. "Be in the present," he said aloud, coaching himself. "Let go and start living."

The advice didn't bring an immediate result, so he tried again. Repetition didn't ease the pain or offer any surge of hope. He supposed it was wishful and absurd to think a deep breath and a few new words would offer instant relief.

He turned around at the sound of an engine, holding up a hand to shield his eyes from the glare of headlights as a big car pulled to a stop at the side of the club. He saw a typical white city taxicab with a familiar logo on the back door. Then a slender woman pushed it open and got out, stumbling a little.

"Hey!" The driver jumped out, as well. "You owe me money, lady."

"I..." The woman frowned at her empty hands. "I don't have money." She wobbled, looking around. "Where—"

"Wait right there!" The cabbie rushed around the car to confront her, and the woman cried out as she tried to get away.

Sensing trouble, Carson dashed forward as the woman tripped and started to fall. He caught her, willing his knee to hold up for both of them. "Back off," he warned the cabbie.

"She owes me the fare."

"I'll cover it." Carson eased the woman down to sit on a discarded pallet. Despite the shadows, he could tell she wasn't well. Drunk or stoned, the visible fresh scrapes and bruises on her face and arms implied someone had taken a few swipes at her recently. "What happened to her?"

"How the hell do I know? She got in the car that way."

Carson looked at the woman. "Is that true?" She only stared up at him, then shied away from the cabbie. "Bring me her purse," he said to the driver.

"No purse." The driver gestured at the empty back-seat. "Just her."

"Where did you pick her up?"

"Near the Penn campus," the cabbie answered, and then asked for the fare again.

That wasn't much help beyond the basic geography. There were a number of reasons for a woman who appeared to be in her midtwenties to be near the University of Pennsylvania campus. Carson reached for his wallet. He handed over enough cash to cover the fare and a tip and sent the cabbie away. When they were alone, he picked up the subtle hitch in her breathing above the muted noises from their surroundings and the occasional raised voices from patrons dawdling in the parking lot.

"Can you stand?"

She stared at him blankly. She had abrasions on her knees and hands, and her left eye was nearly swollen shut. "Escape?"

"Yeah, you made it," he replied. Pretty clear she was one of the people who sought out the secondary purpose of the club—asking Grant for help out of tight or sticky situations. "What's your name?"

"Alex-Alexander?" She managed to squeeze out the name through a raspy voice. Laboring, she raised her closed fist toward his hand. When he opened his palm, she dropped a crushed matchbook into it.

Carson stared at the Escape Club logo for a moment, then flipped open the cover. Seeing the name Alexander scrawled on the inside, he pocketed the matchbook.

Grant trained all of them to respond swiftly and without question if anyone showed up and asked for Alexander. Carson berated himself for making her wait this
long. Her appearance was enough to prove she was in
trouble, with or without the matchbook and code name.
"Come on." He reached out a hand to help her up, and
she stared at him.

"Escape," she repeated.

"Yes." His throat felt raw just listening to her laboring
over each word. "You're safe now." He needed better light
and supplies to administer first aid, which he suspected
was the least of her worries. "Come with me." Grant
would know what to do. Carson had to get her inside the
building before the staff left for the night.

He knelt down on his good knee, putting him at eye
level with her. Her good eye was glassy, and without
his penlight, he couldn't be sure her pupil was properly
responsive. She might be high right now, but he didn't
see any typical signs of habitual use on her arms. He
resisted making more assumptions. Only the right tools
would give him an accurate assessment. "Let's go inside
to see Alexander. You can trust me."

He held out his hand and waited for her to take it. He
helped her stand, but she wobbled with her first step. Exasperated, he scooped her into his arms. Her arms came
around his neck automatically, and her head dropped to
his shoulder as he carried her the short distance to the
back door.

He could feel the toned muscles of her legs under the
thin fabric of her skirt. He'd helped his share of addicts
on the job, and the safe bet was she wasn't one. Relieved
no one caught him struggling with both her and the door,
he called for help once they were inside.

Grant appeared in the hallway first, followed by other members of the staff.

"She asked for Alexander," Carson said, though it was pretty obvious. "A cab just dropped her off."

"My office," Grant said, taking in the details with that penetrating gaze. "Bring us the first aid kit, a blanket and bottled water," he called out to others.

Carson made it down the hall without dropping the woman. She wasn't heavy. He situated her in one chair and pulled the second around to face her. He pressed his fingers to her wrist, taking a pulse while he waited for the first aid kit to arrive.

She squinted against the brighter light in the office, but she didn't fight him while he evaluated her. Every physical indication was she'd been in a fight with someone bigger and stronger than herself.

Her sluggish responses to his questions bothered him. When the first aid kit arrived, he pulled on gloves and took a closer look at her noticeable injuries. The swollen eye was nasty and the color was going to be vivid, but he didn't think there was a fracture. He used a penlight to test her pupils, being cautious as he manipulated the swollen eye. Both pupils responded but were almost as listless as her speech. With her dark hair and eyes, excellent bone structure and warm golden skin, she'd be lovely under healthy circumstances. There was additional swelling along her jaw, there were bruises on her neck and her wide mouth would be lopsided for at least a day or two. He struggled against a sudden, familiar rush of anger at whoever had used her for a punching bag. Despite answering numerous domestic violence calls, he'd never become immune to the results.

"Who hit you?" he asked.

She tried to shake her head, but he had her face trapped in his hands as he gently prodded again at the black eye.

"Easy. Just take your time," he said.

"I don't know."

He'd expected that answer. Victims rarely outed an abuser at the first opportunity. He reached for antiseptic to clean the split skin above her eyebrow. "Where were you before you got into the cab?"

Her good eye went wide, then closed, her features tightening with pain or shame. "I…I don't know."

"No problem. Just relax." Carson didn't try to coax more answers out of her. He tended the scrapes on her knees and hands and left the question-and-answer part of the program to Grant. "You're safe now. That's what matters."

She glanced over his shoulder to the doorway with her good eye. "Okay."

Once her wounds were clean, he really thought the cut above her eye needed stitches more than the glue and small bandages in the first aid kit. Grant came in and offered her a bottle of water and a bag of ice, then retreated. She passed the basic concussion protocol, but he thought she should be evaluated by a physician anyway.

"What's the word?" Grant asked, stepping into the office again.

"Some good news. Nothing points to a serious concussion," Carson replied as he peeled off the gloves. "Still, she should probably go to the hospital."

"No!" The bag of ice landed in her lap, her hands clutching it tightly. "No hospital." She tried to scoot the chair back out of his reach, but in her weakened state, she didn't get far.

"Relax." Grant, perched on the edge of his desk and arched an eyebrow at Carson before turning back to their guest. "Put the ice back on your cheek," he said, motioning to the ice pack in her lap. "Now take a breath," he added when she'd done as he instructed. "Why did you come here to the club?"

"No hospital," she repeated, wincing as she shook her head. "C-can't go to a hospital."

Carson signaled Grant to back off. Her breathing had turned rapid and shallow, and her pulse had leapt into overdrive.

"Okay, hospitals are not an option. I get it. Just relax. You're safe here with us." Grant's tone was full of soothing calm. "How did you hear about Alexander?"

Her gaze dropped to the floor, and her eyebrows dipped low over those wide brown eyes.

"I—I don't remember." She swallowed.

"That's not unexpected based on your injuries," Carson said quietly.

"Carson would know," Grant added. "He's a paramedic and I'm a former cop. You don't know us, but we are trustworthy. Can you tell me how you got hurt?"

She ignored Grant, staring at Carson with her good eye, the other hidden by the ice pack. "You're Carson?"

"Yes. Carson Lane." She didn't look familiar to him, but something in the way she studied him, something about the way she said his name, made him uneasy. "Have we met?"

"I don't know." Under the denim jacket and pale blue T-shirt, her shoulders shuddered as she sucked in another breath and tremors set in.

Carson looked around. "I'll go find a blanket or something."

"I'll do it." Grant moved faster than Carson, leaving him alone with the woman again.

A dozen questions rolled through his mind, but considering her physical and emotional state, he kept them to himself. He wished she would at least give them her name.

Grant returned with a blanket and Carson draped it over the woman's narrow shoulders, tucking it around her and pulling it down as far as it would go to cover her legs. Her feet were likely still chilled, but it was the best they could do at the moment. She needed real medical attention at a hospital. Was she afraid of one particular hospital or all hospitals?

"Do you have a wallet or purse with you?" Grant asked, settling behind his desk this time rather than on it.

Fat tears spiked her dark lashes and rolled down her cheeks. "I don't think so. I can't remember anything." She clutched the ice pack in her lap again.

"Only the matchbook," Carson answered, showing it to Grant. Every instinct hammered at him to make this better, but he didn't know how.

"Hmm." Grant was doing something on his computer, likely checking for any breaking reports involving a woman of her description. "No missing persons," he murmured almost to himself. "I could run prints."

"She's been through something," Carson said. "If she doesn't want to talk about it…" He left the implication hanging out there. He wished there was a woman around who could ask if she'd been raped. He wasn't comfortable with those questions in this particular setting. "She doesn't know what day it is, not the year or season."

"What is the last thing you do remember?"

Grant's query was met with another fat tear trailing

the others. "I remember getting out of the cab. Seeing you." She turned that good eye to Carson again.

He knew concussions could mess up a person's memory, but she didn't have symptoms of that problem. This sounded more as if there had been significantly more emotional trauma involved. Without a battery of tests, there was no way to know the validity, cause or even prognosis of her amnesia.

He reached out and took her hand. "You need to be seen by a doctor."

"Please. *No*. I…" She struggled with something and gave up. "I don't know why. I just know I *can't* do that. No doctors, no hospitals. Whatever you've done for me is enough. I'll be okay."

Carson disagreed. The stark terror in her good eye at the mention of more comprehensive medical care worried him. Had she been attacked at a hospital or possibly escaped a psych ward?

"How about this?" Grant said with infinite calm and patience. "Carson can keep an eye on you for a few hours. Just until morning."

Carson gawked at his boss. "You can't be serious. I'm no doctor."

"A point in your favor based on the patient's preference. You can handle the observation through the night, right?"

"Anyone here can do that." Someone else, anyone else, should have done that. Grant's wife, Katie, had been at the club earlier, and rumor was she always waited up for Grant to get home. The two of them would be a better team to help this woman through the night than Carson.

"You're the most qualified. You know what symptoms require her to go to the ER." Grant held up a hand as the woman protested. "Whether you want that or not, I'm not taking a chance you'll get worse after coming to us for help. Carson is the best person to watch over you tonight."

She sighed, her lips tight.

"I understand it's uncomfortable, and I'm open to another option. Would you like us to take you home or call a friend or family member for you?"

A fresh bolt of panic shot through her like white-hot lightning streaking through a dark sky. The sensation left her gasping. She knew what they were asking. She knew what it meant to call someone. She just couldn't remember the numbers or names that would connect her to someone familiar. The concept of family made her feel marginally better and a thousand times worse, though the word didn't induce quite as much dread the way *friend* did. Alexander was the name on the matchbook, and Grant and Carson were here and had been kind to her. Those three names were the extent of her world.

She fought against the tremors of fear skipping through her body. She wanted answers as much as the men asking the questions.

"No. I guess not." She studied the man named Grant sitting behind his desk, struggling against the idea that she should know him. The hard jaw and thick build gave off an air of no-nonsense toughness, but his warm brown gaze didn't induce any fear, and the gray hair salting his temples added a trust factor.

Dropping her gaze to the floor again, she said, "I can't tell you where I live. I mean, I don't know the answer." She fisted her hands in frustration, and her short fingernails bit into her palms. "I don't know who to call. The names..." Her breath rattled in and out of her chest. How could her head feel so full and empty at the same time? "The names are just gone," she finished in a hoarse whisper.

The man who'd cleaned the blood from her face scooted closer. "Pushing to remember won't help. You need to let your brain rest and give your body time to recover."

Carson. His name was Carson. She clung to the new detail as she tried to find something familiar. She didn't recognize the silver band on her thumb or the soft floral fabric of her skirt skimming her knees. Wiggling her toes inside her scuffed blue ballet flats, she wondered why her feet felt so sore and achy.

They'd asked for her name and information about her circumstances, and she wanted to cooperate. At least she *thought* she should cooperate. But where the information should have been, she had only a dark, blank canvas.

"I don't remember getting into the cab. Before that is just a blank." What the hell had happened to her? "I remember getting out, feeling woozy. The matchbook," she said, her gaze locking onto the item at the edge of the desk. Something nudged at her mind, like light seeping around the edges of a door. "I don't think it's mine. I don't know why I have it or who gave it to me."

She pressed the heel of a hand to her temple near her good eye. Her head felt caught in a vise while her pulse throbbed in her lip and over her battered eye. Her raw throat resisted every word she spoke.

Carson's palm covered her other hand, peeling her fingers off the arm of the chair. "Relax. Don't fight for it. You've clearly been through an ordeal." He sounded so sure and steady, and his gentle touch calmed her.

"My brain feels like oatmeal." She could see a pot of oatmeal in her mind, and she could almost smell the homey scent of the dish blended with cinnamon and chunks of warm apples. "How do I know oatmeal and not my own name?"

"There are several things that can cause this situation." He cleared his throat, his gaze sliding away for a moment. "I'm confident your memory will return soon…" he said, looking her in the eye.

She heard the hesitation where he would have used her name if either of them had known it. "You're confident?"

"Would you like a second opinion?" he asked with an eager spark in his hazel eyes. "You'd learn more from a full CT scan and workup."

Her heart kicked against her ribs at the thought of a hospital. "Your opinion will do," she said. "No hospitals." Her feet shifted. Every instinct she had told her to run, but where would she go? Her body ached from head to toe. She'd never outrun the able-bodied people here even if she could think of a direction. "Please, don't make me go." She was probably only making a bad situation worse, and she was definitely taking advantage of strangers who had better things to do, but she didn't have another option.

"Take it easy." Carson encouraged her to have more water.

She drank deeply, washing away the dry-cotton feeling in her mouth.

The older man, Grant, made several notes on a card, then wrote a few more lines on a second card and slid that one across the desk to her. "You can trust Carson to take care of you tonight. Why don't you check back with me tomorrow morning?"

She blinked at the jumble of letters and numbers on the card, utterly overwhelmed. She could read it, but it didn't mean anything. There had to be people she knew, people who knew her. *Had to be*, she thought, despite the void in her head. Could she trust what was happening to her now? Her sole possessions included her clothing, a matchbook and now this card. Her acquaintances were limited to the two men in this room until her brain decided to cooperate again.

She was as eager as they were to learn how she'd ended up here.

Carson seemed to understand what she couldn't articulate. "It's going to be fine," he said. Picking up the card and matchbook, he placed both items into her palm and curled her fingers around them. "If you'd be more comfortable staying with a woman—"

"No." The word burst out of her, and tears welled in her eyes, blurring her vision until she blinked them away. "You." She gulped, knowing she had to calm down. "I trust you." An absurd claim, considering she'd just met him.

If her declaration surprised him, it didn't show. His steady hazel eyes held her gaze. He didn't look like a creep, he'd tended her wounds with kind hands, and the matchbook indicated that someone trustworthy had sent her here.

"Then let's get going," he said.

She nodded. No other choice without her memory. She placed her hand in his and let him guide her out of the office, keeping her head down so she wouldn't be overwhelmed by the lights.

He proceeded slowly down the hallway, and his fingers gripped hers a little tighter as he pushed open the back door. The yawning darkness and the smells of the river sent a tremor down her spine. This was the only familiar territory in her mind, and the bleak fact made her want to curl up and cry until the world made sense again. She managed to keep moving, thanks to the anchor of Carson's strong hand enveloping hers.

His palms were calloused and rough. Something inside her cringed from a memory of similar hands. When she tried to pluck at that thread, it dissolved.

"Easy," he said, opening the door of a big gray truck. "Need a boost?"

"I can do it," she said, trying to convince herself as much as him as she stepped on the running board to get up into the seat. He checked to be sure she was settled before he closed the door.

She caught her reflection in the side mirror and gave a start. Her face was a mess with the swelling and bandages and deep bruises. At least she knew she wasn't supposed to look this way. In the mere seconds it took for him to get around the truck and into the driver's seat, she fought back a swamping fear of being alone. The reaction startled her, and again something felt wrong about her reaction.

Everything about everything felt wrong, inside and out.

"Where do you live?" she asked as he started the truck. His answer meant nothing to her, and she watched a foreign world drift by in the dark as he drove through the streets. "Have you lived here all your life?"

"Born and raised here in Philadelphia," he answered, giving her vital information without making her feel stupid. "I've traveled a little, but I haven't found another place I'd rather call home."

At the next intersection, he turned off the main road, and she wished for daylight so it might have been easier to remember any possible landmark. He'd told her not to push it, yet she couldn't stop herself from trying.

"How do you know so much about my, um, situation?"

He shrugged a shoulder. "As a paramedic, I've treated more than a few victims who struggled to remember what happened at the time of their injuries. The brain often blocks out facts until we can handle them, physically or emotionally. The best term for it is trauma-induced amnesia."

"That's what you think is wrong with me?"

"Without better testing, I can give you only my best guess." He turned down another street and then into an alley tucked between rows of tall houses with only the occasional light in a window to give signs of life.

"And people recover? They remember who they are?"

He slowed down a bit more. "I don't usually hear the end of the story." He reached up and pressed a button over the rearview mirror. The big garage door opened, a light coming on inside. "My job is to stabilize patients so they can be transported and turned over to a doctor's care." He backed into the garage and cut the engine, hitting the button again to lower the door.

Another shiver raced over her skin at the mention of a doctor. Her palms went damp and her breath backed up in her lungs. "Guess I don't like being closed in."

"We won't be for long." He opened his door, and light flooded the truck. "That's an important detail you've remembered."

She slid out of the truck and straightened her skirt. "Do you live alone?" she asked as they walked across the narrow backyard to his house. Some distant part of her mind thought she should be wary of heading into a stranger's home, but her intuition overrode that.

"Yes. If that's a problem, I can call one of my sisters."

"No." She didn't want to meet anyone, not looking like this and not at almost three in the morning. "Well, yes, I'm uncomfortable, but don't do that."

Something in his face clouded over, and he seemed so sad, although she couldn't figure out why she would recognize that emotion in him when she didn't recognize her clothes, her reflection or any aspect of her circumstances.

He opened the back door and flipped the switch on the wall, flooding a gorgeous kitchen with light. It was decorated in muted blue tones and pops of sunny yellow. "There's one better option," he said, giving her a long look.

She knew that he meant the hospital and he believed she'd be better cared for there. Thankfully he didn't say the words again. She stepped closer to the central island, admiring the clean lines and tidiness of his kitchen.

"The full house tour can wait." He led her toward the front of the house, up the stairs, pointing out a bathroom on the way to a guest room with twin beds on either side of a centered window, covered by a decorated pull-down shade. He walked into the room and turned on a bedside lamp.

The soft glow lent a cozy atmosphere to the room, at

odds with the strange turmoil in her head. Unless she'd lost her sense of direction as well as her memory, the view through the window would overlook the backyard. "This is…" Too many emotions clogged her throat. His kindness and compassion and generosity overwhelmed her. "Thank you," she managed after a moment.

"No problem. I'll get you something to sleep in." She hovered at the doorway while he moved to the opposite end of the hall and disappeared into another room, returning quickly with a T-shirt and sweatpants. "Probably too big for you. I'm sure my sisters left something closer to your size. They use my place for wardrobe overflow. Feel free to check the closet or dresser for better options."

She took the clothing he offered. "Thank you."

He tucked his hands into his pockets. "Anything you need, just ask. I'll be checking on you a few times through what's left of the night."

"You will?"

"Just a precaution. You might not even notice."

He'd mentioned that. Or Grant had. Not that it mattered. Exhaustion pushed at her from every side, and she thought it might be easier to give in and fold to the pressure. "You have to do it?" She was torn between wanting to be alone and being terrified of the same situation.

"Yes." He backed up a step, hand on the doorknob. "Get some rest. I'm right down the hall."

Rest. What an easy thing to say, but she didn't think it would be nearly as easy to accomplish despite her rampant fatigue. With the clothing in her arms, she sat down on the edge of the nearest bed. The fabric smelled freshly laundered, and under that, she caught a whiff of the man who'd helped her. *Carson.*

He had a crisp, honest scent. *The scent of safety*, she thought. Curling up on top of the denim-colored bedspread, she hugged the clothing close to her chest and stopped trying to think about the infinite details and information missing from her mind.

Chapter 2

Carson slept in short cycles, much as he did during the overnight rotations on the ambulance rig. Observation protocol wasn't fun for either the injured person or the one doing the checking, but it had to be done for her safety.

The first time he'd gone into her room, he worried about startling her, but she hadn't yet fallen asleep. Or changed into the T-shirt and sweats he'd given her. In her position, he probably wouldn't have done that, either. Though he tried, he couldn't imagine the challenge of her situation and her complete lack of self-history and awareness.

The remainder of the night went on in a similar fashion, with him padding down the hall and rousing her gently, exchanging a few words and then heading back to his room. He'd chosen a few questions she could answer with her limited memory, and her answers were consistent with each check. While that was great news for her health, he'd breathe easier if she would agree to be seen by professionals.

He recognized his frustration stemmed from the invasion of privacy. He hadn't had a woman stay over since well before the ambulance was ambushed, and his current houseguest was about as far removed from a date with a happy, sexy ending as a man could get. She was, in essence, a patient, and more than once as the hours ticked toward dawn, he was grumpy that Grant hadn't sent her home with one of the women on staff at the club.

At the 8:00 a.m. check, he let her curl up and go back to sleep while he returned to his bathroom to shower and shave. After tugging on comfortable jeans and a shirt emblazoned with the logo from the last 5K he'd run for a charity event, he opened his bedroom door.

The woman—his patient—stood there looking lost, her hand raised to knock. Her bruises stood out in stark relief against her skin, and he mentally ran down options to reduce the swelling. "You're awake." He gave her his best reassuring-paramedic smile.

"I am," she agreed. "Thanks for keeping tabs on me."

"Just doing my job," he said quickly. He didn't want more thanks. He wanted to hand her off to a qualified doctor. "Are you hungry?"

Her warm brown eyes lit up as she held a hand to her midriff. "Yes, I am."

That was another good sign. "Any memories come back to you yet?"

She gave a small shake of her head and pushed her hands into the pockets of her denim jacket. He suspected she was clutching the business card and matchbook.

"I'll get some breakfast going." He'd make something soft and easy to chew as he was pretty sure her jaw would ache like crazy today. "Anything in particular sound good?"

Her dark eyebrows flexed into a frown. "I can't remember having any favorites."

"You will," he replied confidently. He would cling to that belief, sure her memory would return, for both of them. "The hall bathroom should have whatever you need. Feel free to raid the closet or dresser. My sisters leave stuff here all the time and they won't mind."

"Are you always this generous?"

"Only with their stuff." He regretted the joke almost immediately as her gaze clouded over. "I'm kidding." He extended a hand to offer comfort, then quickly pulled back, reluctant to send any mixed signals. At this point he was basically her doctor, and he needed to maintain that distance. "Take a shower, and I'll redress and treat the areas that need attention when you come downstairs."

"Okay."

As she turned and walked down the hall to the guest room, he realized she was barefoot. The sight charmed him. He ducked back into his bedroom and tried to stifle the awkward blend of empathy and pride that in the midst of her crisis, she trusted him enough to ditch the shoes.

Unwilling to have another encounter in the hallway, he waited until he heard the taps running before heading downstairs to start on breakfast. His own stomach was rumbling loudly by the time he started oatmeal, so he heated a skillet for bacon and cracked a few eggs into a bowl, whisking in pepper and a dash of salt and wondering if he should add dill and thyme the way his sisters did.

He set out raisins, brown sugar and a small pitcher of milk to go with the oatmeal. Better to give her options, he decided, than force her brain to struggle and puzzle over what she preferred.

The second round of bacon was sizzling in the pan when she appeared in ankle-length yoga pants and a souvenir shirt from the October music festival the Escape Club had anchored last year. Her glossy, damp hair was held back with a clip at the nape of her neck, and her hands were hidden in the pockets of the denim jacket. She'd slipped her shoes on.

"It smells good in here," she said with a lopsided smile.

"Let's hope that's a good sign things will taste good."

She stepped closer to the stove. "You made oatmeal."

"Is that a problem?" She'd mentioned it last night, and he wanted to support anything familiar.

"No." She didn't look convinced.

"It's a go-to comfort food in my family." He tipped his head to the table. "We usually add apples, but I'm out. There are raisins and other toppings to make it interesting. I also have eggs and bacon going."

"I remember the aroma of oatmeal with cinnamon and apples, but I can't put any faces or names with it."

"You will in time. It sounds like a positive memory," he pointed out.

"It does." Her eyes glistened with a tear-raising emotion, but she didn't elaborate or let the tears fall today.

She ladled oatmeal into a bowl, added various toppings sparingly and stirred it before taking her first bite.

"That's delicious. Thank you," she said, adding another spoonful of brown sugar.

"You're welcome." He turned the bacon in the skillet. "You don't have to thank me for every little thing. We stick by each other at the Escape Club, and we help out when and where we're needed."

"That extends to people like me?" She took a seat at the counter, cradling her oatmeal bowl in her hands.

"Yes, it does." He pulled out a tray of bacon and eggs he'd kept warm in the oven.

"Even when you don't know who you're sticking by?"

He nudged a plate toward her. "Fill up as you please." *Treat her normally*, he thought. They didn't know her name, and it was better if they ignored that elephant-sized detail for now.

He watched as she chose one slice of bacon and a small portion of the scrambled eggs. While it was possible she was cautious until she knew what she liked, he had the distinct feeling that someone had raised her not to waste food. As helpful details went, it didn't rank very high on the list, but it was something to keep in mind. She murmured approval of everything she tasted and went back for seconds on the oatmeal.

"Did you get any rest last night?" he asked as he set the machine for a second cup of coffee. She'd turned down the offer of coffee, sticking with water.

"Some, thank y—" She cut off the gratitude with a self-deprecating quirk at the corner of her mouth. The move made her wince. "Some."

"Would you like another ice pack for the lip or the eye?"

"Arnica oil," she said, her entire body perking up. "You apply arnica oil to heal bruises." She grinned and gave the oatmeal a stir. "I'm going to sit here and be thrilled I know that."

"Okay," he agreed easily. "I don't have any, but I can make a call. My oldest sister is big into alternatives to standard medicine."

Her grin faded. "Arnica is an alternative?"

"It is to me," Carson replied with an abbreviated laugh. "One more reason I'm glad I stopped at being a paramedic rather than going on to medical school. My sister and I fight enough as it is."

She savored the last bites of her oatmeal. "I don't think I have a sister." Her eyebrows furrowed a moment. "Or a brother. Thinking about siblings makes me feel strange." She tapped a finger over her heart. "Not sad, but not happy, either."

He leaned back against the counter, his mug of fresh coffee steaming as he raised it to his lips. "Your injuries alone would play havoc with your emotions. Compound that with whatever ordeal has your memory locked down, and it's not a surprise that you're not sure how you're feeling about any of this."

"I feel like I can trust you, Carson." She gave him a lopsided smile as she used his name. "I'm basing all my reactions on that one point."

No pressure there. "I suppose you need to start somewhere."

"Right." She twisted the paper napkin in her hands. "Now that it's daylight, could you take me for a drive around the city? Please?"

"Sure." He took another gulp of coffee. "The cab driver said he picked you up near the Penn campus. We could start there and then head over to meet Grant at the club. He'll want to see how you're doing and share any information he's found through his contacts."

"All right." She gathered up the dishes and put them on the counter, systematically scraping each dish into the trash, then setting it in the sink. "What kind of contacts?"

"He was a police officer and is still friends with people all over the city," Carson explained as he loaded the dishes into the dishwasher. He urged her to have a seat while he finished the cleanup. "I'm sure he has people checking missing person reports or any reported domestic troubles."

"That sounds smart."

Hearing the catch in her voice, he glanced over his shoulder, then rushed to her side when she swayed. "You're pale." He'd thought it would help her to know Grant and others were working to figure out the mystery of her identity. "I'd feel better if you'd let a doctor look you over."

"No."

"Not a hospital, but what about an urgent care office?"

"No." She lifted her hands to either side of her neck and he watched her dig her fingers into the series of muscle attachments along her spine. "I saw my reflection and I know I look like hell, but a doctor is out of the question. The idea makes my stomach curdle."

"Arnica oil won't help the memory issues," he said.

"According to you, nothing but time will do that." Her hands trembled when she lowered them, fisted them and shoved them into her jacket pockets once more. "I don't know why. I just know I can't ignore this instinct."

"Okay." Caught by his own argument, he held up

his hands, palms out. "I promise I won't force the issue without real cause."

She arched an eyebrow. "That's a blurry term."

"*Real cause* as defined by arterial bleeding or broken bones." Confident she wouldn't fall off the counter stool, he went back and closed the dishwasher, then swiped a finger over his heart in an X. "I promise."

"Thank you," she said with that unbalanced grin. "I won't even take that one back."

Before they set out to drive around the city, he insisted on giving her an ice pack for the eye and lip while he sent Grant a text message outlining their plan. Next he sent a text to his sister Renee, asking where he could pick up some arnica oil. Naturally she was so excited about his interest, she offered to deliver the oil personally before she even asked why he needed it. Thank goodness he and his companion were heading out for a few hours. Even as he thought how typical his sister's response was, he slid a glance at the woman at the counter, wondering who was out there worrying—or not worrying—about her welfare.

He hoped Grant learned someone was out there searching for her. She struck him as a good person, and when she smiled, he imagined how that expression would light up a family conversation. It would be criminal if she was as alone in the world as she felt right now.

Done with the ice, they stepped out of the house into a gorgeous spring morning that seemed infused with hope and upbeat energy. He caught her taking in every detail and visual cue as they walked to the garage. He could remind her not to tax herself, but what was the point? She was managing the situation better than he'd expected. Whoever she was, he'd bet this ability to adapt and roll with life's ups and downs was part of her nature.

So what kind of hell had she survived that her brain resorted to amnesia as a self-preservation tactic?

Much as she'd done last night, she peered at the passing neighborhoods and buildings lining the streets as he drove across town. He took his time, avoiding the expressways, but nothing elicited a significant reaction as he meandered around and through the Penn campus. On a hunch, he circled the university hospital. She seemed to stick by that claim of trusting him, because she didn't bother to remind him she refused testing or an evaluation.

He let her toy with the radio as he doubled back and headed for the club situated at the edge of the Delaware River, this time taking the expressway.

"It's an interesting city," she said, studying the view. "I wonder why it doesn't feel like home."

"Maybe you're new." Or maybe being attacked in her hometown had pushed her mind into a drastic safe place. "You might even be a tourist."

"Hmm." She sat quietly, her toe tapping in time with the music on the radio station she'd chosen.

Whoever she was with her memories intact, he was glad she preferred classic rock today. Carson changed his route, thinking about the idea of her being a tourist. It would explain no immediate outcry from friends or family.

He drove past the zoo and the famous steps of the Philadelphia Museum of Art, then looped back so they could cruise past Liberty Bell Park. Nothing seemed to break anything loose for her, so he gave up and aimed for the club. He'd hoped by now Grant would have found some sort of clue.

Carson's cell phone rang, interrupting the song on the radio as they passed Independence Hall. Hearing the system tell him it was Grant Sullivan, Carson answered with the hands-free connection in the truck. "Hello, you're on speaker," he answered. "We're only a few minutes away."

"Good," Grant said. "How are you both feeling?"

"Tired," Carson admitted. He motioned for the woman beside him to speak up.

"Calmer," she replied.

"Have you remembered anything yet?" Grant asked.

"Nothing but arnica oil," she said.

"I'll explain when we get there, Boss."

"Great." Grant didn't sound too thrilled. "What's your ETA?"

"Five minutes," Carson replied.

"Even better." Grant ended the call, and the music filled the cab once more.

"He knows something." She'd pulled the matchbook from her pocket and traced the edges with her fingertips.

"If that's true, it will only help you," he said.

"Unless I'm the reason for my troubles," she murmured as she turned away from the reflection in the side mirror.

"What are you talking about?"

"Maybe I've done something horrible. There's a lump of dread right here, Carson, in the pit of my stomach. You said the brain takes drastic action in terrible situations. What if I'm the real problem?"

"I don't believe that." Carson drove down the pier

and parked in one of the spaces reserved for deliveries near the kitchen door.

"You don't know me!" Her voice rose with each word. "I don't know me."

He put the truck in Park and pushed his sunglasses up to his hair as he scrambled for the right words. "You told me you were testing every new reaction and feeling off that one spark of trust you experienced overnight."

"Yes, I trust *you*." She sucked in a quick, shallow breath. "I don't trust myself." She gripped the seat belt, as if by holding on tightly she could stay in the truck rather than face the unknowns outside. She squeezed her eyes shut. "Nothing makes sense."

"Relax and breathe." He encouraged her as she inhaled deeply and exhaled a few times. "You trusted me by relying on intuition. It's the same for me. No, I can't claim to know you, but I'm almost certain you aren't a criminal or that you brought any of this on yourself."

She sent him a sideways glance. "I think that sentence would sound a lot better if you could use my name."

He smiled at her and reached over to release her seat belt, easing her grip so it could retract completely. "You're probably right, but it wouldn't feel any different saying it." He waited for her to meet his gaze. "Whatever Grant has or hasn't learned about you, you won't have to face it alone."

With a single tense bob of her chin, she stopped arguing, and the color seeped back into her face. It was little relief as he replayed his words, hearing the implied promise. He'd committed himself to her cause, despite the nonexistent facts. He dropped his sunglasses back to the bridge of his nose, knowing he'd stand by the promise, at least until her memory returned, if for no other reason than he didn't have the heart to backpedal now.

"You won't have to face it alone." Carson's comforting promise steadied her as much as his presence while he held open the nightclub's back door for her. Her body felt like one giant ache from her toes to the top of her head with various sore spots throbbing in between. She felt as if she'd been in a car wreck and realized with a manic laugh inside her head that she might have been.

The thought caught her off guard. Did she know what a car wreck felt like? "Are my injuries consistent with a car accident?"

Carson paused as the door swung shut behind him. Behind his sunglasses, she could tell he was giving her a thorough once-over. After a moment, he shook his head. "Unlikely. Or maybe it's safer to say that if you were in a car wreck, it was after someone beat the hell out of you."

"Okay." She caught back the thank-you that danced at the tip of her tongue, not wanting to make her sole ally in this mess any more uncomfortable. Her intuition told her gratitude was a key part of her personality, but she had to find some of the other missing pieces to go along with it and balance it out.

Down the hall, she heard a symphony of voices, none of them familiar. Yet something about the noise tickled a memory. Voices raised in agreement or discussion were an important clue to who she was. The sounds rose and fell as they passed the kitchen and walked toward Grant's office. There were voices there, too. Both male, engaged in a more moderate discussion.

Carson stepped in front of her, a protective movement she appreciated. "Hi," he greeted the men inside.

Grant and the other man stood up, and Grant motioned them forward. "Come on in. Carson, you've met Detective Neil Werner, right?"

"Sure."

From her position just behind him, she saw the tension snap across Carson's shoulders. She cursed her faulty brain, having no way to discern if she was the cause. Grant waved them in, his gaze catching on her, as if he wasn't sure what he should call her. Suddenly uncomfortable, she wished the floor would swallow her up. Something else she was learning about herself was that she didn't like being a burden or creating drama.

The detective stepped forward, offered his hand. His palm dwarfed hers, but his grip was gentle and warm. He was clearly dedicated to fitness as his broad shoulders strained against his suit. The close-cropped dark blond hair, the crow's feet framing his soft blue eyes and the creases bracketing his mouth created a general sense of friendliness.

"As you're surely aware, Grant reached out to me in an attempt to help you. Have a seat." He gestured her toward the chair he'd just vacated.

Sitting down, she noticed she was effectively hemmed in. No way out, except through the three men. The knot of fear in her belly loosened as Carson sat down next to her. Catching the quick glance between the detective and Grant, her pulse kicked into overdrive. "You know who I am."

The detective's mouth curved into a faint smile. "Turns out your fingerprints are on file with the police."

"I have a criminal record?" Shock coursed through her, cold and hard. She turned to Carson, but before she could release him from his rash promise, the detective waved a hand.

"No, no," Werner assured her. "Your, ah, employer keeps fingerprint records as part of their security protocol."

That sounded promising. "Who do I work for?"

The detective leaned back on Grant's desk and studied his hands for a long moment. "After what Grant told me, I consulted with an expert before I came out here," he said, finally meeting her gaze. "They think it's best if I don't force your memories onto you right now."

"That wouldn't help the amnesia?"

"So I'm told," he said. "Your name also popped up in the course of a different investigation this morning." He looked at Carson, arching his eyebrows. "I'm at a loss. I really don't know how to proceed here."

"Gently," Carson suggested. "The simpler the better."

"All right." Detective Werner tugged at one ear, his mouth twisting to the side. "Does the name Melissa Baxter ring any bells?"

She shook her head and glanced at Carson. He only shrugged. "No, sir," she replied.

"How about Noelle Anson?"

"Sorry, another blank." She repeated the names in her head, willing some reaction or recognition to come forward. "Are either of those names mine?"

Werner squinted and winced. "Noelle's body was found just up river early this morning. Her security badge from her place of employment was in her pocket, so we followed the lead, asked questions. Her coworkers and members of the security staff there remember seeing you with Noelle last night. The descriptions and fingerprints on Noelle's personal belongings match up with you."

"You're saying my name is Melissa?"

"Melissa Baxter," he confirmed with a serious nod. "You're seen several times with Noelle on the security camera records, as well. Anson's coworkers claim you were close friends."

Why couldn't she remember a detail as simple, as essential as her name? None of this information felt familiar or gave her an intuitive sense of rightness. A thousand questions chased each other through her mind, questions about herself, this friend and her workplace. The detective had the answers, yet she suspected hearing them wouldn't help.

She was locked out of herself, and the dread was building. She didn't feel like a Melissa, couldn't dredge up any feeling for the dead woman. She stared at her hands as a buzzing sound filled her ears. Were they saying she was a killer? A warm hand covered hers, and she blinked rapidly to find Carson leaning close, watching her. No judgment in his hazel eyes, only a calm and comfort.

"Take a breath," he said.

She tried, hiccuped. "I can't remember anything about any of this. Have I killed someone? Would I kill a friend?"

"No." The absolute confidence in his voice brought a rush of stinging tears to her eyes.

"You sound so sure," she whispered.

"I am."

"Carson, we can't—" Grant began.

"She is *not* a killer." Carson cut him off emphatically. "If you thought that, you'd be reading her her rights and pulling out the handcuffs."

Grant's chair creaked as he rocked back. "What are you thinking here, Werner?"

"I'm thinking Ms. Baxter needs a proper medical evaluation so I can get some real answers about her condition as well as the victim's. The river took enough evidence already."

"Look at her," Carson said. "She's a victim, too."

"All the more reason for a doctor to find out what's up with her memory. You can go along for the ride if you like." The detective stepped toward the door but didn't open it.

"No hospitals." Her heart pounded against her rib cage as desperation and fear swamped her. She clutched Carson's hand. "I'll cooperate with the police, I swear it, but no hospitals. Please."

"Apparently her abject terror at the idea hasn't changed from last night," Grant said. "I know you need leads, Werner, but it doesn't seem as if Ms. Baxter has any to give you right now."

Carson stood up, tugged her up with him. He kept his body between her and the detective. "I'm taking her home to rest."

Werner didn't budge. "Hang on a minute."

"Do you have cause to hold her?"

"Hell, yes!" The detective folded his arms over his chest. "Best I can tell, she's the last person to see her friend alive."

She cringed at his tone, at his insistence that she was somehow linked with a dead body they'd pulled from the river.

"As soon as her memory returns, we'll call you," Carson said. "Pushing her and stressing her out will only delay her recovery and your investigation."

The detective muttered a curse under his breath. "She's clearly been through some trauma. I want a doctor, not some washed-out paramedic, to tell me she's not faking this amnesia thing."

"Watch it, Werner." Grant's voice had dropped to a growl. "You're in my house," he added, coming to his feet. "You told me you wanted a conversation and you said you'd go easy with a woman who is more likely an eyewitness than the killer."

"Come on." Werner's hand gripped the doorknob hard. "I need to speak with her alone."

"No," Carson and Grant said in unison.

She watched the exchange, fascinated and horrified all at once.

"When you have a weapon with her fingerprints on it or a cause of death Melissa could manage, come on back," Grant said. "Until then, we'll keep an eye on her. You have my word. Carson and I will help her through this, and when her memory returns, you'll be our first call."

"Damn it, Sullivan. That isn't good enough."

"It will have to be for today." Grant flared his hands. "This is awkward, to be sure." He moved around to open the office door, adding his stocky body as another obstacle between the detective and her. "You keep working the case on your side, we'll work it from this side, and I'm sure we'll find justice for everyone in the middle."

"That's a thin line, Grant," Werner said. "We go way back, but this is pushing the friendship."

"We'll get through it." Grant pulled the door shut behind him as he ushered the detective out of the office. Their voices faded away.

"Am I a killer?" she asked herself in the long silence that followed.

"No." Carson put his hands on her shoulders and studied her face with his intriguing hazel eyes. "You have a headache."

The man had a gift for noticing the details and medical assessment. "Could it be a reaction to suppressed guilt?"

He threw his head back and laughed. It was a beautiful sound that rolled over her and took a little of the weight of the terrible insinuations from the detective with it. "Not a chance. You're just trying too hard to figure out if you're Melissa and what that means."

"Wouldn't you?"

"Absolutely," he admitted. "I'm sorry. I didn't bring you here to sandbag you."

Before she could reply, the office door opened and Grant returned. To her relief, he didn't close it again. "Well, that couldn't have gone much worse. How are you holding up, Melissa?" His gaze jerked to Carson as he slapped a hand lightly to his mouth. "Is it okay to call her that?"

She answered, "We have to call me something. Might as well use my given name."

"Sit down. Relax," Grant said. "Werner has agreed to give us—you—a little time and breathing room."

It wasn't as comforting as he probably meant it to be. "Meaning?"

"Go home, rest, let yourself heal," Grant said. "I made Werner give me your information."

"So, which home?" Carson asked.

"Not mine," she said quickly. "I mean, if I have a choice. I know you can't babysit me forever, but—"

"My place it is." Carson patted her hand again. "As I said, we'll stick it out together. I have a feeling the detective knocked a few things loose in there." He tapped his own temple. "But I'd rather you didn't rush it and risk more trouble. You shouldn't be alone when things do come back to you."

Grant agreed with him. "Just keep me in the loop and I'll deal with Werner."

She let Carson guide her out of the office, turning back to Grant at the last second. "Can you tell me where I work? Maybe it will help me remember something relevant."

Grant looked past her to Carson, got the nod to share. "You're a conservator at the Philadelphia Museum of Art."

The information didn't create any spark of recognition, only left her feeling more detached as though it all related to a stranger. She locked onto the one detail she could put in context. "We drove by earlier, right? With all the steps?" she asked Carson.

"Yes. You didn't seem to recognize it."

"Can we try again?" She couldn't give up. Not while the police were searching for the truth about the murder of a woman who was apparently her friend.

Though Carson was reluctant, they left the club behind for another drive past the museum. Though the song wasn't familiar, the rock music on the radio was a welcome background noise for her whirling thoughts. The beat was hard and steady, the bass grounding her when it felt like her life was flying about her in ragged pieces. "Do you think anyone at the museum would recognize me if we went in?"

"I'm sure they would, if we found the department you work in. It's a big place."

"And I could be anyone," she said. "What if I've missed work?" For reasons she couldn't fully express, it troubled her to think that the fallout of having amnesia would cost her her job. "It makes me queasy to think I've missed work."

"That's a good sign on several levels..." His voice trailed off awkwardly.

"Why do you hesitate to call me Melissa when you let Grant and Detective Werner give me other details?"

"Because I don't want to plant more ideas or thoughts in your head. It's just my opinion, but I think it's best if your memory returns as naturally as possible."

"How is it you know so much about amnesia?"

"I don't know that much. My experience on the ambulance hardly qualifies me, though I've seen people who can't recall how they were injured," he replied. "The detective isn't wrong to suggest you see a doctor."

She understood the concern and couldn't suppress the goose bumps that shivered over her skin at the thought of it. "Did you ever want to be a doctor?" she asked, shifting the focus away from her.

"I considered it at one point. I thought I'd enjoy the challenges."

"You'd be great." She wasn't sure why she knew it, but she believed his careful hands and comforting manner would be an asset in the medical field. "What changed your mind?"

"College and medical school are expensive. I started out as a paramedic, thinking I'd work my way through, and then found out I loved the first-on-scene piece of the process."

Based on the strain in his shoulders and the hard set of his mouth, she thought there was more to it, but prying seemed rude in light of everything he was doing for her. Really, as soon as she remembered who she was, she would be out of his life. Ideally she wouldn't be trading Carson's guest room for a jail cell. Whatever had him convinced she wasn't a killer, she appreciated his unwavering belief and willingness to stand by her before they had any definitive answers.

"Anything?" he asked as they drove by the museum's iconic run of stairs like the monument it was.

"No." She blew out a sigh. "Maybe we should go in for a little bit."

Carson shook his head. "Not today."

"At some point I'll be late for work."

"True. And when we reach that point, we'll deal with that." He aimed one of those quiet smiles her way. "I'm sure the detective will let them know what's going on."

He might have done so already. There wasn't much she could do either way until someone told her about her life or she remembered who she was. What type of work did she do as an art conservator? When she tried to think about a job, she couldn't pinpoint any precise task or familiar routine or responsibility. As it was, she was useless to everyone. She laced her fingers together, wondering what it would take to break through the walls in her brain.

"Are you working at the club again tonight?" She studied the scenery, hoping for some familiar clue.

"No," he replied. "I was on the schedule, but Grant will have covered the shift by now. He's made you my sole priority."

"Then what are we going to do with the rest of the

day?" Despite his encouragement to rest her mind, she didn't want to go back to his house and hide from the world and the trouble she couldn't remember.

"Good question." He gave her a long look while they were stopped at a red light. "Is the sunlight bothering you?"

"No." Another part of the observation process, she supposed.

"In that case, let's go to the zoo."

"The zoo?" She circled a finger around her face. "Looking like this? I'll scare little kids."

"So, you have a vain streak. How interesting."

She laughed when she caught his teasing tone and the smirk on his face, although she wondered what she would be like, how she'd feel about Noelle and everything else, once her memory returned. "You're right. Not about the vain thing, though that's possible. I feel like I can agree with you that I didn't kill her. My friend," she added, testing the theory in her heart, in her head.

"Good."

"Promise me one thing." She studied the silver band on her thumb, twisting it around and around.

"What's that?"

"If we're wrong and I am a killer, promise me you'll take me straight to the police station."

She liked that he took his time, mulling over her request for several blocks before he offered an answer.

"We're not wrong, but you have my word, Melissa."

However things worked out for her, whoever she was when her brain started cooperating again, she suddenly hoped she would be a person Carson had reason to believe in.

Chapter 3

Carson dug through the glove box for a second pair of sunglasses, relieved that one of his sisters had left a pair behind at some point. He wasn't embarrassed by Melissa's battered face and didn't want her to be, either, but he felt that the less they advertised it, the better. For both of them.

He'd been working through the blurry pieces of Melissa's puzzle Detective Werner had given them. Hearing her name and that of a close friend hadn't triggered any reaction for her. Yet. The brain was tricky terrain, and he wished she hadn't been forced to hear even that much before she was ready.

Her friend had been dumped in the river by a killer who hadn't bothered to remove any identifiers. Not a good sign. In Carson's limited experience, that meant the killer wasn't worried about being identified, and yet no one had come after Melissa. Had she escaped from the situation Friday night, or had she been left for dead?

If Noelle's coworkers knew she and Melissa were friends, how long would it take before the detective or reporters searching for a story plastered Melissa's face across the media?

He decided to take his own advice and not push himself. It wasn't his job to solve the case, only to keep an eye on Melissa. "If you feel weak or sick," he said as they neared the ticket booth at the front of the zoo, "let me know and we'll go."

"Are you second guessing this outing?" she asked when they'd purchased their tickets.

"Not really," he replied. "Fresh air and sunshine will do you good. And being active should help you ward off sore muscles, too." He handed her the zoo map.

"Is it so obvious?"

"Only to a trained observer." He smiled, pleased when her mouth curled up and her eyes sparkled in return. They veered left, meandering by the hot-air balloon and down the tree-lined path toward the African Plains exhibits. Between keeping an eye on her and the families around them, he discovered the fresh air and sunshine were giving him a boost, too.

It was soon evident they both enjoyed people watching, or at least, this side of her enjoyed it. When they sat down to a late lunch, she was full of questions about both the nightclub and his adventures as a paramedic. Whether it was because he expected her to be a short-term intrusion in his life or out of respect for her situation, he found it easy to talk with her. Before long, he'd shared a couple of the strangest calls he and Sarah had handled.

"Why did the detective call you washed-out? Wait." She held up a hand before he could think how to evade the question. "Don't answer that. It was too nosy. I must be a real pain in the butt at parties," she added absently.

The remark had him laughing until his sides hurt. First time since Sarah's death that had happened. "Only Sarah could make me laugh that hard," he admitted when he finally caught his breath. "It's a reasonable question."

"You still don't have to answer." She tore a french fry in two and nibbled on one piece.

"I want to," he said, surprising himself that his immediate reply was true. "Sarah died on a call just over eight months ago." 255 days. The math was automatic. "She was shot by thugs determined to rob the rig. I couldn't st-stabilize her."

"That must have been awful, Carson. I'm so sorry."

"It was the worst night of my life." He rolled his shoulders against the flood of sympathy. At least the sunglasses hid the pity surely lurking in her pretty brown eyes. "I haven't gone back to full-time since, though I sub in for paramedics once in a while."

"You don't want to get close to another partner."

He nodded. "I appreciate you not adding your voice to the chorus of people telling me to get back in the saddle."

She shook her head. "I can't imagine how hard it must be for you. No clue why, but I don't think I've ever had a partnership as deep as you clearly had with Sarah. I can see what she meant to you."

"Still." He balled up the paper from his burger and held it in his fist while he searched for his composure.

"Were you more than friends and coworkers?" She waved her hands. "You don't have to answer that."

"No," he answered, anyway.

"Make me another promise." She wrinkled her nose as she leaned closer. "Please?"

"We'll see." He wasn't sure making promises to her was the wise thing to do.

"When my memory returns, ask me the most personal, embarrassing questions you can think of. I mean it," she added when he laughed. "I deserve every single one of them."

"What's your favorite color?" he asked instead.

"Purple," she replied instantly. "Wait. How did you know to try that?"

"It's one of the questions I asked you last night, just to see if the answer stayed the same."

"Did it? I was so exhausted, I barely remember you coming in."

He grinned at her. "Yes."

"I'll take that as a good sign and the first piece of me coming back." She bounced a little in her seat.

"We'll find out soon enough, I think."

"You're a good man, Carson. However I wound up at the Escape Club last night, I'm glad you were there to help me out."

"Any of the staff would have done the same," he said, ducking the praise. "Grant trains all of us to be aware and help discreetly." With every hour she seemed more at ease, despite her lack of personal history. Her ability to roll with her circumstances baffled him and, to his shame, stirred up a little resentment. He felt constantly battered by his memories of the night Sarah died.

His knee was an achy distraction by the time they finished their circuit and returned to the main gate, but he was glad they'd come. She was moving better and seemed refreshed overall. He offered to buy her a shirt from the gift shop, to add to the few possessions she could call her own, but she turned it down, claiming she owed him enough.

"Do you want to go by your place for clothing or anything else you might need?" he asked as they returned to his truck.

"We probably should. Do you know my address? Good grief, that sounds so weird to ask."

"I'll get it from Grant." Carson sent the text and had a reply before they left the parking lot. She lived only a few blocks away from the museum, and when he told her, she eagerly gazed out the windows.

"Something pulls me to that building," she said, twisting around in her seat when they passed the museum again.

"It's designed to pull attention," he agreed.

"More than that. I'm going to take it as a good sign that maybe this version of me isn't too far off from the real me."

"I've never believed anyone could stray too far from their basic nature." He felt the curiosity in her gaze and focused on the driving.

"You don't believe people can change?"

"Habits? Sure. People can and should grow through life," he said. "I just think some people are inherently nice or awkward or have a built-in mean streak. They can mask those traits, learn to use them, but they can't alter what's ingrained."

She made a little humming sound and started drumming her fingertips on her thigh. "What traits define you?"

Cowardice, he thought, immediately aggravated by the first word that popped into his head. "I'd define myself as helpful and compassionate." *And, gee, didn't that sound exciting?*

"Based on our short acquaintance, I'd agree." She whistled. "This is so weird, knowing concepts and stuff without knowing who I am or where I come from."

Carson was inordinately relieved to shift the subject into the safer territory of her. "You'll get there, Melissa." He'd decided to use her name. It wasn't as if they could put that genie back in the bottle, anyway. While pushing her could be counterproductive, the sooner she recovered, the sooner he could resume his routine. He'd been smart to stick with being a paramedic, a job in which he could treat and transport and hand off the patient for long-term care. Spending these hours with Melissa—a patient—through her recovery was messing with his head and tempering his resolve to avoid connections. Talking with her exposed that raw, gaping hole where his best friend had been and left him vulnerable to every emotional assault.

He parked at the curb and studied the corner lot and the three-story home that had been converted into separate apartments. "Do you want to go inside and get some things? According to the address, your apartment is on the third floor."

"I don't even know how to get inside," she pointed out, shying away from the window.

"We can ask a neighbor or look for where you hid your spare key. Most people do that."

"A key, right," she whispered, stuffing her hands into her pockets. "Why don't I have my key? I don't remember if I trust my neighbors. I must. I live here, right?" Her teeth caught her lip, and she hissed at the pain. "This is a bad idea." Her gaze raked the street, her house and back again. "I can't do this." Her breath came in shallow sips. "Nothing here feels right. This isn't home. It's wrong." She closed her eyes tight, curling in on herself, and wrapped her hands around her head. "Not home. My head hurts, Carson."

Her sudden reversal scared the crap out of him. He understood memory lapses from trauma, understood some people never recovered all the pieces relating to a violent event or accident. Several of the first responders he counted as friends had blank spaces and never remembered all the details of severe injuries that had occurred. Still, he'd never seen any of them experience the stark fear stamped all over Melissa right now.

He released her seat belt and dragged her to his side of the truck cab. Her body shook like a leaf in a hard wind. Out of better ideas, he wrapped his arms around her, silently willing her to calm down as he searched for the right thing to say or do.

"Easy. Just breathe." He muttered more nonsensical suggestions, most of them probably useless, until eventually her body gave in and relaxed. "It will be fine. It's all going to be fine." A lie if ever he told one, since he had zero idea how any of this would work out for her.

At last she pushed back from him, blotting her face with the cuff of her denim jacket. "This isn't home, Carson."

"Okay." Maybe she'd moved and hadn't updated her information yet. Although it wasn't a definitive reason to take her to a hospital, he'd have to let Grant know about her panic attack at the sight of her house. "Can you tell me what home looks like?"

"No," she murmured. She scooted back to the passenger seat and snapped her seat belt. "I'm trying. Can

I please abuse your hospitality a little longer? And borrow more clothes from your sisters?"

"Sure thing." He was thinking he should probably call his sisters in to give her someone else to lean on. It was only a matter of time before he made a mistake and let her down.

She pulled the matchbook from her pocket, then the business card. "I didn't have a purse. Today every woman I've seen has been carrying some kind of purse or tote. What happened to mine?"

He wished he had an answer. Carson pulled away from the converted house and decided to take the long route to his place. Whether it was the scenery, lack of a formal destination or some other reason, being on the move seemed to soothe her. "After an accident or an emergency, a lot of female patients ask that question," he said after they'd left her neighborhood. "About the purse, I mean. It's a kind of lifeline. Grant and Werner will already have people on alert for action on your credit cards or identification. You may feel alone and disconnected, but there are people in your corner."

"People who have no way of knowing if I'm worth their effort," she said.

He reached over and covered her hand with his. "You're worth it."

She just shook her head, her dark hair swaying over her shoulder. "I hope you're right."

"It is absolutely normal to be scared, Melissa. I can't imagine what you're going through." He was definitely a coward, wishing he could wipe out his final memories of Sarah. He'd tried everything to forget, to no avail. He understood how the department chaplain and others wanted to help, but that horrible night wouldn't fade.

"That house was really my address?" she asked, drawing him away from what had become a familiar slide into despair.

He cleared his throat and focused on her. His personal problems would be there after her situation was resolved. "According to the records that popped up with your fingerprints." She sounded stronger with the distance from her apartment. "Maybe the record needs to be updated."

"Home isn't one place," she whispered a few minutes later.

"Pardon?"

"I don't know, but it feels right. Home isn't one place," she repeated. "Home is..." Her voice trailed off, and she groaned. "It was right there, a glimpse of my memory, and I lost it."

"For now. I think that's a good sign you'll make a full recovery." He glanced over and saw the frown tugging at the corner of her mouth. "Relax. Paramedic's orders."

He saw the ploy worked when she smiled at him. "Thanks for putting up with me."

"No problem." And it wasn't. He hadn't been all that comfortable with the idea at first, concerned that she might need medical attention more than his observation. While he didn't think she was completely out of the woods yet, he wasn't worried that they were doing more harm by honoring her wish to avoid hospitals.

Her panic wouldn't help her amnesia recovery or anything else. "Let's go see if my sister came through with the arnica oil, and we'll just take it easy for the rest of the day."

"You can do that?"

He nodded. "Can and will." With luck, having Melissa at the house would be enough of a distraction to ward off the loneliness and flashes of Sarah's voice and face that he dealt with day in and day out.

Melissa found an absurd comfort and sense of peace in her head and her heart when she saw the small, dark bottle of arnica oil on Carson's kitchen counter. The note from his sister left him shaking his head, and she wondered again if she was an only child. Or maybe she was an orphan. The detective hadn't mentioned that she had any family in the city, only a job and a friend. A dead friend.

Swallowing the lump in her throat, she took the oil to the downstairs bathroom and smoothed the oil onto the battered skin. When she finished, she stretched out on the couch to watch television in Carson's den, again relaxing per paramedic's orders.

She learned that resting a brain wasn't as easy as it should have been, especially for her, with no memories, responsibilities or guilt to get in the way.

Though she didn't feel tired, she discovered the afternoon had slipped away and the sun had set when she woke to warm, savory scents drifting on the air. She stretched and sat up, trying to feel like Melissa Baxter. Giving up on that exercise after several wasted minutes, she walked into the kitchen and found Carson hunched over his phone at the island.

Though he turned and smiled, she caught the shadows of sadness in his hazel eyes. "Something smells fantastic," she said.

"It's Becky's famous lasagna. She's the chef in the family."

"Did she come by to check on you?" She bit back the query of how much he'd shared about her. Maybe his family was simply trying to make sure his forgetful patient, who was also a possible murderer, hadn't decided to take a second life in as many days.

"Yes. They've all been hovering more after…after Sarah died."

"Oh." That must have been a nice feeling, to have someone care and hover and check in. "Do you think the detective is keeping me away from my family?"

"Huh?" Carson tilted his head. "That's a good question. I don't see how that would help his case or you, either, but I can double-check with Grant if it bothers you."

She studied the label on the bottle of arnica oil. Had someone cared enough to teach her about this trick, or was it something she'd taught herself? "I'm not bothered, exactly. I guess I'm just trying to figure out how much trouble I'm in."

"Stop trying to figure out anything and let your mind rest. If Werner had some valid evidence that you killed someone, you'd be in custody, amnesia or not."

"Right."

At Carson's direction, she tossed fresh salad greens together with a blue cheese dressing that appealed to her taste buds after tasting the options he had on hand. She set the serving bowl on the table while he served each of them a hearty square of the cheesy lasagna.

Carson made small talk about the Escape Club and how and why Grant Sullivan had opened the place. It made her sad to hear he'd been wounded in the line of duty, but she smiled at the man's triumph over the situation. "You should hear him on drums," Carson said. "He could've made a career out of that."

"Why didn't he?"

"The man is third-generation cop. It's hardwired into his DNA. If I had to guess, the music is his release valve and serves him better that way."

Every conversation she had created more questions about who she was and what might be hardwired into her. Did she have passions and release valves? Generations of family she'd followed into her career at the museum? She liked music, but she didn't think she played an instrument. She'd had a great time at the zoo with both the animals and people watching. Did that mean she worked with the public?

"I can practically hear the gears turning in your head." Carson pointed his fork at her plate. "Focus on the food, just the food for now."

She did as he asked, simply in honor of the way he'd upended his life for her. "Is this the house where you grew up?"

He shook his head. "My parents are too glued to their empty nest to vacate. They finally remodeled after my youngest sister moved out. I got to pitch in because they used a friend of mine in the fire department for the interior updates. They claim the house is now fortified and ready for grandkids to wreck it."

"Are there grandkids?"

"Two so far, courtesy of Renee and her husband. She's the one who brought over the oil."

"Oh, I should thank her for that."

Carson chuckled. "Trust me, the fact that I asked for it is all the encouragement and praise she needs."

Melissa grinned at him. "You work with a construction company in addition to shifts at the club and your job as a paramedic?"

He nodded, and something niggled at the edge of her mind, as if that movement should have been familiar.

"You could say the release valve for me is demo day on a construction site."

She studied his face and hands, remembered the strength in his arms when he'd held her during her meltdown in the truck. "I can see that."

"Can you?"

She grinned, as curious about her observation as he seemed to be. "Nothing more objective than a stranger," she quipped. "Good grief. That sounds like something I heard as a kid."

"I think your parents must be unique people."

She'd hoped he would toss out more theories so she could see if they fit, but he dug into his meal instead. She did the same, although the silence was companionable and comforting.

"Your eye is looking better," he said as they took care of the dishes together. "Not as puffy and definitely not as colorful. Renee won't let me live it down."

When they finished the meal, Melissa covered the lasagna pan with foil and slid it into the refrigerator while Carson loaded the dishwasher. "Your sister has a gift," she said, pressing a hand to her stomach. "That was divine."

"Agreed." At the sink, Carson dried his hands and folded the towel over one of the hooks at the end of the counter. "Is your headache gone?"

"Yes, thanks to you."

"See? There's one more reason I'm sure you're not the problem child in this equation."

The remark caught her off guard. "What do you mean?"

"You're thoughtful, kind and quick to show gratitude."

"Are you saying that in some subtle effort to encourage my memory?"

He shook his head. "I only want to reinforce that you're in a safe place when your memory returns."

She appreciated the gesture and his efforts, so much that she had to blink back a rush of tears. Crying didn't seem like something she normally indulged in, and it felt as if she'd hit her quota outside what they'd been told was her apartment.

"Feel like a movie?" he asked.

"Sure. As long as you choose."

"Can't remember any favorites?" he queried with an easy smile.

"Not so far." The idea of watching a movie made her feel lighthearted, as if it was some kind of rare treat. That didn't make much sense if she had her own place, but whatever. She had to let her mind come back online at its own pace.

Carson chose a romantic comedy his sisters loved. The blend of action, romance, laughter and fun held her attention. She relaxed, curled into the corner of his big couch and just let the story wash over her. When the credits rolled, she was smiling and full of good feelings with only the smallest twinge of a headache behind her eyes. "That was a great idea."

"I'm glad." He walked over, ejected the DVD and returned it to the case.

His entertainment system switched over to the television broadcast, and she recognized the anchors on the news. Considering that small revelation progress, she begged Carson to let her watch for a few minutes. Suddenly her face filled the screen along with her name. Melissa froze as a picture of Noelle Anson followed, along with overhead views of the place where the body was found. The view changed again, showing a reporter standing outside a hospital where Noelle's coworkers had created a makeshift memorial.

She heard Carson's voice, muffled and distant, then closer. The reporter's voice died and the television screen went black. Carson held her shoulders and gave her a little shake. "Melissa! Melissa, breathe."

Had she stopped breathing? His hands were on her arms, rubbing briskly. She was so cold and trembling again.

"Breathe. Slow and easy," he said over and over. "Look at me now. Come on."

She followed the sound of his voice, struggled to co-operate with his requests. Her eyes locked with his, registering the abject worry in his hazel eyes. "What is wrong with me?"

"Trauma. It leaves a ton of wreckage."

She heard the experience and pure sympathy in his voice. If he could get over what happened to his ambulance partner, she could fight back from this abyss to help her friend.

"Did they say they were looking for leads?"

"Yes."

"Looking for information on me?"

"They said they were looking for people who saw you together last night."

She had a sudden fear that this mess would cost her the museum job. On instinct alone she knew that kind of fallout would be awful for her. On the heels of that, she felt dreadful that she'd apparently lost a good friend and was selfish enough to worry about her work rather than a woman's life. "I'm a terrible person," she muttered.

"You didn't hurt your friend."

"I want to believe you. I almost do. But my friend is dead, and inside—" she tapped her fingers over her heart "—I'm actually worried about my job." She couldn't look at him. It was bad enough to say it all out loud. She couldn't bear to see the judgment in his eyes.

Carson tipped up her face so she had to look at him. "That's human, Melissa."

"I don't even remember what I *do*." Her voice cracked on a borderline hysterical laugh. "I don't—"

She gasped when Carson tugged her to her feet and nudged her along to the kitchen.

"Chocolate. You'll have something sweet, and then we're going to bed."

"What?" The image of being in bed beside his lean, warm body gave her mind something new and tempting to latch onto. An utterly inappropriate choice, but she couldn't reel it back in.

"I, ah. I didn't say that quite right. Have a seat." He guided her to the counter stool. "I have it on good authority, which adds up to pretty much every woman I know, that chocolate fixes everything. So you'll have chocolate and then you're going up to your room and sleeping. You don't have to worry about me interrupting you at all tonight."

"Okay." Sleeping alone in the twin bed didn't hold as much appeal as sleeping beside him, but it was the smart solution. He was taking care of her, and she'd have been crazy to give in to the attraction pulsing through her blood at the moment. "Chocolate sounds perfect," she managed.

A slice of cake appeared in front of her. It was airy and nearly black, and the aroma alone eased her frayed nerves.

"Ice cream?" Carson had a small pint of ice cream in one hand, scoop ready in the other.

"No, thank you."

"More for me," he said with an easy shrug. He topped his slice of the dark cake with a generous scoop of ice cream and then returned the remaining ice cream to the freezer. He raised his fork in a dessert version of a toast, and they dug in.

The cake was amazing, the rich cocoa flavor melting in her mouth. "Your sister again?"

"Yes," he said. "But this is a family recipe. My mom used to make this all the time because it's so fast and easy."

"This?" She turned her plate, wondering how something so intense and delicious could be easy. "If we find out I like to cook, I want the recipe."

"Deal."

She believed he'd honor that deal, just as he kept his word and insisted she head straight up to the bedroom as soon as she finished her cake. He refused her offer to take care of the dishes, practically pushing her up the stairs.

In the bathroom, she washed her face, brushed her hair and teeth, and changed into the T-shirt he'd brought in for her last night. So much had happened in the past twenty-four hours.

This time she pulled back the covers and slipped between the sheets, but sleep eluded her. Staring up at the dark ceiling, she thought about Carson's confidence in her, even without her memories. She prayed her mind would cooperate soon. The police needed to know who had killed her friend and beaten her up. She had to remember, no matter what those memories revealed about who she was and how she was involved.

Chapter 4

When he heard the guest room door close with a quiet click, Carson picked up his phone and called Grant. He had to leave a message, no surprise this close to midnight on a Saturday. The Escape Club had become one of Philly's hottest spots for great music.

Less than ten minutes later, his phone hummed with an incoming call, and a picture of the neon-blue club logo filled the screen. "You guys okay?" Grant asked as soon as Carson picked up. "Has she remembered anything?"

"Nothing helpful. We drove around a little and spent some time at the zoo as a distraction."

"Yeah, Detective Werner mentioned that."

"What?" Carson asked. "You're saying Werner put a tail on her? On us?" And Carson had been oblivious. While he wasn't exactly Melissa's bodyguard, he felt responsible for her, and the discovery unsettled him.

"I assumed he'd have someone keeping track of her," Grant pointed out. "She's the best connection to the victim. Werner pestered me with questions about how being a tourist would repair her brain. I told him you knew what you were doing."

Carson wished he had that much confidence in himself. "Thanks for standing up for both of us. Forcing her to a hospital or doctor would've been the worst move."

"What happened that you're so sure?"

Leave it to Grant's cop instincts to pick up on every nuance. "Hang on." Carson had heard a creaky floorboard overhead and paused to listen. Satisfied she wasn't coming back downstairs, he told Grant about the panic attack near her apartment. "She's really struggling to remember. It's obvious she wants to help, but this kind of thing can't be forced."

"If you say so."

"Either she moved since that address was added to her security file, or she's blocked out more than we know. Werner might want to see if there's been any sign of trouble at her place. Unless someone comes forward who *does* know her we can't be sure."

"You pulled her out of the panic attack?"

"Eventually," Carson said, still amazed he'd been successful. Maybe his similar panic attacks had helped him help her. If that was the case, it was the only silver lining he could find in that cloud of personal grief. "She's tough, whoever she is. I'll give her that."

"Good." Grant sounded relieved to hear it. "I don't like this at all."

Carson agreed. "We caught the report on the eleven-o'clock news that the cops are asking for any witnesses to step forward. That didn't help matters."

"They posted her face on the news?" Grant muttered an oath. "I'll follow up on that. Do you need me to hand her off to someone else, now that she's out of the critical observation time?"

And then what would he do? The idea of playing hot potato with a person with Melissa's memory issues put Carson on edge. "We'll manage," he said. "She trusts me." No matter how disquieting he felt having her in the house, he wouldn't abuse that trust.

"We all do," Grant replied.

Carson didn't reply. The deeper meaning, the bigger implication in Grant's voice, made him uncomfortable. They trusted him, but they didn't know he was a loose cannon.

"Keep me posted, Carson. And if you need anything, call."

"Sure thing."

He stood there for some time, working up the energy to fight his knee on the climb up the stairs, belatedly realizing it didn't ache. It had given him plenty of grief at the zoo, and he'd forgotten to down the ibuprofen when they got back. *Crap.* He knew enough about the mental and emotional side of injuries and trauma to understand what that meant. Hell, he'd probably known the knee was more of a psychosomatic condition for at least a month or two. Sarah had been gone for 255 days—256, now that it was past midnight—and this was the first pain-free moment he could recall.

Had it been the chaplain who'd calmly made a perceptive observation that Carson's ongoing knee pain was a personally inflicted penance? Yeah, that sounded like something the chaplain would say. Grant would've clearly stated Carson was milking the injury as an excuse—and had done so a few weeks back.

Slowly he did a couple of deep knee bends, even a careful one-leg effort, and didn't feel so much as a twinge. In the near silence of the house, he could almost hear Sarah laughing at him. He shut off the kitchen light and headed for the stairs, striding confidently. It would feel good to sleep through the night.

The sudden scream ripped through the quiet and yanked him out of his thoughts. His body stormed into immediate action and he took the steps two at a time, desperate to reach Melissa's room.

At the closed door, he hesitated for a split second, ready to knock or call out, when she let loose another bloodcurdling wail. He turned the knob and pushed the door open, his eyes raking the room for the source of her trouble. A slash of light from the closet cut through the room through the cracked door. The window was closed and she was alone, her legs tangled in the bedding. A nightmare, he realized, had her locked in a terrifying grip.

Her soft whimper and wrenching plea put a lump in his throat, but the next scream forced him forward. He couldn't let her ride this out alone. Moving close to the side of the bed, he called her name softly and placed a hand on her shoulder as he'd done when his youngest sister had had nightmares as a kid. Melissa was chilled, her skin clammy under his palm. Murmuring assurances, he waited for her to wake up or ease back into a restful sleep.

To his surprise, she rolled over and clutched his hand in a grip strengthened by fear of her nightmare. Her body thrashed, fighting some invisible enemy while a cold sweat glistened across her forehead. He kept up the soothing nonsense despite the fire blazing through the bones and tendons in his hand. Finally her hold went lax and her breathing evened out, and he eased back to straighten the sheets.

Her eyes popped open. "Carson?" Though she looked right at him, he didn't think she was awake.

"Yes, it's me."

"Take me with you." She lifted her arms to him. "Please, don't leave me here with him."

Not awake at all. Her mind was caught in that strange twilight no logic could touch. He brushed her hair back from her forehead and temples, which were damp with sweat. "I won't. I'll stay right here with you, Melissa. Go to sleep."

"Don't leave me," she pleaded.

"I'm right here." He smoothed a thumb over the creases of worry furrowing her brow.

Her hand caught his again and held, gently this time. "Call me Lissa," she murmured in a small voice as her eyelids drifted shut.

"Lissa." He tested it out, deciding the abbreviated nickname suited her. Determined to keep his word, he fished his cell phone from his pocket and set it to Silent, turning off his alarms. When he trusted she was settled, he pulled his hand free from hers and, stripping off his shirt and socks, he kept his jeans on and crawled into the other bed.

The awareness snuck up on Lissa as she came awake. First the dull throbbing in her head, evidence of a restless night, followed by the room that didn't smell at all like the lavender potpourri she kept in her bedroom. She slid her arms across the mattress, and although she was alone, she found the edges too quickly. The bed was too small, and the jersey fabric of the sheets no match for the crisp, smooth cotton she preferred. Her alarm obviously hadn't gone off, as it was well past dawn and the morning light was coming from the wrong angle. At her place, the window would be on the wall to her left, not by the headboard as it was here.

Panic pulsed through her in one hard jolt.

When it passed, reality trickled in. Sitting up a little, she pushed her hair back from her face and turned away from the window. Bumping her cheek, she remembered taking a hard blow from a frighteningly calm man. He'd asked her questions she had no hope of answering. There was more. She could feel the details of recent days floating around in a thick fog in her mind.

Fisting her hands in the sheets, she closed her eyes and tried to wrangle the onslaught of facts. Some things were clear. Others she couldn't pin down. She was Lissa Baxter, a conservator at the Philadelphia Museum of Art. She was under the care of and sleeping in the home of Carson Lane. He'd been the man who'd found her and treated her injuries when the taxicab had dropped her off at the pier.

The Escape Club, she remembered. Noelle, her best friend, had mentioned it. Told her the staff there helped people dealing with overwhelming or tough situations. She'd also mentioned a guy by the name of Alexander, though Lissa couldn't put a face with the name.

"You're awake."

She jumped a bit at the voice, though it was familiar and warm and gritty from sleep. She turned to find Carson propped up on one elbow in the twin bed opposite hers. His was the voice of security, the anchor she'd clung to when her mind had been adrift. "You slept here?" she asked.

"Yes. During your nightmare, you asked me to. How are you feeling?"

"Sorry to impose." She didn't recall asking him to stay, but she was glad he had. "I remember more of the, um…problem."

Carson sat up, swinging around to perch at the edge of the mattress, his torso and feet bare, and the top button on his jeans open. "Which part?"

It took her a moment to answer. It wasn't fair to be faced with such a handsome distraction at the lowest time in her life. "I remember my name. Melissa Baxter. I know what I do at the museum, and I know my best friend was Noelle Anson."

He stopped in the process of scooping his tawny hair back from his face, and she enjoyed the still-life composition of his arm, his biceps. She knew from experience his lean and defined ropy muscles packed serious strength. "That's a great start," he said, dropping his hand back to his side.

"I think I have more than a start," she admitted. "Though I know I don't have all of it."

As much as she dreaded remembering all of what happened in Noelle's final hours, Lissa hoped there was more in her head than the little bits trickling out around the edges of the protective armored vault her mind had created.

"Come on," Carson said. "I'll fix us breakfast while you talk it through." He pushed to his feet and started for the door.

"Was your ambulance part food truck?"

"Huh?" He turned around and the golden scruff on his jaw created a sexy shadow, but the lack of good sleep was apparent in his befuddled hazel eyes.

"You automatically offer comfort with food."

"Oh." His lips curved in a self-conscious smile. "Lane family habit, I guess."

She thought a family habit of comfort and active acts of kindness and compassion sounded amazing. A family habit like that explained his sisters dropping off lasagna, fresh salad and cake along with the arnica oil he'd requested.

"Well, I'm a happy beneficiary." She threw back the covers before she remembered she'd worn only his shirt to bed. She felt his eyes on her legs, and her cheeks heated with embarrassment. Dumb reaction, considering he'd probably seen people in all manner of dress, undress and disarray. Still, when he'd seen her at her worst, she hadn't known enough to be humiliated, and now she did. She brazened through the awkward moment. "Why don't you grab a shower and I'll go down and start the coffee?"

"But you've had a rough night, and—"

"And what I've remembered isn't going anywhere," she finished for him. She didn't have the details the detective surely wanted, but she hoped Carson could help her sort out what she had remembered. "It would be nice to mull things over for a few minutes, with coffee, before we start analyzing and fitting the pieces together."

His eyebrows dipped with his contemplative frown as he studied her. "If you're sure?"

"Absolutely. Take your time." Ideally her attempt at a casual-sister impersonation had been effective. When he walked out of the room, she made her bed, then the one he'd slept in, catching his masculine scent clinging to the sheets. She tugged on yesterday's borrowed yoga pants and darted downstairs to make coffee, then scampered back upstairs to the hall bathroom and cleaned up in record time.

Seeing his bedroom door still closed, she headed back down to the kitchen. Poking around the space, she sought out options for equipment and ingredients, eager to do something nice for him for a change.

The coffee had finished brewing and she was gathering ingredients when he walked into the kitchen, looking like a man headed out for a run or to the gym for a basketball game. Or maybe he was just ready to run far away from his wacky houseguest.

She didn't want to overstay her welcome, but she found that along with recalling her family dynamics, her upbringing and how she'd landed in Philly, she also recalled the man who'd rescued her was definitely her type. Trim, athletic, easygoing and smart was almost too much of her type. *If only we'd met under different circumstances*, she thought with an inward sigh.

"So, I remembered I do like to cook." She filled a tall coffee mug, leaving room for him to stir in a spoonful of sugar and splash of milk as he'd done yesterday.

"Great news." He took a deep gulp of coffee and held her gaze. "Are you good at it?"

The question caught her off guard and she laughed, happy to release the tension bubbling in her system. "I don't recall any complaints," she replied. She swallowed the lump stuck in her throat and added, "Let me just put this out there. I remember my fifth birthday party with stunning clarity, but I don't remember exactly what happened to Noelle on Friday night."

"Do you recall meeting her?"

"Yes!" She seized on the positive point. "We met in college here in Philadelphia. Is that a good sign?"

He nodded, took another long pull on the coffee. "You added something to this," he said, staring into the mug.

"A dash of cinnamon. It's how I always make coffee. I should've warned you. Is it a problem?"

"No, it's good." He set the mug down and leaned back against the counter. "What else do you remember?"

"About the nightmare?"

He went to the fridge, opened it and stared. "About anything."

After a minute, she gently guided him out of the way. "My epiphany and your sleepless nights aren't a good mix. Have a seat and I'll cook breakfast while you drink more coffee." She needed to keep her hands busy, to create her own anchor for her swirling thoughts. Leaning on Carson indefinitely wasn't the best option for either of them. On top of the crises they were each coping with, she had a mile-wide independent streak, and he had a steadiness and compassionate calm nature she found irresistible.

"I've remembered I'm an independent person," she said. "When I'm not dealing with amnesia."

"That has to be a relief for you." He topped off his coffee and stepped to the other side of the counter, sliding onto a stool. "What are you making?"

"Egg sandwiches." She turned, arched her eyebrows. "Fast, filling and you had all the ingredients, so I assumed it would be okay."

"Notice I'm not arguing with you." He rolled his hand, urging her to keep going. "You were saying something about remembering?"

She felt a smile curl her lips, saw a ghost of a smile flit over his face in silent reply. Suddenly she had a flash of a similar expression on his face at the zoo, right after she made him promise to ask her the nosiest question imaginable when she got over the amnesia. Thank goodness he hadn't done so yet.

"As I said, independent person, just as my parents raised me." She organized the ingredients she'd gathered before he came downstairs. "Also, I was an only child and we traveled a lot. I envy you your sisters and how you were born and raised in the same town."

"Hmm. I used to wish for my sisters to disappear. Is the travel what triggered the anxiety at your apartment yesterday?"

She liked the way he phrased it, as if she hadn't just dissolved into a puddle of misery. "I'm sure of it." Turning up the heat under the cast iron skillet she'd found in a cabinet, she tossed fresh greens in a bowl with a bit of oil and a dash of lemon juice, then placed bread slices into the toaster. While the eggs fried, she thought about how her life had been a series of blending what was available into something memorable and delicious no matter where they were living. She'd loved it, until she discovered she needed more stability than her mom and dad could offer.

Waiting for the eggs to cook, she said, "My parents are archaeologists. They encouraged me to go to college, of course, but I baffled them when I chose to stay longer and put down roots here in Philly rather than go into some kind of field work."

"You don't have any family here?"

She smiled at his bewilderment, layering a slice of cheese on each slice of toast, then the greens. When the eggs were ready, she slid them on top of the greens and added a sprinkle of shredded Romano cheese. "No." She handed him his plate along with a napkin and fork, then prepped her own. "By now they should be on a dig in Montana, unless their work at a site in France went long." She glanced over her shoulder, caught his scowl. "Don't you dare feel sorry for me, Carson. I have a job I love and great friends at work and outside work."

Thinking of her best friend, it was a helpful discovery that she'd cried herself out during the nightmare. Noelle, as an emergency room nurse and a student of life, had always been pragmatic about death. She'd been dialed into the present, squeezing the most out of every moment, and she wouldn't have wanted Lissa wallowing in tears.

"No pity here," he countered. "Just drinking coffee and eating this amazing breakfast." He took a big bite to prove it.

"And you're wondering about the nightmare," she said, cutting into her sandwich. "Me, too."

"You were screaming," he pointed out.

"Based on the pieces I have rattling around my brain, I don't doubt it."

Needing the food, she resisted looking too closely at the images flashing through her mind so she wouldn't lose her appetite. None of it made any sense, and until it did, she didn't have to embrace any of the ugly recollections as conclusively real. "I'm a serious history nerd, I love superhero movies, and I go by Lissa with all my friends."

"So you said last night. *Lissa*, I mean." His gaze roamed over her face. "It suits you."

"Thanks." She held her cup in both hands, wondering where to begin with the rest of it that wouldn't make them both sick. "I don't know what happened to my purse that night, but I remember what it looked like."

"There's a breakthrough," he said with a grin.

That vibrant expression did wonders for him, easing the sadness that seemed to haunt his candid gaze. "I even remember my bank account number."

"Good." He slid off the stool to his feet and rubbed a hand over his flat belly. "That was amazing. Thank you."

"You're welcome. I also remembered where I keep my spare key for the apartment. We were at the right place yesterday." At his arched eyebrows, she explained. "The spare is in my office. We can swing by when the museum opens today. I can ask security to walk me downstairs. Maybe you'd like me to show you around, give you the inside scoop?"

He grimaced. "We'll see. Our first stop should be the police station and a chat with Detective Werner. Even before your apartment, but especially before the museum, for any reason. He has someone from the department tailing you. Us."

"What?" The idea was a shock, and her stomach threatened to rebel. "Since when? Do they think I'm a suspect?"

"Easy," he said, carrying their plates to the sink. "No sense being aggravated after the fact. Grant told me about the person assigned to us last night when I gave him an update. Before your nightmare started," he added. "Have you remembered enough to be confident that you're innocent?"

"Yes and no." She shook her head and peered into her coffee, unable to meet his gaze. "There are bits and pieces that must be from that night. I don't think I killed her—not directly, at least—but I don't remember much about who did."

He brought over the coffeepot and filled her cup. "It will all come back."

After the nightmares last night and the flickers of memories today, she wasn't sure she wanted to know, even though it was absolutely necessary. "If we go to the police station, they'll expect answers. I really don't have any."

"Yet." He loaded the dishwasher and dug out the salt to scour the cast-iron skillet. "You've done a fine job of talking all around the actual nightmare. Go ahead and tell me what you can and we can make a better plan."

"Okay." She took a breath and wrapped both hands around the warm coffee mug. "I remember going home from work to change clothes. I called a car service and went to meet Noelle at the hospital near the Penn campus as she was getting off work." Her right hand flexed and fisted as she recalled the feel of her purse strap in her hand. "We were going out for girls' night."

"Were you meeting anyone else? More girlfriends?"

"No," Lissa replied, her mind pushing more disjointed details to the front. "I got there without any trouble. It was like the stars were aligned because her shift had gone well and she was ready to go. We were headed for the parking garage when a man caught up with us. Closer to the hospital than the garage, I think."

"Take it easy."

She couldn't do that. Noelle needed her to bring the killer to justice. Lissa pressed fingertips to her temples. "He was rude to her. To us." She shuddered at the rush of images, the horrible threats, the sharp bursts of pain.

How much was real and how much stemmed from her vivid imagination? "He had two friends with him."

"How often did you go out on girls' nights?"

"About once a month. We spoke all the time, every day, by text, phone, whatever was easiest. We've been that way since college. Official girls' night was once a month, and we had movie nights at my place as needed."

"What were her favorite movies?"

"Noelle was a B-movie horror-genre junkie," she replied. "The wackier the better for her." Lissa laughed a little at the bittersweet memory.

"And you like superheroes," Carson said with a wide smile. "You were an eclectic pair."

"True," Lissa allowed. "But we were sisters at heart. It sounds sappy, but it's the best description. We were both only children eager for an unbreakable sibling connection." She treasured the kind sympathy in his eyes, appreciated the way he encouraged her to honor Noelle's memory. "She was a good person. And so are you for letting me ramble on."

"Would you be more comfortable talking to the detective at the club, or even here instead of at the police station?"

"I'm willing to speak with the detective anywhere, but I'd really like to do it in my own clothes, if you don't mind. Although your sisters have excellent taste, I feel like I've intruded enough on you and them." And she was fortunate the sizes had been close enough to fit well.

"It's not a big deal at all. I'll change and be ready in five minutes. Unless you want me to shave?"

"Scruffy is fine with me."

A grin flashed across his face and launched a flock

of butterflies in her belly before he turned and loped back upstairs.

She couldn't wait to get back to her own space, to wear her clothes and sleep in her queen-size bed. While she didn't yet trust all of the images in her head about Noelle or the trouble they'd met, she trusted herself again. It was a tremendous comfort to be out of that fog of anonymity. Identity and memory were two things among a growing list that she would never take for granted again.

Carson finished his second cup of coffee and sent text messages about their plan to both Grant and Detective Werner while Lissa called ahead to the museum and arranged for someone to escort her from the employee entrance to her work space down in the first sublevel.

He wasn't exactly unfamiliar with the museum, inside or out. Everyone within the PFD received extensive training on the landmark building, which seemed to have specific circumstance notes and exemptions for fire safety layered into every square inch. He and Sarah had answered more than one call here, but that was an entirely different experience than walking in as Lissa's guest today.

Following Lissa into the rear entrance, he mentally ticked through the understated security measures, but the guard's boisterous greeting startled him. Lissa made introductions, and after the guard gave her a temporary ID card, Carson trailed after the two of them. The two behaved as if they'd been friends from birth and separated for years rather than a couple of days. She soothed her friend's worry after the news report as the three of them headed for the lower level where Lissa worked.

As they walked along, Carson noticed she used first names with everyone they met along the way and he recognized sincere, friendly affection aimed toward her in return. Everyone they met was relieved to see her, making sure she was okay, and it was clear no one here believed she could have been involved with anything illegal. It seemed the only child who'd grown up without roots had firmly planted herself here.

He wasn't sure why he took comfort in that awareness, since he was only a temporary fixture in her life. Once she was out of this trouble, they'd go their separate ways, and it wasn't likely their paths would cross again. It was common sense, yet it left him feeling hollowed out. What was his problem? More than a little aggravated, he blamed his swinging reactions on a lack of sleep.

There was a wholesome energy to Lissa, grounded with an unmistakable integrity in her dark eyes. As she flipped on the light in her office, her enthusiasm for her work played across her face, turning a beautiful woman irresistible as she gave him a brief explanation of what she did for the museum while she retrieved her spare key to the apartment.

"So you're the CSI of old documents?" he asked, putting her explanation into the most familiar context he could come up with.

"Yes!" Her beaming smile wobbled and faded. "That must bore you to tears." She stuffed the key and both hands into the pockets of her denim jacket.

That nervous tell she had left him searching for a way to make her laugh. "Not at all." And he meant it. "That's actually pretty cool."

"I think so. My parents were all for it, until they realized I didn't want to graduate and go back to traipsing around the world from dig to dig, doing what I do here for them."

"The support dried up?" She was hardly the first kid to take a detour from a parental plan.

"Not intentionally. I make it sound terrible, and it isn't." She sighed as they walked back to the elevator. "I know they love me. That's always been a constant. They definitely appreciate my skills and what I do. They just don't understand how the wanderlust from both sides of the genetic code skipped me so completely."

Carson smiled, pushing the call button. "We always think of the apple falling close to the tree and forget how many roll away."

"Roll away and become new orchards." She wrinkled her nose. "Sorry if that pushes the metaphor too far. Eighteen years of playing in the oldest dirt of the world's most remote locales was long enough."

"It's fine." He enjoyed traveling, but he had a hard time imagining her background. The elevator car arrived and they stepped in. She pushed the button to return to the ground floor. "I bet you're ready to get back to your apartment," he said.

"Yes, please." Her head bobbed and her eyes sparkled. "Your sisters are probably ready to know they won't be sharing their clothes anymore."

"Isn't that accepted practice with females?"

She elbowed him. "It can be, but it's polite to ask rather than assume. Noelle and I—" Her mouth closed, lips clamped together to hold back the words and emotions.

"You can talk about her. You should," he added.

"Is this official advice?"

"Advice can be both helpful and official," he said, holding the door so she could exit the elevator first. They left the cool, dry climate-controlled air of the museum and entered the warmth of the midspring morning, giving the city its first hint of the summer to come.

She climbed into his truck and buckled up. When he had done the same and started the engine, she shifted to face him. "Okay. I'll talk about her. Noelle and I used to share clothing and lament the differences in our shoe sizes. She was an amazing friend and an excellent nurse. I can't think of any reason anyone would hassle her. I have to remember it all and fast."

"You'll get there, I believe it more with every hour. But why are you in a rush?"

"If the case goes cold and the killer gets away because I can't remember the details, I'll never forgive myself."

"Pushing yourself isn't the answer." He pulled out of the parking area and, now that he knew what he was looking for, he saw the unmarked car fall in behind them. "Your body is still healing."

"The detective will want answers. *I* want answers."

"They'll come," he said. "You know who you are. Just yesterday you weren't convinced even that would happen. Between what you have recalled and what the police have found, they will find justice for Noelle."

A few minutes later, Carson pulled to a stop on her street once more. He pointed out their understated police escort to Lissa. "Do you want me to say something to him?"

"No." She'd left her sable hair loose this morning, and it rippled like silk as she shook her head. "Won't the detective call him off? They must have better things to do than keep an eye on me."

Carson wanted to reassure her and yet he couldn't lie. "Hard to tell how long he'll be around. It probably depends on what they uncover and when, regarding Noelle's case."

"Right." Her mouth firmed into a determined line. She pushed open the truck door and hopped out. "I am ready to be back in my place again," she said when he joined her on the sidewalk. "Probably as ready as you are to be rid of me."

He didn't know what to say, so he let her lead the way up the short walk to the front of the house. Her building had once been a stately single-family home perched at the top of a gentle slope. Now it was subdivided, and the landlord must have made bank for the location on the large corner lot with the shade and shelter of mature trees and even three off-street parking spaces. Down the rest of the block in one direction he saw the more common row houses marching along. In the opposite direction around the corner were more homes like this one, most of them clearly subdivided.

"Tidy place," he said, following her up the narrow sidewalk and steps to the front porch.

"The porch is considered a community area." She paused at the porch rail and looked up at him, trouble brewing in her gaze. "How is it I couldn't remember any of this yesterday? I mean, seriously, that old spring rocker was my contribution."

"The brain is a strange place." He shrugged a shoulder and walked over to the chair. "It's in great condition."

"I restored it," she said, with an exasperated huff. "I put my sweat and elbow grease into it. Noelle and I found it when we were out junking one weekend. Sandpaper and a little TLC followed by primer and a gallon of paint. How could I forget I *did* that?"

He took a closer look at the chair. She'd chosen a soft, sky blue color and painted a daisy chain along the back. "Did you paint this freehand?"

"Yes."

"Wow. Nice work." He caught her blushing at his praise. "Why go to all that trouble and leave it in a common space where you can't use it as often?"

"Two reasons." She pulled the house key from her pocket and toyed with it. "First, sharing is caring," she quipped. "I like seeing my neighbors enjoy the chair, too."

"And second?"

She grinned and spun the key around her index finger. "I have a second one upstairs."

That grin on her face was as lovely as a clear sunrise on the Schuylkill River after a grueling night shift. And the admission shifted something inside him. They weren't precisely friends, but he thought they might get there with time. "We'd better get moving if we're going to meet the detective at the station."

She opened the door and explained the house had been divided into three apartments, one per floor. The landlord reserved the basement for maintenance and storage. Carson had pitched in with his friends on projects that both created apartments and restored homes to the original single-family state. Subdividing projects weren't always as well done as this one seemed to be. Although the stairwell to her apartment was narrow and steep, it was sturdy. "I'd like to know who built this," he murmured to himself.

She stopped short at the landing and turned. A step

above him now, she was at eye level when she shot him a hard glare. "You're not thinking of breaking up your house?"

"Not a chance." He'd put in too many long hours on it to chop it up, even if he could double his income by way of the rentals.

Sunlight streamed through the window at the top of the stairs as they turned in to the small sitting room of her apartment. She'd dealt well with the challenges of the pitched roofline and arranged her furniture so guests wouldn't bash into the low angled ceiling. "Nice space," he said and went straight for the restored chair near the window that overlooked the front yard. "You were right about this." He rocked back a little, testing the coiled springs. "Comfy."

"Isn't it? I know the apartment is miniscule, but it was exactly what I needed and the price was right."

"Always a plus." From here he could see straight into her galley kitchen and the doors for both bath and bedroom. "My friend Daniel Jennings would love to get a look at this place if you wouldn't mind giving him a tour."

"Why's that?"

"He's a firefighter, and he runs a construction team when he's not on shift for PFD," Carson explained. "He loves to see projects like this done right."

"That's fine with me. I could probably convince my neighbors to open up, as well. I lucked out in that department," she added. "There's an awesome retired couple on the ground floor. Both teachers. They do a ton of traveling to keep up with the grandkids. The guy who lives on the second floor is in his thirties and is a game design and development professor. He and his partner are huge supporters of the museum."

Carson had never known that much about his neighbors. "Dan would really appreciate it."

"Um. Do you mind if I, ah, just duck aside for a few minutes?" She gestured to the cracked bedroom door. "Help yourself to whatever you like. I'll be quick if you want to touch base with Detective Werner and let him know when to expect us."

"I can do that." Pulling out his cell phone, he left an updated message with the detective. Sunday morning might not be ideal for another interview, but Carson knew from Grant's reaction that the cops were eager for a solid lead on Noelle's killer. When bodies were found in such public locations, the media scrutiny magnified the typically high-pressure task of finding a killer.

Personally, he wanted to take a swing at the man who'd blacked Lissa's eye. Carson knew there were all kinds of nasty people in the world—hell, in the city— but he held a special loathing for bullies who hit women. He'd seen enough on his calls to recognize the pattern of a fist in the bruising.

The pipes rattled a little, and he assumed she'd turned on the water in the bathroom. He wandered over to the kitchen and opened the fridge, hoping for a bottle of water. Finding several, he helped himself as he looked around the space. It gave him a good sense of her, and fit the woman he was coming to know, both before and after her memory returned.

She was resourceful. This place was within an easy walk or bike ride to the museum. Taking the third floor made an expensive neighborhood more attainable. The quirky, clever decor she'd used only underscored her ingenuity and emphasized her determination to make her own way. Whatever hang-ups she'd carried as a kid or the distractions her parents had, she'd turned into a capable woman.

He jumped at the sound of a buzzer. He crossed through the sitting room and pushed the call button on the panel near the landing. "Yeah?"

"It's Werner." The detective's rough, impatient voice clashed with the serenity of Lissa's home.

What the hell? They'd planned to meet him at the station. "I'll be right down," Carson said. He gave a shout to Lissa to let her know the new plan before he went downstairs to let the detective inside. There was probably a way to unlock the door with the keypad, but going down in person bought her a few more moments to brace for the interview.

Werner was pacing from the porch rail to the door, clearly eager to get inside and speak with Melissa. "Has she told you what she remembers?" he asked as soon as he crossed the threshold.

"Yes." Carson purposely kept his reply vague.

"Can she give an ID?" Werner forced Carson back another step. "Have you made a sketch?"

"We haven't gotten that far."

The detective halted in the cramped entry. "What do you mean?"

"From what she's shared with me, it sounds like only a few pieces of that night have come back to her so far, and she doesn't seem to trust them."

"So I'm wasting my time here," Werner grumbled.

"You know where the door is," Carson said.

"Ease up there, Galahad." Werner started up the steps. "I've made some progress just from her fear of hospitals," he admitted when he reached the landing. The detective looked over her small home with a cool, assessing gaze, and Carson wondered how much he learned about the woman based on the address and the room.

She stepped out of the bedroom wearing faded jeans and a flowing top that left her shoulders bare and fluttered at her hips. The bold strokes of copper slashing through black reminded him of sunlight striking her dark hair. Although she tried to smile, it was tight at the edges, and her dark eyes remained cautious. "Hello, Detective. We were planning to meet you at the station."

"This was quicker for me. Are you ready to cooperate, Miss Baxter?"

"Careful," Carson murmured under his breath.

"I hope what I've pieced together will be helpful," she replied, ignoring the barb.

Carson admired her cool reserve. The detective unbuttoned his suit coat, revealing the gun in his shoulder holster as he pulled around a ladder-back chair from the dining set and took a seat. Carson sat with Lissa on the love seat she'd covered with a blue-and-white gingham slipcover. As he expected, the detective made a note on the move.

We're a team now, Carson thought, eyeing him. *Deal with it.*

"I'd like to speak with Miss Baxter alone."

"No."

"You're not her doctor or her lawyer," Werner said. "You can't claim client privacy or privilege."

"I'm the closest thing she has at the moment," Carson shot back. "And I know she doesn't have to cooperate with you. Weren't you saying something to me about finding a lead at the hospital?"

"Really?" Lissa perked up.

"Not a lead, precisely. Your fear of hospitals in light of Noelle's work made me curious. I've been taking a harder look at the people there, but she didn't seem to have any enemies."

"Noelle got along with everyone. She was gregarious, compassionate and a quick study. The emergency room is a perfect fit for her. *Was*," Lissa corrected herself after a beat.

"Her coworkers claim you stopped by often."

Lissa bobbed her chin slowly in agreement.

Werner leaned forward, elbows on his knees. "So why were you so afraid to go back to a place you know well when you were hurt?"

"I don't know. Did you ever find my purse?"

"Yes," the detective answered without elaborating on where it had been found. "We have it stored with the other evidence gathered in the case. Your phone, cash and cards were all in there. You can come down and claim them at any time and double-check if anything is missing. Now let's hear it."

Lissa took a deep breath. "A man gave us trouble, hassled us as we walked from the hospital to the parking garage after Noelle's shift. We'd planned a night out. A club and appetizers, maybe a movie. We hadn't decided."

Carson didn't like the cloud of doubt on the detective's face. He bit back the questions and interruptions only so she didn't get hauled into the police station as a suspect.

"According to the hospital employees on duty with Noelle that night," Detective Werner began, "she spoke to you during a break. She hadn't finished her shift at all."

Lissa's eyes darted from the detective to Carson, and he saw the flare of panic in her deep brown eyes. "Maybe I'm confused and mixing up the timing with another night." Her eyebrows drew together, and her teeth worked over her full lower lip, avoiding the healing split from the night she was attacked. "I clearly know who *I* am, and I remember my parents and details from my childhood, as well. I know where I work, how I got through college and how I was hired into my current position. Everything about the night Noelle died is still a bit blurry around the edges. I'm sorry."

"Uh-huh." The detective braced his elbows on his knees, his pen tapping against the page in his notebook. "Just let me hear the rest."

Carson gave a start when she reached for his hand. He let her hold on as she told the detective the fractured pieces she'd remembered.

Werner sighed and closed his notebook and sat up straight. "This isn't much to go on and far less than I'd hoped for."

"I'm aware," Lissa agreed. "I'll keep you informed as more details come back to me."

At Werner's snort of doubt, Carson leaped to her defense. "This is a good start," he said. "And it's a strong sign that she'll recall more details with better clarity." He hoped it wouldn't mean more terrifying nightmares for her in the process. He turned to the detective. "How is it three men came after two women on the street and no one saw anything?"

"People saw Melissa," Werner replied pointedly. "The rest seems to be up for debate."

Her hand flexed in Carson's. "You're looking at me as a suspect?"

"No." Werner shook his head, resignation stamped on his features. "It would have been easier if you'd been treated and had a definitive, official medical record of your memory trouble."

"Grant and I can attest to her condition when she showed up at the club," Carson offered.

Werner snorted again. "Stand down, Lane. I'm aware of the good Grant does for the community beyond the music. But a full workup could have been helpful, y'know?"

"They respected my fear of going back," Lissa said. "The attack had to have happened there, rather than on the street as I'm recalling it." She rubbed at her temples. "Where do I factor into your investigation?"

"Well, so far as we can tell, you didn't kill her," Werner said. "The injuries she sustained were delivered by someone bigger and far more brutal," he added, with another glance around the cheery apartment. "That being said, I'd appreciate it if you stayed in town."

"Of course," she agreed. "And I will let you know as soon as I remember anything that makes sense."

"How about you call when you remember anything? Let me make sense of it." When she nodded an agreement he turned to Carson. "Get me a sketch if she recalls enough."

"You have my word."

The detective stood and buttoned his suit jacket, the gun discreet once more. "Walk me out?" he asked Carson.

They went downstairs in silence and stepped out on the porch and into the gentle spring warmth. "Look, anything at all she remembers," he said. "I'm serious. I need to know."

"You've made that crystal clear." Carson folded his arms over his chest. "I'll stay in touch with her. Check in occasionally."

"How about closer than that?" Werner rocked back on his heels. "I don't have anything definitive, but there are some nasty rumors under the rocks I'm turning over."

"You just said—"

Werner's gaze drifted past Carson, up and down the street. "She's not a murder suspect, I can't keep her under surveillance much longer and I don't have enough right now to justify an official protective detail."

"What are you asking me to do? I'm just a washed-out paramedic."

Werner had the grace to wince. "Sorry about that," he said. "Look, she trusts you. If you care about her, you need to stay close until I get a handle on this case."

"Care?" Carson protested instantly. "I barely know her."

"Exactly." He aimed a finger at Carson. "It takes innate compassion to do what we do. I'm not saying walk her down the aisle, man. I'm saying she might need someone to stick close, be a friend. Oh—" he reached into his suit jacket, on the side opposite the gun "—here's the information for her friend's funeral service. I'm sure Miss Baxter will want to say goodbye."

Carson winced, knowing the detective was right on that point, at least. He'd also been around long enough to read between the lines. "You're trying to get out of here without saying it, but Melissa is a target, isn't she?"

"We both know only the lowest form of humanity is capable of something like this, Lane. I doubt the killer gives a damn about the nuances of amnesia or plans to give her time to remember anything we can use to catch him."

"And that said, you still can't offer her any protection?"

The detective rolled his shoulders. "I'm aware the facts suck. I joined the force to protect people. The minute I have enough to take action, I'll take it."

Carson knew by reputation and his connection to Grant that the detective was one of the good guys, but he was aggravated all the same. He went back inside, locked the door, and climbed the stairs to Lissa's apartment.

This entire situation had spun out of control. He didn't want to stay close to her, didn't want to worry over a woman who was little more than a stranger. It wasn't fair to either of them. If things went sideways, he wouldn't be any good to her.

He could almost hear Sarah calling him a chicken and scolding him for being afraid of letting Lissa get too close.

He didn't *want* anyone close, despite what he'd been thinking earlier about being friends with Lissa. She had a target on her back, and he was no bodyguard. He could not take the risk that he'd like her and have her torn out of his life. He wouldn't survive losing another friend that way.

The only answer was to maintain a polite, professional distance, even while he kept an eye on her.

Chapter 5

Lissa heard Carson's footfalls as he marched back up the stairs. He and the detective had definitely exchanged words outside. She didn't want to be the source of trouble for him, and now that she knew who she was, knew how to take care of herself, Carson didn't need to waste his time hovering over her anymore.

"Everything okay?" she asked as he stepped into the apartment.

"Yeah." He rolled his shoulders and hooked his thumbs in his back pockets. "Werner can be a jerk. That's all."

"I'm sure it goes with the territory. Maybe we should try and do a sketch for him."

He arched an eyebrow. "Are you confident in the description yet?"

"Not really," she confessed. She tucked her hair behind her ears, wondering what to do next. "I thought having a starting point or reference could help."

"The wrong description could throw off the entire investigation."

He had a good point. "Thanks for taking me to the museum and staying for that interview." She braced for the solitude that was coming, reminding herself that she'd always thrived on her quiet and alone time. "You probably have at least a dozen things to do. Thanks again for helping me."

He took a step closer, and his eyebrows furrowed. "Are you kicking me out?"

"That's not how I'd put it. I'm just—"

"How will you get to work tomorrow?"

Startled by the question, she frowned at him. "I'll walk or take my bike."

"No."

She gaped at his no-room-to-argue reply. "Then I'll call for a ride."

He shook his head. "It's easier if I take you."

He didn't seem too happy about it. In fact, his hard expression implied he'd rather pull out his own teeth than stick around. Had the detective lied to her about being a suspect? "Why don't you tell me what suddenly crawled under your skin?"

He opened his mouth and slammed it shut. "Me. My problem." He held up his hands in surrender. "Didn't mean to take it out on you. Sorry."

That wasn't even close to the whole story. She folded her arms over her chest. "I'd rather have the truth than a half-assed apology."

"I haven't lied to you," Carson insisted. "It wouldn't do any good."

And yet he didn't elaborate. Exasperated with both of them, she went to the kitchen to see what she could throw together for lunch. It seemed as though Carson was staying even though his body language said he wanted to run and never look back.

"Hey," she called over her shoulder as she studied the contents of her refrigerator. "Do you think amnesia recovery and hunger go together? I've been starving all day."

"Your body craves fuel for the recovery process," he answered after a long silence. "We can go hit one of the Sunday buffets if that sounds good."

He'd come up right behind her. Definitely not much of a challenge in her small place, but his nearness put her on edge, had her hormones revving. "No, thanks." That would feel too much like a date for her comfort. The last thing she needed was to let an ill-timed attraction spiral into a misplaced crush. "I'd prefer to cook. I hope burgers are okay." Opening the freezer, she grabbed a package of hamburger patties she'd prepped and frozen. "And you haven't seen the best feature of this apartment yet."

He gave her another skeptical eyebrow arch and turned a slow circle. "I'll take your word."

"Good." She pulled veggies out of the crisper and buns from the pantry. Setting everything on the limited counter space, she couldn't stop the stab of envy she felt for his kitchen. "Can you at least confirm that whatever is bugging you doesn't come down to the detective believing I really am a suspect?"

"You're clear on the murder, but he'd love to crawl inside your head and see what you saw that night," Carson answered.

"That makes it unanimous, I suppose." When he offered to help with the meal, she gave him a knife and cutting board and set him to slicing tomatoes and onions while she prepped the rest of the picnic she was planning. "If I'm not a suspect, then I must be a target," she said, watching him closely. "Why else would you feel obligated to stick around?"

He set the knife down carefully and turned to face her. "In a word, yes."

The brief answer came out of him with such honesty and concern, she melted. Her parents hadn't stared at her with such abject worry since she was a small child. Her fingertips tingled with a sudden desire to kiss him while yet another thank-you danced on her lips. How had she been so lucky to stumble into such a decent man when she'd needed help? "You can't stand here and tell me you intend to protect me until the killer is in custody."

"That exactly what I intend."

"I'm flattered, but—"

"It's got nothing to do with flattery." She couldn't be sure if that was attraction or frustration sparking in his gaze. "It's the right thing to do. You don't have family around and your best friend is d—gone," he amended quickly.

"She's dead," Lissa said. "It's okay to be blunt."

"It's also okay to be kind."

He'd been exceptionally kind to her. Only a person with a special gift would take in a stranger in her condition. Just because she'd learned to depend on herself out of necessity didn't negate how much she enjoyed being self-sufficient. But still, there were long, lonely pockets of time, even after she and Noelle had bonded, after she'd made friends at work. Loneliness gave her no right to trample all over Carson's life. "You have a life, Carson, and I understand you have more important priorities than keeping tabs on me."

"Not really." He shrugged and turned back to the cutting board, snapping the strange sizzle arcing between them.

With a hard mental shake, she told herself she was relieved. There were more pressing matters to deal with than her undeniable fascination with him. "You must have substitute shifts coming up."

"Nothing's written in stone. I can find plenty to do on a construction site to match up with the hours you're at the museum."

She didn't like the sound of that. He was a paramedic, not a jack-of-all-trades. She nearly said the words and stopped herself. It wasn't her place to judge his choices. For all she knew, he was better at construction than he was as a paramedic. Maybe he even enjoyed it more. She had to remember she didn't know him and he had no reason to trust her opinions or concerns.

Gathering the supplies they'd prepped and serving ware onto a big tray, she tipped her head to the fridge. "Grab a bottle of water for me and whatever you'd like to drink and follow me. You'll love this."

Balancing the loaded tray with one hand, she employed the skills gained during her years as a waitress and opened the narrow door that led up to the roof. Built as a fire escape, she basically had her own private balcony and container garden, though her neighbor on the second floor had easy access if he wanted to climb up the fire escape.

"Holy cow," Carson said. "This is incredible."

A breeze ruffled his gold-streaked brown hair, and she wished she could run her hands through it, feel the silk of it against her skin. She had to dial it down before she did something foolish. "Isn't it?" She set the tray on the small table tucked against the wall of the house. "They don't even charge me extra rent."

"Wow." A smile curled his mouth. "You've made the most of every inch of it."

"Thanks. Usually it's just me." Noelle had been her only visitor up here. They'd shared coffee and sunrises after her marathon overnight shifts at the hospital or, more often, moonlight and wine and late-night conversations.

Lissa ignited the compact propane camping grill she'd set up on the open corner of the platform. "It won't take long to cook these up," she said, reaching for the plate of burger patties.

Carson seemed to have forgotten the food, thoroughly distracted by the view. "It's like a secret tree house."

"Noelle and I would come out here with a bottle of wine and stargaze sometimes."

Carson cleared his throat. "Detective Werner gave me the information for her memorial service. It's this Tuesday afternoon." He handed the notecard to her.

She read it and shoved it into her back pocket. "The service is here," she murmured. "Naturally her parents would want to make things easier on her friends and co-workers." She had to swallow the lump of grief lodged in her throat. "They must be devastated." She gazed out at the trees, seeing only Noelle's beautiful smile. "And wondering why I haven't called."

"Amnesia is a valid reason for your silence," Carson pointed out, handing her the bottle of water.

"Bringing her parents closure is a valid impetus to remember every detail."

Within the limits of the small balcony, Carson only

had to shift his body to put his arm around her shoulders. "Give it time."

She eyed the burgers, but it was too soon to turn them. Instead she relaxed into the comfort he offered. "It feels selfish to have it all mixed-up and jumbled when I want to be helpful."

He reached back for one of the folding lawn chairs and kicked it open for her. "You *will* help in due time. The police have solved crimes, even murders, without eyewitnesses before. If you never remember, it will be fine."

"It's pretty obvious that the attack must have been terrible, but I survived it. She didn't. She deserves justice." Lissa wasn't convinced she'd ever remember the critical details, and yet she had no way of controlling what her brain was doing with the lost hours of Friday night.

Thankfully, while the burgers cooked, Carson changed the subject, asking about her career at the museum and how she became interested in becoming a conservator. An understandable attempt at distraction, and she appreciated his effort.

When her enthusiastic rambling slowed down, he picked up another thread of conversation as they ate, telling her stories about how Grant had met his wife, Katie, during his hunt for the nightclub a few years back and built it from nothing into the current trendy place. He talked about the various bands they'd had in recently and some of the events coming up in the summer.

"I can't believe that was your first visit," he said. "Grant went out of his way to create a perfect signature cosmopolitan for ladies' night."

She and Noelle hadn't made clubbing a priority, although they enjoyed going out and catching live groups or trivia nights at bars near the hospital campus. Something about that niggled at her mind but wouldn't come into focus. She stopped forcing it and voiced a question that had been bugging her since the detective's visit. "How did I get that matchbook?"

"If you still don't remember, it must have come from someone at the hospital," Carson said. "Or someone you met that night," he added.

"I'm hoping it's a clue of some sort," she said. "We should have let the detective take it for fingerprints."

"We still can turn it over as evidence when we go to pick up your purse."

"Maybe." She finished her water and started cleaning up. "They might find it as useless as my foggy memories, the way I've been holding it like a good luck charm."

"Let me handle cleanup." Carson moved around her, nudging her back into the chair.

A sharp bang sounded in the next second, immediately followed by a metallic screech near her head. She swiveled to see a menacing black puncture in the aluminum siding that framed the door.

"Gun! Get down!" Carson yanked her beneath him and covered her body with his as two more gunshots ripped apart the quiet day.

"Are you hit?" she rasped, her breath shallow. Trapped, she could feel his heart hammering against her arm. "Carson?"

"Inside!" He pushed up on his arms, giving her room to squirm away. "Go." Another two bullets whizzed past them.

"Carson—" She tugged open the door and scrambled into the stairwell. She didn't have long to worry as he crashed into the small space with her and pulled the door closed.

Another spate of bullets bit through the door, and beams of sunlight spilled through the holes, casting crazy shadows.

They rushed into her apartment and bolted that door. She searched for her cell phone, then remembered yet again that it was in her purse at the police station.

Carson was already on his phone, reporting the incident. "Stay back from the windows," he snapped at her.

She sank to the kitchen floor, her back pressed against the cabinets. It was the nearest windowless place. Through the pounding of her heart, she heard Carson give her address. Then suddenly he was on his knees in front of her.

"Are you hurt?" He pushed seeking fingers through her hair, down her neck and then smoothed his palms across her shoulders. "Turn around."

"I'm fine."

"Turn around," he said, even as he moved her, his hands skimming over her ribs and abdomen.

She caught a flash of red on his arm. "You've been shot. I'm fine."

"No. Not my blood." His hands swept down her back. "Your blood. Let me see your legs."

"My legs are fine," she said, twisting back to face him. "Carson, stop. You're hurt."

"No." He didn't stop searching her for injuries. "You need help, Sarah." His skin was pale, and he was taking in rapid sips of air as if his lungs wouldn't inflate all the way.

"Carson, I'm Lissa." She reached up and held his face, waited for him to see her. He gazed at her through glassy eyes, but she knew he saw his former partner. "Come sit by me." She took his hand, struggled against his natural strength boosted by his fear. "Please, Carson. Just sit with me."

His breath caught, stuttered. Then, on a deep inhalation, he sat down. He held her hand so tightly, she thought the bones would snap, but she refused to complain or move. This wasn't her first encounter with a person in shock or even having posttraumatic stress reaction. Traveling the world with her parents, she'd witnessed accidents on the dig sites and seen natural disasters tear apart villages along with more common domestic violence producing emotional aftershocks.

At least from this angle, she could verify the blood on his arm was seeping from a shallow wound. Either he got caught on something on the rooftop patio, or one of the bullets had nicked him. The good news was she didn't think the injury would require more than basic first aid, a couple of stitches at most. A dreadful chill slipped across her skin. Unless that wasn't the only wound. Nothing else within her view of him was bleeding, and she clung to that small shred of hope while they waited for whomever he'd called in.

She spoke to him with gentle reassurances, in much the same way he'd talked her out of her recent meltdowns. Finally, his body stopped quaking as the adrenaline rush subsided. Later she would think about being afraid of the shooter. Right now, she'd be strong while Carson shook off the terror and loss he was reliving.

Minutes ticked by, each one longer than the last, until finally she heard sirens screaming down the street. Someone pounded on her door even as Carson's cell phone rang from the floor beside him. "Come on." She bumped him with her shoulder. "We have to let them in."

He didn't move. She twisted to her knees, letting him keep the death grip on her hand as she put her face close to his. "Carson." She kept her voice firm but calm, mimicking his method. "We're going to stand up now and let the police help us."

He blinked slowly, then rubbed his eyes. When he looked at her, then down at their joined hands, she knew he was back. "Lissa." He released her immediately. "Crap. Did I hurt you?"

"You saved me," she said, kissing his cheek. The scruffy stubble scraped her lips, making her want to linger over the contact. More shouts and pounding came from the door downstairs. "Wait here." She pushed to her feet and ran for the security panel, unlocking the door before they destroyed it. "Upstairs," she called down as uniformed people surged into the narrow stairwell. "Minor wounds only."

They were surrounded in seconds. Paramedics treated Carson at the kitchen table while two men from the fire department exchanged words with him, then wandered back out since they weren't needed. A moment later, she heard the fire truck drive off. A pair of uniformed police officers came up next and took their statements before going up to the rooftop to look things over.

It was no surprise to Lissa when Detective Werner showed up next. Thankfully Carson's wound had been dressed and he'd regained his composure as they explained everything once more for the detective. Apparently a neighbor down the street had called 911 about the gunshots moments before Carson had called in the trouble.

"Now can she have a protective detail?" he asked. Werner hesitated, and Carson swore.

"What is the real issue here, Detective?" Carson asked.

"Available resources, to start." He waited for the crime scene unit to walk on through and up to the roof, and they were alone again. "The three of us can believe this incident was related to the trouble on Friday night, but until we have confirmation of a bigger problem, Miss Baxter has just been in the wrong place at the wrong time."

"Twice in less than seventy-two hours?" Carson glared, his hands balled into fists at his sides. "I don't think anyone believes in that much bad luck."

"Should we make some sort of public statement or do an interview explaining my amnesia?" she offered. "Would that help?"

"Absolutely not." The detective planted his hands on his hips.

"Because you want to draw them out," Carson accused. "You want to use her as bait? That's crazy."

The idea didn't hold much appeal for her, either. Lissa folded her arms over her chest, trying to lock down the tremor building in her system before it took hold and became obvious to Carson and everyone else. She definitely wanted justice for Noelle, but the stunt on the rooftop had brought the immediate danger into undeniable focus. She swallowed, knowing she should leap at any opportunity to help and struggling against the fear.

Werner's pale blue gaze narrowed. "You're out of line."

"Same goes," Carson said. "Seems we've reached an impasse."

"Why don't you come down to the station," Werner appealed to Lissa. "You can look at some photo arrays, and we can build a description if one of the faces clicks for you."

"Oh, yeah, that'll erase the target from her back, for sure," Carson grumbled. "Whoever fired that gun at us knows neither of us got a look at him today, which means we can only be at the station to give you a statement and information about Friday."

"Which I will happily do when I remember," she said. Nightmares or not, she had to find those lost hours. She knew the odds weren't good, if only because of the way Carson kept reassuring her not to force the issue.

"When or even if you remember isn't enough," Werner muttered. "Once they process the scene, it might give us another lead."

"Wait." Carson's eyebrows knit into a deep scowl. "Give us one second, please?" he asked Lissa.

She shook her head. "I'm in this all the way. Just say whatever is on your mind."

The debate over how much to share played out in the set of his mouth, the troubled expression in his eyes. "You think the men who killed Noelle and beat up Melissa can be tracked down by the ammunition used here," Carson finally said.

"It's possible," Werner replied, not looking at Lissa. "The techs pulled a .40 caliber bullet out of the door frame. We'll know more after the lab takes a look. More still when we find the gun and identify the shooter."

The color drained out of Carson's face again, and he slumped into the nearest chair. "What could that mean?" she asked, stepping closer to him. "Are you okay?"

"There's a gang running in Philly that prefers .40

caliber ammunition. It's too common, so they often, not always, mark their bullets for hits to send a message," Werner said.

"Wouldn't that make them easier to arrest?"

"You'd think," Werner said. "Sometimes they leave an unspent bullet behind. Sometimes we find a marked shell casing. Without corroborating evidence or eyewitnesses, it's an uphill battle in court."

None of that explained Carson's sudden despair.

"Not quite nine months ago," Werner continued, "that signature ammunition was used in an ambulance robbery that ended with the death of Carson's partner, Sarah Neely."

Carson hid his face in his hands, and she wanted to comfort him, but all she could do was stand there and feel helpless. "How exactly did Noelle die?" she heard herself ask as if she was standing just behind her body rather than in it.

Werner shook his head and gave her a pitying look. "Let's just say a marked .40 caliber bullet lodged in her heart was the last straw."

Her stomach lurched, and she had to concentrate to keep her knees from buckling. "I see."

The detective studied her. "Do you?"

She leaned away from the blatant doubt and frustration in the detective's accusing gaze. "You think Noelle knew the killer. That I know who attacked us."

"Yes." He bobbed his head. "According to everyone she knew, *you* were her best friend. You're not doing her any favors by hiding details of her personal life from this investigation."

Her head swam. Noelle was *not* a criminal. She had no reason to consort with violent criminals who used signature ammunition. In the ER, she treated too many gunshot victims to support thugs who dealt out that kind of pain. Images passed through her mind of Noelle out dancing, sharing fun dinners with coworkers, the utter exhaustion on her face after troubling shifts packed with emergencies and crises at the hospital. Why would Werner or anyone else suspect Noelle was involved with her killer? Lissa wanted to defend her best friend, but her throat had gone dry and the words stuck there, useless.

"Well?" the detective pressed. "Tell me what you remember before I haul you in on obstruction."

"Take it easy, Detective," Carson said. "He's blustering, Lissa. Don't let him get to you."

Her ears buzzed as she tried to find some fact to point to, some recent memory that would shatter such an outrageous theory about her best friend. "You're wrong."

"About which part?"

"You're wrong," she repeated, not recognizing the rasping sound that was her voice.

Without realizing how it happened, she found herself in Carson's warm arms, his heartbeat a calm, steady comfort under her cheek. Had Noelle managed to get tangled up with the wrong people? It didn't make any sense, but it felt as if there were more gaps in Lissa's memory than facts.

In low tones, male voices talked over her head, and she just didn't care anymore. She'd been attacked, battered and now shot at. Her best friend was dead, and though most of her past was clear, she'd exhausted herself trying to dredge up the most important pieces of her memory that were still missing.

"You're safe." Carson's voice was a quiet murmur at her ear, a soft descant to the enormous screaming heartbreak inside her. "He's gone. Let it out," he said. "We're alone now."

Lissa had no sense of time, no sense of anything but the paralyzing fear and sorrow that came at her in ceaseless waves. Carson's soothing voice, his patient ministrations, his lean body supporting hers were all she could comprehend until finally everything faded to a velvet-coated, starless black.

Propped up by throw pillows, Carson watched Lissa sleep, her body safely caught between his and the back of the love seat, her head on his chest. He was confident they were two of the most broken people in the city today. First his panic attack during the shooting, and now her breakdown. She'd snapped. He'd seen it coming when the detective kept peppering her with information about marked bullets, suspicions over Noelle's associates and his attempts to press and intimidate Lissa.

The outburst that had started with a raspy denial and mild trembling had given way to tears and a flood of emotional energy. A flood he thought was long overdue after the few glimpses he'd gleaned of the hell she'd escaped. She'd clung like a burr through it all, and tucking in beside her on the love seat had been the only solution.

Naturally the detective considered her escape from the attack as suspicious as everything else regarding Noelle's death, despite the evidence that Lissa hadn't committed the murder herself.

At least Werner had left two officers in a marked car parked on the street as a protective measure until Lissa was well enough to move. Carson had no intention of letting her stay here, where memories of Noelle haunted her and they were only one small stairwell away from the roof where they'd been attacked.

Once she woke up, she could pack a few things and they'd make a plan. They could move back to his place, or find a motel, or whatever made her feel comfortable and safe. As soon as they reached a decision, he'd call Grant and bring him up to speed. Maybe Grant would apply his perennial cop instincts or possibly his wife's real estate resources and offer a better solution to protect Lissa from both the criminals determined to silence her and the stubborn, resolute detective.

She stirred in his arms, snuggling closer, her arm sliding over his waist. He smoothed a hand over her glossy, dark hair, struggling to recall the last time he'd been so relaxed. It was well before Sarah's death—that much was certain. While the circumstances for this particular revelation epitomized bad timing, he discovered an odd pulse of hope in his system. That small hope was undoubtedly for Lissa's recovery. After his collapse during their emergency, he knew better than to harbor any hope for himself.

He remembered it as if watching a bad television segment. He'd been belligerent, ordering her about at the first sound of gunfire. He recalled seeing the blood staining her shirt and trying to find a wound that wasn't real. The only blood had been his, a minor graze from one of the bullets. He knew the gunfire had dragged him down into that abyss, knew he'd clawed for control and lost the battle. Lissa's voice alone had pulled him back out again, and she'd managed that rescue before his peers arrived and found him acting like a maniac over a negligible scratch.

He owed her.

If she needed him to stay right here so she could sleep, this was where he'd stay. He wasn't sure what to make of his sudden determination and didn't care to sort it out right now. Aside from his occasional substitute shift for the PFD, he hadn't done anything noteworthy since Sarah died. The woman in his arms needed help, and for some inexplicable reason, Lissa kept latching onto him.

Why couldn't he see her in the detached way he viewed other patients? Bringing her to his home for observation that first night was part of it, yes, but there had to be another factor.

He stroked her hair, keeping them both relaxed as the thick silk sifted through his fingers. His phone vibrated on the end table, and he reached back to check the display. His supervisor, Evelyn, he noticed on the caller ID, probably calling for an upcoming shift. He didn't envy her job, but she could find someone else this time. Carson refused to risk putting more than a few minutes of distance between Lissa and himself until Noelle's killer was caught and behind bars.

As he thought about it, his muscles involuntarily tensed up, and Lissa's breath hitched for a cycle or two before she relaxed again. Carson kept his own breath soft and even, and as recent events caught up to him, he dozed off.

He came awake, disoriented and chilled, to find himself alone on the love seat. Lissa had replaced her soft, warm body with the poor substitute of a soft crocheted throw. "Lissa?" he called, sitting up.

"In here." Her voice carried from the bedroom.

He rolled to his feet and stretched, popping stiff joints. Taking a detour, he stopped in the bathroom and splashed cool water on his face before tapping on the open bedroom door.

She turned, her gaze not quite meeting his. "Did I wake you?"

He shook his head, not inclined to admit it had been her absence that had brought him awake. "How are you feeling?"

"Foggy, but better. I must have made quite a scene."

Her eyes were puffy and red-rimmed, but she was packing an overnight bag. "It got Werner out of here, so you won't get a complaint from me."

Her lips twitched at one corner. "That *is* a plus." She sat down on the corner of the bed and tossed the shirt she'd been holding into the luggage. "I didn't remember anything new."

"Did I ask?"

"No." She pushed the heels of her hands across her forehead, clearly trying to wipe away a headache. "I'm not as patient as you."

"And I'm not being hounded by a homicide detective."

"Let's not forget the killer. Assuming Friday night and this afternoon are linked."

He was sure of it. "No, we can't forget the killer." He leaned into the doorjamb, watching her. "That brings us to why you're packing. Is there somewhere you'd like to go?"

"It's logical to leave, right? I'd rather not go, but it's logical." She brought her knees to her chest and wrapped her arms around them. "I don't see how leaving changes anything."

He understood her reluctance, but he wanted her far away from the rooftop incident. *For my benefit or hers?* He focused on her and the traits, both big and small, that she'd revealed in the short time since recalling her name and background.

"You've put down roots here. I understand that," he said. "No one is forcing you out of town."

"Then I want to stay. Here."

"Lissa." He took a deep breath. "There's a crime scene upstairs. Logic indicates you're a sitting duck if you stay."

"And if I go, how long before whoever killed Noelle finds me? He could lie in wait and take me out at the museum for all we know."

Carson winced at the scenario that popped into his head. "Do you have any vacation time?"

"I will not run like a scared rabbit."

"Okay, okay." He held up his hands in surrender. "Think of it as less running and more strategy. Why stay here where the killer knows he can get to you?"

"Noelle's parents need closure. The community needs this guy off the street, whatever his crime of preference. Staying here puts us in the driver's seat."

"Driver's seat?" He snorted.

"I'm not running." She stood up and started unpacking her suitcase. "I'm close to work. I know the area. I have memories of Noelle here. All of that has to help."

Her voice cracked, and he hurried forward into the bedroom. "Got it." The apartment itself wasn't an active crime scene, and more than likely the roof had been processed and considered cleared once the bullets were recovered. He only hoped they matched the signature bullets so Werner had a lead other than Lissa's memory. "Will you leave long enough to help me pack some things at my place?"

Her chin fell. "You don't mean to stay here?"

"I'm not leaving you alone until this is settled."

"But—"

"I'm not running, either," he said, mimicking the grit she'd shown. "Haven't we covered this?"

She needed only a bit more convincing, and fifteen minutes later, he was explaining their plans to the policemen who'd been stationed on the street. At his place, Carson packed up the few things he would need, including a suit for the funeral on Tuesday. To buy some breathing space, he sent his sisters a text that he was helping out a friend for a few days, and then he updated Grant.

Although judging tone in a text message wasn't easy, the reply from the Escape Club owner didn't give Carson the impression that Grant was pleased with Lissa's decision to dig in her heels and remain at her apartment. Carson handed Lissa the phone. "He's not thrilled with either of us."

"Yikes," she said, cringing at the terse message. "You should return to your regular schedule. I'll be okay."

"We've covered this," he reminded her through clenched teeth. He wasn't going through it again. "Let's grab some dinner and talk about your plans for tomorrow and the rest of the week."

They chose a Greek restaurant Lissa favored, and Carson was as happy with the set up at the cozy family diner where he could see everyone as he was with the generous portions of soup, spicy gyros and cool *tzatziki* sauce.

They made a quick grocery list while they waited for the check and then completed that errand before heading back to her place. Between them they made it upstairs with his duffel and the grocery sacks in one trip. As she put things away in the kitchen, he went back down to his truck for the suit he'd covered with a garment bag.

He wasn't a cop by training, but paramedics were taught to stay observant despite a crisis. He'd been an epic failure for Sarah on that front, but he was doing all he could not to repeat that failure with Lissa. He could almost hear the PFD chaplain asking if Lissa was a surrogate for Sarah's memory. Carson didn't want to believe he was using an innocent woman to make up for such a dreadful error. That was impossible. No one could replace Sarah or fill the void she'd left behind.

Lissa is not a stand-in, he thought, taking time to walk the perimeter of the house, getting a feel for the area and routes to neighbors. She'd come to Escape Club for help, with or without her memories, and Carson knew how vital it was to maintain the reputation the club had as a safe place for the community.

Grant, using the code name of Alexander, had a reputation for helping out people who slipped through the cracks of typical law enforcement assistance. Lissa definitely fit that bill.

Carson circled back to the front door, knowing the cops had canvassed the area and looked for any sign of the shooter's location. Still, as he walked to his truck, he felt exposed. It didn't take special training or extra intuition to know someone wanted to keep Lissa from talking about what she'd seen that night. Until she regained her memory or the police found the killer, that someone was going to have to get by Carson first.

Chapter 6

Lissa woke early Monday morning, feeling something was off and quickly realizing it was the faint snoring from the man sacked out in her sitting room. She muffled an inappropriate giggle at the hitched breath and groaning sounds. The apartment wasn't really big enough for two people, but Carson hadn't let that hinder his determination to stay over. The guy was really too good to be true, barreling through a situation that clearly made him uncomfortable, just to keep her safe. If ever there was a man meant to rescue people, it was him.

She slipped her short cotton robe over the camisole and shorts she slept in and made a beeline for the bathroom, unable to resist sneaking a glance at his sleeping form. At rest, the persistent tension that lined his forehead and tightened his jaw was gone. It was so tempting to creep closer and steal another touch of that full lower lip, the way she had yesterday evening when she found herself in his arms after her meltdown. Quickly she closed the bathroom door, cringing at the squeaky hinge, and hurried through her morning routine so she would be out before he woke up.

"Good morning," he said when she opened the door again.

His deep voice, rough around the edges, slipped under her robe and warmed her skin as effectively as the lingering steam from her shower. "M-morning," she stammered. They'd circled around each other for three mornings now, and she was afraid she knew exactly why the first greeting of every day was becoming more of a challenge than a familiarity. "Um, it's all yours," she added, sidestepping to her bedroom and closing the door.

She caught her reflection in the full-length mirror near her closet and nearly laughed out loud. He wasn't a date. He wasn't here because he liked her or wanted to sleep with her. And who could blame him, with her wet hair bundled into a towel, no makeup, the remnants of a black eye and a robe that had seen better days? He was here to help protect her from a killer until her brain cooperated and she could give Detective Werner the information he needed.

As she dried her hair and dressed for work, she wondered how often people in official protective custody developed unwise attachments to the people guarding them. There had been more than a few movies and books with that theme, and in light of recent days, she was starting to feel more sympathy for the characters in those stories.

If only her nightmare could be resolved in the course of a two-hour movie or the three hundred action-packed pages of a book. She'd dreamed of Noelle all night long, but only the good times, nothing helpful about the night that mattered more than any of her other memories.

Dressed, she started on her makeup. It was careful going with concealer and foundation to hide her black eye, but she didn't want to field questions about the injury all day long. At least the swelling was nearly gone. She paused in the process of carefully applying her mascara and forced herself to think about the last conversations she remembered with her best friend.

There were always things going at the hospital, good and bad. Noelle had been the type to vent the worst and then let it go. Her ability to compartmentalize had made her particularly good at her job and helped her advance. She had her eye on a move to Children's, but it was a ways off on her life plan.

A knock on the door had her checking the bedside clock. "Crap." She'd dawdled in here so long that she'd have to skip breakfast or be late for work.

"You okay?" Carson asked.

"Yes. Just a second." Too easily she pictured him leaning a shoulder against the doorjamb. Sliding into her shoes, she picked up the purse she'd chosen to replace the one she'd lost to police custody and walked out of the bedroom. "I'm ready," she said.

He leaned back, his gaze drifting over her from head to toe. "You look terrific."

The compliment caught her off guard. "Thanks." She caught a gleam in his eye, and for a moment she thought he would kiss her. A happy image of domestic bliss rippled through her, swiftly evaporating in the savory scents of bacon, cheese and egg.

"Breakfast," he said, pushing a wrapped sandwich into her free hand. "I'll carry the coffee."

"You made breakfast." She stared at him as she inhaled the delicious aroma. "For me."

"We bought groceries to use them, right?" He cocked his head. "Do you normally eat at work?"

"Yes. No." She shook her head. "I mean, yes, this is why we bought groceries. I just didn't expect this."

"Let's go," he said, urging her toward the stairs. "Being on time is you, right?"

She laughed. "Yes. Very me." She noticed his hesitation at the bottom of the stairs, knew he was checking the porch and street for visible risks.

Unable to stop herself, she peered over his shoulder, seeking anything out of the ordinary. As he moved, she followed, letting him lock the door since he would keep the key while she was at work.

While he made the short drive to the museum, she wolfed down the sandwich and scalded her tongue on the piping hot coffee, but it was worth it.

"I have time to pick up your purse from Werner while you're working today," he offered, pulling into the parking lot they'd used yesterday and stopping at the curb since he was dropping her off. "If that's okay?"

Okay? It will be fantastic. She knew she was being a coward, but she wanted to avoid Werner until she had some substantial information. "That would be great." She stuffed the last bite into her mouth and licked her fingers before she remembered her manners and used the paper napkin.

His gaze tracked the movement, and her heart skipped into overdrive.

"That was perfect," she said. "Thanks."

He grinned, the expression slow and too sexy. "You're welcome." He cleared his throat. "Do you mind if I get another key cut for the apartment?"

"Fine," she said once she'd swallowed. "Oh. Oh, no." She pressed her hand to her lips and tried to breathe through the sudden, choking panic.

"What?" He looked around, checking the mirrors first and then twisting in the seat. "What's wrong?"

"The key. Noelle h-had a key."

He checked the mirror and pulled into the first available space, slamming the gearshift to Park. "Breathe."

"I'm trying. What if…" She couldn't bring herself to finish the sentence.

"I'll walk through with the police, and I'll get the locks changed first thing."

The list grew in her head. She should call the landlord for permission and find out what was compatible with the security system. Her mind started spinning until she found her hands cradled by his. "Carson," she began, looking up into his face.

"I'll handle it," he promised. He lifted her hands to his lips. "Have a good day."

The silly move soothed her, smoothing out the anxiety before it could swamp her again. She reached for the door and turned back. On a whim, she leaned over and kissed his cheek before she changed her mind. "I'll call from the office when I'm ready to leave."

"I'll be here," he promised.

He would be, just as he'd handle the locks and her purse, too. Overwhelmed with enough gratitude to embarrass them both, she pushed open the door and forced herself out before she did something really stupid. "I'll…um… Okay, bye." She imagined she could feel the warmth of his hazel eyes all the way into the building, and she refused to spoil the fantasy by turning around.

Once she'd run the gamut of good mornings and general concern after her face had been plastered on every local news outlet, she settled at her desk to review what needed to be dealt with today. She had the tasks in mind when an instant message from her boss, Elaine Jasper, popped up on her monitor: Stop in and see me ASAP.

Lissa stowed the purse that held little more than her temporary museum ID card, lip balm and twelve dollars she'd found in her dresser, and headed over. Lissa knew she'd been blessed by a good boss, as bosses went. Elaine could communicate up and down the food chain, ensuring their department was always picking up choice assignments from the art world and continually well-funded. Not an enviable task by any definition, and a challenge Lissa hoped to be prepared for in another decade or more. Right now she preferred the hands-on challenges more than the bureaucracy.

Elaine glanced up and smiled when Lissa came into view. She was a petite woman with an hourglass figure and a personality that stood ten feet tall. Her blond hair was always styled in a sleek bob unless they were working on a project. Then it was always pulled back and covered by a wrap she made look stylish better than anyone Lissa had met.

Elaine rounded the desk, sincere concern clouding her brown eyes. "Are you okay?" She held Lissa at arm's length, tsk-tsking over the fading marks Lissa had covered with makeup. The woman had a knack for spotting the fake or forged. "I listened to your voice mail last night, but I want to hear the whole story, face-to-face."

Once Lissa was seated, Elaine closed the door and

pulled up another guest chair rather than returning to her side of the ruthlessly organized desk. "Tell me what's going on."

"I can't tell you much more than I did on the voice mail." She laced her fingers together. Even knowing this conversation was inevitable, it was hard to get the words past the lump of grief and gritty fear lodged in her throat. "Noelle and I were attacked when we went out Friday night. I survived. She, um... Well, you know from the news reports that she didn't."

Elaine patted Lissa's white-knuckled hands. "I'm so sorry. I know you were closer than sisters. You didn't have to come in today."

"I need the distraction," Lissa admitted. Though it might have been fun, and the view superb, she couldn't have sat back and watched Carson work all day. Thinking about the key that might very well be in a killer's hands, she couldn't bear the idea of puttering around alone at the apartment, waiting for the next bad thing to find her. "Noelle's family scheduled a memorial service here in town for tomorrow," she said.

"We won't expect you to come in at all, then. I mean it," Elaine added when Lissa tried to protest. "Grieving takes time. It's better not to fight the process."

Lissa swallowed and gave a weak nod of agreement.

"Whatever we can do to make this easier, just say the word. You're part of our family. Lean on us. We're happy to support you."

It wasn't the first time she'd heard the phrase or felt the sincerity behind it, but the words just seemed to slip past her logic and sink into her heart this time. *Family* was a beautiful, powerful word, and while she loved her parents and appreciated the opportunities they'd provided, she'd never quite fit in with their lives. No question they loved her, too. They simply thrived on their work. Everything for her first sixteen years had revolved around their schedules. They believed that hard work was good, learning was a lifelong pursuit and immeasurable value was rooted in the past. After her first semester of college, she'd learned she wasn't built for that lifestyle.

"I would have called earlier, before the news broke," Lissa explained, "but I had trauma-related amnesia until yesterday morning."

Elaine gasped. "That must have been terrifying."

"It wasn't fun. Unfortunately, I still don't have full recall of the attack. I haven't been much help to the police."

Elaine leaned back and pursed her lips, her fingertip tapping the arm of the chair. "What's the last thing you clearly recall about Friday?"

"So far, it's our staff lunch on Friday. I remember all the chatter over the new additions to the American art gallery. We ordered from that new chicken salad place." The worried frown on Elaine's face warned her she'd messed up something. "What?"

"Chicken salad was two Fridays ago. Last Friday we ordered cheesesteaks because—"

"David wanted 'real man' food," Lissa finished as the fractured memory fell into place. "Oh, man. I know I had amnesia, but is everything in my head supposed to be this screwed up?"

"What did the doctors tell you?"

"To take it easy and give myself time to recover." Carson was close enough to a doctor that Lissa didn't feel guilty for fibbing about technicalities.

"It would be smart to follow that advice."

"Maybe, but I'd like to try to work. If it's too much and I get a headache, I'll go home early."

"Promise?"

"Absolutely." Lissa smiled, hoping the expression gave off more confidence than desperation. Here, behind the impenetrable walls of the museum, she felt safe from the person apparently bent on eliminating her along with her memories.

She returned to her desk, her head only a bit achy as she tried to piece together events of what was now a missing week. Last night, Carson insisted that she take care today not to overdo it. It was easy to assure him she'd be smart when she was riding the high of defiance by remaining in her apartment after the shooting on the roof. Of course, having Carson stay with her gave her courage a crucial boost.

Now reality set in. She wasn't nearly as together as she'd believed. In the wake of remembering Noelle had had a key to her apartment, Carson's suggestion to leave made more sense. With the near misses and frustrating discussions, it shouldn't have surprised her that her thoughts were bouncing and skittering like marbles tossed onto a concrete floor. Every time she tried to concentrate on one thing, it rolled out of her grasp.

After an hour of writing and rewriting a single email, she gave in and headed upstairs to the canteen for a coffee. She kept seeing chunks of time with Noelle, overlaid with flashes of Carson's smile, or worse, his stark, flat gaze when he'd been lost in his own nightmare.

She couldn't blame the scattered focus solely on Elaine's concern about her mixing up Friday lunches. She'd noticed similar gaps since she'd woken on Sunday with full recollection of who she was.

Back at her desk, the aromatic coffee filled the space, and she reviewed the team task list, looking for something mundane and physical she could contribute so the day wouldn't be a total waste. She found two video articles on preservation techniques Elaine had asked the team to view for later discussion, as well as several reports that needed to be logged into the system.

She took notes on the videos and managed to enter the reports with deliberate precision. Checking the clock, she saw she had a few hours left to the typical workday. To avoid email or social media, she poked around online, researching amnesia for a bit, before turning her flighty attention to Carson and Grant. Soon she was engrossed in a series of articles and police reports documenting crimes against first responders in the city. She read every scrap of information available about the attack on the ambulance that had changed Carson's life and killed his partner.

That led her to Sarah Neely's obituary. The tributes from her friends, family and colleagues gave Lissa a picture of a vibrant, tough woman who had been respected and loved.

Lissa had the impression that if Sarah and Noelle had known each other they would've been friends. Thinking of Noelle's memorial service, she did a search for the obituary, posted this morning by the funeral home assisting Noelle's parents with the arrangements. They'd done a lovely job with a challenging task, and Lissa's heart swelled as she read the long list of accomplishments her friend had racked up through her short life. The family directed donations in lieu of flowers to the children's research hospital Noelle had hoped to work for some day. Lissa immediately made a donation through her online bank account, but when she tried to add her comment to the outpouring of sympathy, her eyes burned with tears, and she clicked away before she lost her composure completely. Somehow, alternating between grief and numbness, she made it through the rest of her day, even updating the team task chart after two attempts. When the instant message window popped up, she clicked over and smiled at the notice from security that Carson had arrived before she'd had a chance to call him. Elaine caught her at the elevator and gave her a hug, letting her know they'd all be thinking of her tomorrow.

For the first time since she'd started at the museum, Lissa was utterly relieved to leave work behind. The late afternoon sunshine felt amazing on her face as she glanced around for Carson. She didn't see him or his truck near the door or in either nearby parking area. Confused, she reached for her cell phone, belatedly remembering that he had picked it up, along with her purse, at the police station. As adamant as he had been about keeping close to her, it seemed odd that he'd call and then not be waiting within sight. Doubling back to the museum entrance, she bumped into a hard and unyielding form. "Excuse me," she said, jumping back from the man she'd plowed into. "I was distracted," she added, utterly flustered. He wore a navy blazer over a white button-down shirt and khaki slacks, and his hair was combed back from his face, making his sharp features even more pronounced, despite the dark sunglasses.

"It happens," he muttered. He studied her as if he expected something more from her before striding off rapidly down the sidewalk.

Did she know him? Not today, she didn't. She couldn't

call the face familiar, and yet those brief seconds had given her a jolt of inexplicable alarm. He'd probably recognized her from the news reports. She tried to blow it off, blaming her reactions on the crazy bundle of nerves and increasing distress she'd been struggling with all afternoon.

Once more she searched the area for Carson. She wanted his calm voice and steady presence, and she didn't care that in her mind she was whining a little. Retreating back inside the museum, she used the phone at the security desk to call and verify where he was waiting for her.

"Perfect timing," he said. "I'm just pulling up."

A chill raised the hair at the back of her neck. She peered through the glass as the big gray truck rolled into view. "I'll be right out."

She asked the security guard on duty about the original notification that Carson had arrived. Linda looked it up while she shared the latest updates on her kids with Lissa. "Here it is. A phone call came in, and he asked us to let you know rather than letting us put the call through. Was that a problem?"

"No." Lissa forced her lips to curve upward into a smile. "Thanks so much, Linda. I'll see you Wednesday."

The guard's sympathy trailed her out the door.

Making a beeline for Carson's truck, Lissa gave a wide berth to the people milling about on the sidewalk. "You didn't call the security office, did you?"

The wide, welcoming smile on his face disappeared. "What happened?"

"Nothing." She said the word with a question in her voice. "Nothing bad," she clarified.

He put the car in Park, ignoring the line of vehicles behind him. "You look spooked. Tell me."

"Can we go?" She scanned the area. "I need some distance. He's long gone, anyway."

The car behind them honked loudly.

"Who are you talking about? What happened?"

She flicked her hands, urging him to move. "I'll tell you if you just get moving." She relaxed a fraction and wiped her palms on her slacks as Carson merged with the traffic. "I got the message you were here, so I came upstairs and outside to meet you." Suddenly what had seemed an innocent mistake took on a bigger significance. She didn't want the strange encounter to be that important, and yet she couldn't deny her intuitive recoil from the man she'd bumped into.

"And?" he prompted.

"And you weren't here. I turned around and ran smack into a stranger. It felt weird and awkward when he stared at me like he thought he knew me."

"Or that you should know him."

"Yes." Her skin went cold all over. "I'm putting it into that context now. I wish I could say 'better late than never.'" She rubbed her hands over her arms and then closed the air vents on her side of the truck cab. "But I *didn't* know him at all. I decided he must have recognized me from the news and was trying to place me."

"There was nothing familiar about him?"

"No," she said, wishing the seat would swallow her whole. She felt as if she was one of the new exhibits on display. "Have the locks at my apartment been changed?" The low-grade headache that had started just after lunch was threatening to become an all-out migraine.

"Yes."

"And my purse?"

He aimed his thumb at the space behind the seat. "I tucked it out of sight, expecting to park and walk in to meet you."

She wished that's exactly how it had happened. Closing her eyes, she tried an old exercise she'd learned in college to reframe the moment, envisioning how the pickup should have gone. It gave her a smidge of comfort. Twisting around in the seat, she pulled out the purse. "Thank goodness," she gushed at the familiar feel of the fabric strap in her hand. She gave in to the urge and hugged it close, thrilled to be reunited with the object.

"Happy?"

"Much, much happier," she said, feeling as if she'd taken another big leap toward full recovery. "Did the detective give you any trouble?" She pulled back the zipper and rooted through the inner pockets. Her cell phone was there, though the battery had died, and her keys, her wallet, her favorite pen and everything else were just as she'd left them.

"You can hook up the phone and get it charging," Carson suggested.

"It can wait until we're at my place," she said.

"We should make one stop before we do that." At the next stoplight, he used the voice command to dial Detective Werner's number.

Lissa smothered her groan of dismay when the detective picked up. Carson did all the talking, asking—directing, really—the detective to meet them at the Escape Club. His next call was to give Grant a heads-up about the impromptu meeting.

She wanted to wilt as they headed out to the pier. "You don't think the man who bumped me was random."

"Not a chance," Carson said.

She closed her eyes, bringing the stranger's face into view. "At least I can give you an accurate description."

"Good." Carson reached over and gave her shoulder a light squeeze. "A sketch and conversation, and we can let the detective figure out if the man fits any part of Noelle's case while we enjoy our evening."

It was a good plan, and she knew he was right. "I appreciate that you refer to this as Noelle's case. Somehow it makes it feel less like my responsibility."

"There's still no reason to believe you were anything but an unwilling bystander in this whole mess."

"From your lips to the detective's ear," she murmured, thinking about her jumbled memories and wondering how to tell him it appeared she was missing an entire week.

"He'll come around." Carson rubbed her shoulder again, and it took all her self-control to keep from leaning in to his touch. "You do realize you may never get it all back?"

She rubbed at the stress gripping her forehead like a vise. "I hope you're wrong, but I understand the possibility. I poked around online, looking for information on amnesia today."

"Did it give you a headache?"

"A little bit," she admitted with a wry bark of laughter. "And as far as my boss is concerned, you're a doctor."

He chuckled as he drove down the pier, parking again near the back door, although there were open spaces elsewhere reserved for employees. The detective's car wasn't in sight. "Ready?"

Not at all, but she nodded anyway. What were the

odds that the man she'd seen was related to Noelle's death? At this point she had no idea, but she knew they had to do everything to find out. Resisting the grim awareness settling like an anvil on her shoulders, she walked into the club with Carson.

Carson wanted to take her hand, to give her some tangible reassurance that it would work out. More than that, he wanted to take her home, but they needed to have this meeting. With luck, the man who'd bumped into her outside the museum would be a helpful lead for Werner's case. Carson didn't care for her being drawn out into the open without anyone nearby to keep her safe. If it had been the killer or someone tied to the killer who'd lured Lissa outside, why let her go after making an attempt on her life yesterday?

Grant greeted them in his office and then went off for a bit while Carson created a sketch of the man Lissa had seen. Grant interrupted once with soft drinks and a tray of appetizers for them. The next time Grant knocked on the open door, Detective Werner was at his shoulder, his face locked in that now-familiar expression of perpetual skepticism.

"We're just wrapping up," Carson said, setting aside the pencil and shaking out his hand. "She's got great recall," he added, just to tweak the detective.

Grant shot him a warning glance as the two men entered the office and the detective closed the door. Beside him, Lissa sucked in a startled breath as she studied the sketch. "That's him." She handed the sketch to Grant as if it burned her fingers, and Grant looked it over before handing it to the detective.

Carson watched the detective's face for any signs

of recognition and came up empty. He made a mental note not to play poker with the detective anytime soon. Maybe the man in the sketch was in the system for other crimes, or he was a doctor or some other authority figure from the hospital who fueled Lissa's current terror of medical establishments. Either way, she'd done more than her fair share today for Noelle's case.

He clenched his teeth over every small crease of pain and worry on her face as she explained what had happened outside the museum.

"He didn't say anything else?" Werner asked when she finished.

"No," she replied with a small, terse shake of her head. "I know he couldn't have been staring at me for very long, but it felt so strange, as if he was waiting for me to react."

"To me, that puts him firmly in the problem-child category," Carson said. "This wasn't a coincidence."

The detective muttered an oath and reluctantly agreed with him. "Your lack of memory may have saved your life," Werner said. "The techs did find one of the marked bullets in the evidence gathered from your rooftop. We're pushing hard to unravel this one. I'll add this sketch to the case file, go through some photo arrays myself and then show them to a few of Anson's coworkers."

"Noelle," Lissa whispered.

"Right." Werner's stoic poker face suddenly gave way, and he looked as weary as Lissa. "I want you both to keep an eye out for this man at the funeral tomorrow." He pushed to his feet and reached past Carson to shake Lissa's hand. "Thank you. I'll be at the station if you need me."

He walked out, and Grant hustled after him before

Carson could ask about formal protection or a safe house. Resigned, Carson shifted in his seat, unsure of the next good move. "What do you need?" he asked.

She didn't look up, her gaze on her hands while she twisted the band of silver on her thumb. "Quiet, I think."

As if on cue, the first band on tonight's card started warming up, and the bass rumbled through the floors. They both laughed, snapping the strain of the past few minutes.

"Then I guess we'd better head to your place," Carson said. Standing, he offered her his hand. The quick sizzle when she put her palm in his came as a surprise, and he knew he should resist rather than savor the effect. She looked up at him with those dark chocolate eyes, tilting her head to the side. It would take the smallest effort to lean forward and touch his lips to hers. Before he'd settled the internal debate between temptation and wisdom, Grant returned.

"You handled that like a couple of champs," he said, striding into the office with a big grin on his face. "I've got the kitchen working up some dinner for you to take home, unless you'd like to stay a while and enjoy the band. Katie's coming by in a bit." He smiled at the mention of his wife. "It's a good group tonight."

"That's really thoughtful." Lissa gave Carson's hand a squeeze. "Home is better for me tonight."

"She is pretty worn out after her day at work."

"That's normal, right?" Grant looked to Carson, got the affirmative nod. "Okay. The beating you took combined with the emotional toll of your loss…" Grant's face softened with sympathy as his voice trailed off. "Let's just say I've been there. It takes time."

Lissa's lips quirked up on one side. "So I've been told."

Carson enjoyed the way she kept her hand in his even though it wasn't necessary. "I wanted to ask Werner about assigning her more protection."

"No need," Grant said, sitting down behind his desk. "I talked to him yesterday evening after the incident at the apartment. When I wasn't satisfied with his answer, I put an alternative in place."

Carson was grateful for Grant and his extensive contacts. "Were you going to mention this alternative to us?"

He grinned. "I just did. Sit back down for a minute." He waved them into the chairs as he settled his stocky frame behind the desk again. "I made a few calls on your behalf," he said to Lissa. "I've asked a friend to work out a protective detail for you. Someone will have eyes on your apartment at all times, and others will be around you, as well. You won't see them, and they won't get in the way of the PPD, but I hope you'll feel better knowing they're out there."

"Thanks," Carson said with feeling. Lissa echoed his gratitude. He could keep an eye on her personally, monitor her health recovery, but he didn't have the skills of real cops or investigators that she needed.

"Who's paying for all of this?" she asked.

Grant shooed away her concern with a flick of his fingers. "Don't worry about it. You won't get a bill, and you sure don't owe me anything. I've been around the city long enough to earn a few favors. People from all over enjoy the Escape Club, both the entertainment and assistance facets of our establishment, and we've learned it all evens out."

When the kitchen called to say the food order was

ready, Grant walked them out. Back at the apartment, Carson handed her the new key while he gathered up the food and her extra purse. He could see the exhaustion rolling off her. It felt more like a mountain than two flights of stairs as they climbed up to her apartment, but the scents from the food spurred them both onward.

As they sat at her small table that visually separated her kitchen and sitting room, eating the classic spaghetti-and-meatball dinner, Carson felt increasingly out of his element despite the generally friendly conversation they were having. What was he playing at here?

She didn't need his constant observation anymore, only an occasional reminder to rest to let her mind and body heal. He could do that by phone, now that she'd reclaimed hers. She was smart enough to stay inside behind the new locks and the security system. There was no need for him to be within arm's reach every minute anymore. And with Grant's private team watching out for her, he felt it was past time to offer to let her have her privacy back.

He told himself it was more than a tidy collection of excuses. He had valid reasons to step back from her. He preferred his space, too. A little distance would help him reclaim his perspective, and having some time apart would help him forget her soft skin and silky hair and the light citrus scent of her shower gel. Probably.

He couldn't forget how they'd met. She was basically a patient, and if there was one cardinal rule in his profession, it was to *not* get involved with the patients. Even if he overlooked that rule, she had too much on her mind already without dealing with the attraction he was struggling to keep hidden.

He couldn't claim to know her well, but he recognized she was a woman who needed a man who didn't flake out and panic at the first sign of trouble. She needed someone dependable who could make a commitment and keep it. He hadn't been that kind of man since Sarah died.

As they were cleaning up from dinner and storing the leftovers, he forced himself to say the necessary words. "I should probably get going. You'll need—" Her stricken expression stopped him cold. "What?"

"Please stay." She took a step toward him and caught herself, her hand gripping the edge of the countertop. "I—I don't want to be alone."

"You're not alone," he pointed out. "Grant's team is outside."

"It's not the same. I—" She bit her lip, stopping whatever else she meant to say.

He tried again. "I know I forced myself in here, but if there's another friend I can call for you, that might be better all around."

"I want you." Her deep brown eyes went wide with embarrassment, and she clapped her hand over her mouth. "I mean, um, I want you to *stay*. If you can. I'm sure it's an imposition and inconvenience." She closed her eyes, pink flooding her cheeks as she waved her hands in front of her face. "Good grief, shut me up."

He caught her hands and held on. "I don't *want* to go," he said when she met his gaze. "I just thought I'd invaded your privacy enough for one day."

"You haven't. You've been the only constant, Carson." She took a deep breath. "Please, if you can, stay one more night."

"You got it," he promised before he could give a more sensible response.

"Thank you," she whispered.

He thought he could lose himself in her gorgeous eyes

as the desire to kiss her surged through his bloodstream again. He fought for control, giving himself a fast, mean lecture on professionalism. His body didn't give a damn. She might have remembered she was single, but that didn't give him the right to take advantage of her while she coped with overwhelming grief and loss.

"You should get some rest," he said, still holding her hands. "Work was harder than you anticipated, wasn't it?"

"Yes," she admitted. "Gnats have infinitely more focus than I did today." Her thumbs stroked absently over the backs of his hands. "Could we watch a movie?"

The small, innocent touches set his skin on fire. "You really should just rest." And he should let go. In a minute.

"Rest is hard when it doesn't involve anything fun."

He slowly tugged his hands free. "Go on," he suggested. He needed her to move before he did something stupid and kissed her until neither of them could remember their own names.

"Not even a movie?"

"Not after the day you've had."

"All right." She turned on her heel, aiming for the bedroom, but she paused at the door. "What if—"

His brain filled in the rest of that sentence with invitations and images that left him so hard and aching he didn't hear her. "Pardon?" he asked, breaking free of the sensual haze to find her waiting for an answer.

A little frown creased her brow. "I asked if we could just sit and talk, with the lights turned low."

Her loneliness was obvious, and he understood all too well what it felt like to lose a best friend. He couldn't deny her request. "Sure, we can do that."

Her smile flashed, and it seemed as if a weight had fallen off her shoulders. "Give me just a second."

She disappeared into the bedroom, and he finished the dishes and dimmed the lights. He should probably have taken out the trash for her but decided it could wait until morning. Protective detail or not, he didn't see the sense in running that errand in the dark. He was sure Noelle's killer wanted Lissa silenced, and Carson didn't pose much of a barrier. No matter how he felt toward Lissa, it came down to ability. Experience had taught him he didn't have the intimidation factor or instincts to drive off a killer.

He turned at the sound of Lissa's bedroom door opening, and his lust returned with an uncomfortable vengeance. She'd pulled on gray leggings that clung to every curve and a pale blue shirt that left her deep brown eyes sparkling. She'd removed her makeup, donned fuzzy socks and pulled her hair back into a loose ponytail that spilled over one shoulder.

She crossed the room and sank into one end of the love seat, her feet tucked underneath her. He settled on the opposite end, propping one ankle on the other knee, and waited, regretting his agreement. How was he supposed to chat with her when every cell in his body wanted her?

To his immense relief, she started the conversation. "At one point today," she said, "I followed my scattered thoughts to Noelle's obituary."

"That couldn't have been easy." He tried to shrink deeper into his side.

She shifted, putting her back to the armrest so she could face him. The movement brought her foot across his thigh. "It wasn't," she replied, apparently oblivious to the war waging inside him. Her shy smile appeared. "But since I remembered my banking log-in, I made a donation to the charity fund her parents set up in her memory." She told him about Noelle's ultimate nursing goal, and he found himself taken right back to how the department had done something similar for Sarah on behalf of first responders.

"It sounds like you had an amazing friend."

"She really was." Lissa took a profound interest in the seam near the knee of her leggings. "I think I have a bigger memory gap than I thought. My boss told me that I misremembered last Friday."

"How so?"

She refused to meet his gaze. "We have a staff lunch every Friday, and I got this past Friday mixed-up with the one before it."

"Even people with no memory issues or trauma troubles do that all the time."

She glanced at him from under her lashes but didn't hold his gaze. "You're right. It just makes me wonder." She inhaled deeply and released the breath slowly, pulling her knees to her chest. "What if I remember something wrong and Detective Werner hauls in the wrong person?"

"That's what evidence and lawyers are for," Carson assured her.

"Do you think evidence and lawyers will be enough if the man who bumped into me today is involved?"

"What exactly are you asking?"

"I don't know." She rubbed at her forehead again. "Did you lose your memory after the ambulance was attacked?"

"No." If only he had, the tragedy might have been

easier to cope with. "It's still way too clear for me most of the time." On a whisper, he admitted the ugly truth, "I'm jealous of your amnesia."

"I bet you are." She rested her head against the back of the love seat and went quiet. "What if I'm not remembering because I don't want to?"

"I don't think brains are generally that cooperative." He uncrossed his legs and leaned forward, bracing his elbows on his knees. He couldn't look at her, not when his failures were rolling like a bad movie trailer through his head again. "Part of me hopes you never remember, or that if you do remember, it won't be the details of your beating or the actual murder."

When her hand landed on his shoulder, he shrugged, but she didn't take the hint. "Have you ever read the police reports from the night Sarah died?" she asked.

"No." He shot her a look. "Don't tell me you have."

"Not to pry. I looked because of the detective's implication that Noelle knew the men who attacked us. Don't you wonder about the connection between those marked bullets used against Sarah, Noelle and us?"

"Might be a useless lead," he said, desperate to get off this topic. "Could be a rival using the marked bullets to throw off the police."

"Or it might be precisely the detail that ties it all together," she said.

"Trust me, it's better to leave this stuff to the cops." He stood up, searching for breathing room, but it was impossible to find in her small apartment. "You're not supposed to be thinking this hard."

She stood up, her footsteps quiet with those fuzzy socks. "I'll go to bed, but I think you have forgotten a few things."

"Like what?" He'd sure as hell forgotten where he'd left his sanity and common sense. He turned his back on her, unable to meet her gaze for fear of the pity he'd see in her eyes. Hell, after the shooting yesterday, he'd lost himself in the terror of Sarah's dying breaths and blood, rendering him useless to Lissa. Thank God Grant had called in a qualified team to protect her.

He gave a start when he felt her arms slide around him, her breasts a gentle, tantalizing pressure against his back. "You were a hero, Carson."

A hero would've saved his partner, he thought bitterly. A hero would have pushed her out of the way and taken the bullet. He could have tackled the robbers or done just about anything that might lead to an arrest and real justice. But no. He hadn't done any of those things.

Her arms tightened, then slid away. "I read the reports." Her voice came from the shadows near her bedroom door. "Because of *your* actions, Sarah's organs saved four different people. Because you, Carson, kept her body going long enough to reach the hospital, four families have more time to live and laugh and love."

The bedroom door closed with a soft click, and he stumbled to the bathroom. He turned on the shower taps and stared at his reflection in the mirror while the water rattled through the pipes.

Was she right? *No.* He'd fallen for the ploy and they'd been ambushed. The department might not have written him up, but if he'd been smart, Sarah would still have been here. Still, Lissa's words echoed in his head. *Four lives saved.*

Had he really done something right that night? It had to be some public relations crap generated by the

PFD. He couldn't remember anything but failing his best friend and partner as her life drained away, her blood going cold on his hands.

Chapter 7

Lissa rolled over in bed and checked the clock, relieved to see it was just past six. Finally she could get up and stop pretending to sleep. She cracked open the door to check on Carson, and her heart stuttered to see the empty room. Then she caught the sound of water in the kitchen sink.

Of course he hadn't left, though he'd had every right to walk out and never look back after she'd prodded at his painful past last night. As if the funeral today wasn't enough emotional upheaval to cope with, it would be worse after the restless night. She'd berated herself through the wee hours for forcing her agenda onto Carson and alienating her only ally. Just because she wanted to help him, to give back in some small way after all he'd done for her, it didn't mean her approach was the help he needed.

She told herself to grow a spine, walk in there and apologize for being an insensitive jerk. If she was lucky, he'd forgive her and they would find a way around the inevitable awkwardness. At the last second, her courage faltered, and she slipped into the bathroom, cursing the squeaky hinge. Leaning her back against the closed door, she realized he'd just finished in here. The masculine scent of his shaving cream lingered in the air, and the small room was still warm and damp from the steam of his shower.

A knock sounded at the door, startling a little hiccup out of her.

"Lissa?"

His voice was right next to her ear, as if he was leaning on the other side of the door the way she leaned on this side. "Yes?"

"Can you hand me my clothes?"

"Your…oh." They were on a hanger, on the hook mounted behind the door. She plucked the hanger off the hook and opened the door. Her intended apology evaporated as she gawked at him.

The view of his bare chest sent her heart skipping. Seeing those defined muscles, the temptation to reach out and touch him, nearly obliterated all common sense. She thrust the hanger with his clothing at him and closed the door before lust got the better of her. Jumping him would only make things worse after last night.

When she'd wasted the maximum amount of time in the bathroom, she listened at the door, trying to figure out where Carson was in the apartment. It didn't matter. The only place to avoid him was here in the bathroom or her bedroom, and the only way to get there was to open the door. Dressed in yoga pants and a camisole, her hair bundled into a clip, she opened the door and tried to find some degree of maturity in the awkward situation.

"I made breakfast," he said quietly as soon as the traitorous door hinge squeaked.

"Thanks." She didn't have to turn around to know he was sitting at the table. "Give me fifteen minutes?"

"No problem."

She took ten minutes to breathe and stretch, hoping to make up for the lack of sleep and bolster her nerve— assuming she had any nerve left. She wove her hair into a braid to keep it out of the way and flowed from one restorative pose to the next. Her breath steadied and her pulse calmed until she felt she might actually survive the challenges ahead.

Pulling a black shirt and her black wrap-around skirt from the closet, she dressed quickly, leaving hair, makeup, accessories and shoes for after breakfast. The only demand she would put on herself today, after she apologized to Carson, was to remember all of Noelle's good qualities. She'd focus on all the happy moments and good times they'd shared. Her friend's smile and laughter would be the wall she used to hold back the tide of sorrow and questions surrounding those final hours.

Out of excuses and time, Lissa opened the bedroom door. Carson was standing at the window overlooking the street, the sunlight streaming around him. His back was to her, thankfully, so she had a moment to gather the thoughts that scattered at the sight of him in his dress clothes. The crisp white shirt highlighted his shoulders, tapering to his trim waist and the dark slacks skimming over his long, lean legs.

He had a presence that filled the small apartment, although aside from her fascination with him, she couldn't point out a single thing as overwhelming. Yet having him here seemed to put everything off kilter. Not in a bad way, if she disregarded the circumstances, just a different way of seeing her space and her life.

She moved and he swiveled around, his hazel eyes pinning her in place. "Hungry?" he asked with an easy smile that made her heart ache. Maybe the overwhelming factor was his infinite patience with her. He had every right to snarl and snap at her, but that steady smile remained in place.

Today would surely drag his recent loss right back to the surface, and she felt terrible about not taking that into consideration when she'd begged him to stay last night. "You don't have to go with me," she blurted into the charged silence. "There will be plenty of people around, so I'll be safe."

His smile faded. "None of those people have an accurate description of the man you saw yesterday."

She didn't know what to do with her hands, and she fiddled with the tie on her skirt. "I don't want this mess to be any harder on you than it has been."

"I won't panic again, Lissa," he replied. "You can count on me."

Her attention snapped to his face, caught the muscle jumping in his freshly shaved jaw. "That's not what I meant." She didn't know how to articulate her thoughts. They were such a jumble.

One eyebrow lifted in challenge as he moved past her to the kitchen. "Let's just eat," he suggested.

She took the hint and dropped the subject. It wasn't her place—they barely knew each other—to change the path he was walking to get over the loss of his best friend and partner. Her mouth watered as he pulled a tray of biscuits from the oven, along with a casserole filled with sausage gravy. "Whoa. My hero," she whispered. "How did you manage this? I'm ashamed to admit I didn't even smell it while you were cooking."

"It was early," he admitted, serving them both.

At the table, the hearty comfort food did wonders for her mood, and she didn't feel quite as jittery. "I've stuffed my purse with tissues, and I'm hoping like crazy her parents aren't expecting me to say anything at the service."

"What you expect from yourself is more important today."

"She was their daughter," Lissa pointed out. "They're wonderful people."

He shrugged and dragged a bite of a golden biscuit through the last of his gravy. "Yes, and you being there will be a comfort to them, but don't cheat yourself out of what you need in order to have closure and say goodbye."

She knew he spoke from a much too recent experience. "I'll keep it in mind."

He studied her over the rim of his coffee cup. "You might also keep in mind," he said, replacing the cup on the table, "grief changes people."

She sensed a deeper warning, a cautious undertone that had nothing to do with his personal pain about Sarah. "You're worried about me."

"Yes, I am."

"Because?"

"Yesterday, the roof, the attack on Friday are all enough factors to put anyone on guard." He folded his arms at the edge of the table and leaned in. "Noelle's parents may be the nicest people in the world, but they've lost a daughter, and you were the last one to see her alive."

"And I haven't even called them."

"You weren't in any condition to do so," he reminded her. "And you're still recovering. I don't want you to feel pressured by them, the situation or anything else that might crop up."

He meant her lost memories. She blotted her lips with the paper napkin and then balled it up in her fist, squeezing it tighter and tighter. "You don't want me to go at all."

"That isn't true. I wish the circumstances were different. The service is important, but I want you to go in there, eyes wide open."

"I promise."

His warning followed her through the morning. No activity before they left the apartment distracted her enough to drown it out. Not even the shoes biting into her heels as they walked into the funeral home could keep that advice from swirling back to the front of her thoughts.

As they joined the receiving line before the service, Lissa stared at the closed casket and the beautiful pictures of Noelle enlarged for display. Her pulse tripped each time the line advanced, knowing she would soon face Dr. and Mrs. Anson, the couple who'd once offered her the simple gifts of acceptance and time her parents had never spared for her.

Suddenly the line cleared and she faced Noelle's parents. She felt Carson at her side, his hand light and warm at her back. She could run if she wanted and he'd help her get away. If only she could take that last step and offer the Ansons a better answer than "My brain won't let me remember who killed your daughter." But her feet were rooted to the carpet, her nose about to burst from the fragrant assault of so many flowers. "I'm so sorry."

Mrs. Anson inhaled sharply and shook her head, drawing Lissa into her arms. "Sweetheart. Oh, sweetheart. We've been worried about you."

Over the older woman's shoulder, Lissa saw Dr. Anson brush tears from his eyes as he came forward and joined the embrace. "You'll sit with the family." His tone left no room for debate.

As sniffles subsided, she reached for Carson's hand. "This is Carson Lane. He took care of me...after."

"Thank you." Mrs. Anson covered his hand with both of hers. "We've been so worried for Lissa since the detective called."

"She's well?" Dr. Anson asked as if she wasn't standing right there, in one piece, the last of the bruises hidden under her makeup. "No one would give me the name of her doctor or even the hospital," he grumbled.

"We tried to call and it went to voice mail," Mrs. Anson said.

"My phone and I got separated," Lissa explained.

Carson smiled at her as he addressed the couple. "She's recovering well. Just a short-term amnesia," he explained.

She could've kissed him for leaving out the rest of the details of her arrival at the club. Noelle's parents had more questions, but they'd stalled the line for long enough. "We'll get out of the way," Lissa said. She didn't want them to have this discussion here, or anywhere, really. The Ansons would only be disappointed in her faulty memory. Dr. Anson moved with them at his wife's nod. "You'll fill us in later," Dr. Anson said. He motioned them to take seats in the front row, reserved for immediate family. "Thank you both for being here. It is a comfort and a relief to both of us."

"That went better than I expected," Carson murmured, handing her a small order of service from the stack on the aisle seat.

"The Ansons are wonderful people." Lissa was baffled by the warm reception. Could it really be that they didn't blame her? She wished she and Carson had been allowed to sit further back, but she wouldn't move even though it felt as if she was on display and everyone was staring at her.

"My apologies if I made you nervous about it," Carson said.

"No." She swallowed a fresh wave of tears as she watched the funeral director cut short the line to start the service. "It's not that. You helped me be ready for anything. Hope for the best, prepare for the worst, right?"

As the funeral director deftly prepared for the service to begin, Dr. and Mrs. Anson approached, holding hands, their smiles wobbling. Dr. Anson seated his wife next to Lissa, taking the aisle seat. Mrs. Anson surprised Lissa again by reaching for her hand.

Lissa tried to concentrate on the service, on the messages designed to celebrate Noelle's life. Hemmed in by Carson on one side and Mrs. Anson on the other, she managed not to lose her composure entirely as a few of Noelle's coworkers stood up to share special memories. It helped to keep reminding herself that her pain and heartache were merely a fraction of what the Ansons were coping with.

Finally they were standing for the last hymn. An organ played as the pallbearers came forward to guide the casket out. Her shoes irritated the blisters on her heels and pinched her toes, and Lissa was grateful for the trivial discomfort as she peered at the beautiful photos of her friend for the last time. As part of the family, she and Carson filed out with Dr. and Mrs. Anson behind the casket.

Noelle's casket was loaded into the hearse and would be transported to her hometown, where her parents would endure more sympathy at one more service tomorrow before they could bury their daughter. The finality of it covered Lissa from head to toe, threatening to smother her. Her friend was gone and the killer free because she couldn't remember anything helpful.

The sunlight felt too bright for the sorrow and waves of black-clad mourners pouring out of the funeral home. At the limo designated for family use, Carson's protests were honored once he promised he would bring Lissa straight to the luncheon at a nearby restaurant.

"How can they bear it?" she murmured when they reached the privacy of Carson's truck. "Why are they being so nice to me?"

"They seem to think of you as their own."

It was a strange concept. "I love them, Carson. They were so kind to me and the example of the kind of family I want to create some day. More than anything, I want to be sure Noelle's killer is brought to justice."

"I understand."

She turned at the hard edge in his voice, studying his profile. He did know exactly what she was going through. "Thanks for sticking it out with me."

"I'm glad you could say goodbye here."

"My boss would probably let me go to the interment tomorrow, but I don't think I can."

"Your decision."

"I'm rambling again and you're—" She broke off, startled when he veered out of the line of cars headed to the luncheon and circled back to the funeral home. "What is it?"

"The man who bumped into you yesterday was at the funeral. I spotted him as we left the chapel."

"Really?" She'd completely forgotten to look for him. "I'm a horrible friend."

"You're grieving." He rounded the block, the truck rocking a little on a sharp right turn. "One more reason for me to be here today."

"What are you planning to do?"

"If we're lucky, he hasn't left yet and we can get some useful information from his car," he said.

"Oh." She was so far out of her element with all of this, overwhelmed by unceasing currents of emotion. She decided to stop being useless and studied the people milling about in the parking lot as Carson cruised through the center row. "I tried to put a name to his face last night or put his face into context, but only managed to keep myself awake."

"I know what you mean." Carson's fingers drummed along the top of the steering wheel. "I was sure that Werner would've figured out the name that goes with that face by now. There!" He kept his hand under the dash as he pointed. "That's him, right?"

She considered the man Carson pointed out. "Climbing into the blue sedan, yes." She opened her purse to write down the plate number but found only tissues, a small tin of mints and the bulletin from the service. "Do you have a pen?"

"Glove box," he replied. "What are the odds we can get a full ID on this guy?"

Lissa didn't answer the rhetorical question as Carson cautiously trailed the blue sedan. She agreed completely with his decision. Noelle's parents wouldn't be happy if they missed lunch, but if this man was even remotely related to Friday's trouble, Lissa wanted to know sooner rather than later, so the Anson family could have peace.

Carson remained several car lengths behind the sedan as it headed for the west side. He'd expected the driver to aim for the Penn campus, where the crime on Friday had likely started. Assumptions like that one made it clear why he was a paramedic and not a cop. He leaped to conclusions without enough evidence and let his opinion cloud his judgment.

"Where does Dr. Anson practice?" he asked Lissa.

"He's a surgeon in Allentown. Well respected."

"Have you always been afraid of hospitals?" He kept his eyes on the blue sedan as he waited for her answer.

"No. My recent resistance must be related to where and how those men came after us. I don't recall any other reasons to detest hospitals or doctors."

She believed that by now, if Dr. Anson had been any cause of that, she would have remembered it along with her other memories of Noelle's family. "How do you think this man is connected? Assuming he's connected."

Carson shifted in his seat, the suit jacket bunching behind him. "He must have known Noelle or the family somehow. He appeared to be alone at the service. He left alone."

"Are we going to follow him all day?"

Carson wanted to say yes and knew it was the wrong answer. He'd been hung up on resolving this since Werner had mentioned the matching bullets. He couldn't bear the idea that Noelle would be targeted by a violent gang that had successfully avoided prosecution too many times to count.

"No." He goosed the gas pedal. "I'll get close enough to read the license plate, and then we can head back to your place or the luncheon. Though I'd vote for your place. I want to get out of this suit."

"Me, too." She laughed. "I mean, I want out of my funeral clothes, too."

"Got it." Though now that image was dancing in his head. He couldn't deny the sparks that went off under his skin when she'd caught him in the towel, but this was the wrong time.

Carson accelerated a little more, and Lissa wrote the plate number on her hand and then called and left a message for the detective. Carson eased back again and took the next available exit from the expressway.

"They're expecting us at the luncheon," Lissa reminded him. "As much as I'd rather skip it, I feel obligated to show up."

"We can do that." He navigated the exit ramp and the lights, pulling back onto the expressway and heading to the luncheon. "We should probably brainstorm some excuses for being late."

They tossed around a few ideas on the way but didn't have a chance to use them. Carson's phone rang, and when he answered, Grant's voice filled the car. "Is Lissa still with you?"

"Yes."

"Right here," she said. "What's happened?"

"The team watching the house saw a woman dressed in black go into your apartment a few minutes ago. Now there's smoke pouring out of the kitchen window."

Lissa clapped a hand over her mouth, her eyes hot with temper.

"I was sure you hadn't dropped her off," Grant said.

"Not a chance," Carson confirmed. He reached over and clasped her free hand. "How bad is the fire?"

"Small and nearly out. The man on-site called it in immediately. PFD is on scene. I get the impression it's not a total loss."

"We're on our way," Carson said.

He slid his fingers up, cuffed her wrist and felt her pulse going haywire under his fingertips. "Not a total loss," he reminded her, a little worried now that she'd stopped speaking.

"Right," she agreed. "I'm okay." She picked up his phone from the console and searched for the restaurant's number from the navigation app he had open. "I'll call the restaurant and ask them to give the Ansons a message."

He listened to her fib about tire trouble. "Well done."

She pushed a hand through her hair, dislodging the combs holding the long tresses up off her neck. "I'll call them once I know they're home tonight," she said as she struggled to fix her hair.

When she gave up and just shook out that mass of sable silk, he was grateful for the distraction of keeping the truck on the road, in his lane. *Down, boy.* In almost any other situation, he could have given in to the sensual allure. And destroyed her trust in him. He flexed his fingers on the steering wheel.

"Carson."

He shot her a look when her voice cracked on his name. Had she figured out where his mind had gone? "What?"

"I just realized the killer must have gone through Noelle's apartment." She broke off on a sputter of fury. "I should've gone there first."

"You were incapacitated, Lissa. The police would have done that by now."

"It doesn't matter. I have to figure out what happened." She sucked in a quick breath when he made the turn and she saw the collection of emergency vehicles outside her house. "I can't take this." She curled forward as far as the seat belt allowed and cradled her head in her hands. "I have to remember all of it."

Whatever memory or misplaced guilt had set her off, the curses were flowing in earnest. Better than tears, he hoped, parking as close to her place as he could manage. He hurried around to her side of the truck and opened her door, drawing her into his arms.

She pounded her fists to his chest, then just wrapped herself around him. The woman was a wreck, and he was helpless against the natural progression of grief compounded by the continued violence aimed at her. While he'd been through something equally traumatizing eight months ago, the men who'd robbed the ambulance and killed Sarah had disappeared. Whatever Lissa had witnessed, they were determined to cause her as much grief as possible before they finished her off.

His blood chilled at the thought. He liked her grit, her persistence and the compassion she showed despite her dreadful circumstances. There was something between them. Maybe it was only the shared connection of terrible loss, but she was the first person he enjoyed talking with since losing Sarah. Damned if he was going to let some gang or murder keep him from knowing her better.

As her grief subsided, he ran his hand up and down her spine. "Better?"

"A little." She tipped her head to peek at the house and the sliver of the third floor they could see through the trees from this angle. "I'm still mad. My neighbors could have been hurt or—"

"Mad is perfect. Your neighbors are fine." He shifted so they stood side by side, his arm around her shoulders. "We're going to figure this out. Me, Grant, Werner, whoever it takes, whatever it takes, we won't give up until we know you're safe."

He pressed his lips to her hair and reached for her hand as they walked to the corner. They headed for the cluster of people milling around on the sidewalk across the street from her house.

"Your things were in there, too," she said. "I'm sorry."

"Nothing that can't be replaced," he promised.

She stopped short and looked up into his eyes, then down at their joined hands. "I want to tell you to get far away from me, for your own good, but I'm too selfish."

Unable to resist, he tucked her hair behind her ear. "If you tried, you'd only learn what a lousy listener I am, and I'm trying to keep my biggest flaws a secret." He recognized his friend Daniel near the truck. "Come on this way. I want you to meet that friend who works construction when he isn't at the firehouse."

Carson introduced Lissa to Daniel, ignoring the quizzical look his friend gave to their joined hands and funeral attire. He sent Lissa a reassuring smile. "You live on the third floor?"

"Yes."

"Great space," he said. "I overheard the chief talking with the landlord, and your neighbors have been notified of the problem." He gestured to the crowd of first responders. "No one was hurt, and it's not as bad as it looks from out here."

Carson glanced up to the window as Lissa did. Flames had charred the window casing, and a black sooty scar rose up and over the roofline. They had caught this one fast. His heart gave a weird kick as he imagined how much worse it could have been if Lissa had been inside at the time or if Grant hadn't kept someone on alert.

Still holding her hand, Carson felt her tension ebb away. "Thanks," he said to Daniel.

"Chief has all the official details. See ya." With a quick wave, Daniel loped toward his fire truck.

They crossed the street and joined the chief, who was speaking with a small group of people closer to the house. Carson was braced for the worst and startled when an older woman with thick, steel-gray curls and ebony skin caught Lissa in a tight hug.

"My landlord," Lissa mouthed over the woman's shoulder. "Mrs. Green, this is my friend Carson Lane," she said when the landlord released her. "He took me to Noelle's funeral today."

"I'm so glad she was with a friend," Mrs. Green told Carson. She patted Lissa's hand. "We'll forget this month's rent, sweetheart." She grabbed Lissa in another hug and rocked back and forth for a moment. "They tell me you can't stay here until after the repairs are done."

"How bad is it?"

"Not bad. You'll see when they walk you through." Mrs. Green fluttered a hand over her heart. "Oh, I'm so thankful. So thankful. It could have been so much worse."

"Thank you," Carson said. He cut the conversation

short when he spied Werner stalking up to the scene. "Looks like the police need to talk with Lissa."

Mrs. Green turned back to the fire chief while a uniformed officer and the detective escorted Carson and Lissa up to the porch, pointing out where the new locks had been forced open. They walked in, and as the acrid stench of smoke and melted paint clogged the stairwell, Carson paused. Did she really need to see this?

"You might not want to look," he warned her.

"My imagination will be worse," she said, motioning for him to keep going.

When they reached the landing, Werner gave a low whistle and Lissa gasped, reaching back for Carson's hand. The apartment had clearly been tossed. Someone, presumably the woman seen entering the apartment, had conducted a frantic search until Grant's man had interrupted. The door to the attic was splintered, and the entire space smelled like a fire pit without the happy-campfire ambiance.

While Lissa fumed over the damages and confirmed nothing obvious had been taken, Carson took pictures on his cell phone and sent them on to Grant. Werner took a few pictures and excused himself quickly.

The reply from Grant came back a moment later. Salvage what you can and bring her to ladies' night.

Carson choked back a laugh. The famous Escape Club cosmopolitans might be just what Lissa needed, the way this day was shaping up. A night out wasn't the conventional post-funeral activity, but he thought Grant had the right idea. Too much quiet to think would only leave her more agitated and frustrated with the gaps in her memory.

He couldn't believe that he, king of solitude and introspection, was about to recommend a night out for drinks and dancing to a grieving woman. It sounded like the epitome of hypocritical, and yet he knew he'd make the suggestion.

"Well, it's official. I need to relocate while they clean it up and process the scene. I'm allowed to pack some clothing, assuming none of it reeks of smoke." Her nose crinkled as she looked at the mess.

"Pack whatever you want," he said. "We can drop it off at a dry cleaner. Be sure to pack your dancing shoes," he said, trailing her to the bedroom. Either the smoke wasn't as bad back here or he was getting used to it.

"Seriously?"

He nodded. "Grant invited us to ladies' night."

She stared at him, eyes wide and mouth agape. "That's absurd," she said, turning to survey her closet. "The last thing I need tonight is a noisy club."

He walked up behind her, not wanting anyone else to overhear and tattle on him for the hypocrisy he was about to deliver. "I know it sounds absurd, but believe me, the change of scenery will do you good. Me, too," he added, hoping to appeal to her innate concern for others.

She spun around, nearly catching him with an elbow, hands planted on her hips. "You expect me to believe you went dancing after your friend's funeral?"

"No," he said through clenched teeth. "But maybe I should have." He took a breath, struggling to find the words that would help her understand the wisdom behind Grant's plan. Instead, his gaze drifted to her mouth, the sweet bow of her upper lip, the tempting fullness of the lower, and his only thoughts were how good those lips would feel against his. "I'll just wait out there."

"Stop." She grabbed his sleeve and held on. "I'm

sorry. That was out of line." Her lips parted as she moistened her lips. While he was mesmerized by that view, one of her fine-boned hands slid up the back of his neck.

Then her lips met his in a tentative and inviting exploration. A wealth of needs exploded in his system and his mouth shaped hers, learned hers as they kissed. He wrapped her close, reveling in the press of her soft, sweet body all along his. She gasped again and his tongue swept into the heat of her mouth, teasing out layers of need and desire.

To hell with the club, he thought. He'd be fine right here for the rest of the night. The rest of the week.

"Miss Baxter?"

They sprang apart like a couple of teenagers caught in the sudden flash of a porch light.

The uniformed officer stepped into the doorway. "We'd like to clear the scene if you're packed."

"Right. Of course." Her cheeks were bright red. "Just one more minute."

"Can I help?" Carson asked, reluctant to stray from her now that he knew the sensuality of her touch, her lips.

She shot him a long look under her lashes. "Better if you focus on collecting whatever you brought over."

She had to know that small taste of her didn't satisfy him in the least. No, it only fueled his desire for her. He walked out with the cop, stopping to grab his gear from the bathroom and toss it into his duffel bag. He was tempted to leave it all here as it reeked of smoke from the fire. Thank goodness they could put it all in the bed of the truck so they wouldn't have to purge the smoke from the truck upholstery, too.

She emerged from the bedroom with a wheeled suitcase, a backpack and an oversize tote. Depositing the suitcase and backpack with him, she carried the tote into the bathroom. A few minutes later, she reappeared and declared herself ready.

The cop escorted them outside. With the emergency vehicles gone, the bystanders had wandered off. They loaded everything into the back of his truck, and she gave a little wave to her landlady before they drove away.

"Grant wants to see us because of the break-in and fire?"

"I'm sure there are several factors," he replied. Should he mention the kiss? Better to let her bring it up, he decided. "We'll drop off your clothes for cleaning and get settled at my place. I assumed my place was where you wanted to stay."

"Yes, that's fine." She laced her fingers in her lap, her knuckles standing out, white against her black skirt.

Maybe she expected an apology, but he didn't see how the kiss was his fault. She'd started it, and he was only human. He shifted a little in the seat, but it was impossible to get truly comfortable.

"I'm *not* sorry," she said abruptly when they'd dropped off the clothes and gotten back in the truck.

"Pardon me?"

"You're really playing it that way?" The question sounded more like a snarl. "All right." She smoothed her hands over her lap, her gaze straight ahead. "I am not sorry I kissed you."

Damn. He had sisters, and he'd known every facet of Sarah's personality, and still the only thing he knew to do with a woman in a mood as sharp and dangerous as Lissa's was to remain calm and confident. Perceived detachment could be as disastrous as focused interest.

"I enjoyed it," he replied as casually as he could manage. "I hope it won't be the last time you kiss me," he added, testing her reaction.

To his surprise, she didn't give him much of a reaction or say another word until they reached his place. She laid a hand on his arm as the garage door rolled up and open. "What about a hotel?"

"A hotel?" He knew his mind was in the gutter, but what was she thinking?

"I'll cover the expense," she said quickly. "You wouldn't have to stay. That would be your choice."

He pulled into the garage, cut the engine and stared at her in the dim light filtering in from the windows. "What are you talking about?"

"I'm a danger to you," she said. "I know you've got this whole rescue-protector routine going on, and it's fantastic. You're great at it. But wouldn't I—we—be safer at a hotel?"

"No."

"Carson." She released her seat belt and swiveled in her seat, stopping him with a touch to his shoulder before he could get out of the truck.

He craved her so desperately that he let her feather-light hand hold him.

"Carson, someone searched my house. I don't want to bring that here, to your home."

"You don't even know what they were after," he pointed out.

"That only makes it more of a risk for you. You didn't ask for this."

"No one asks for this kind of crap." He took her hand in his, mesmerized by the differences. Her slender frame made her seem delicate, but there was fire inside her and a steel will he admired.

"There's more," she said. "Full-disclosure time."

"God help me."

Her lips tilted in a shy smile. "I wanted to be mad after I kissed you."

"I noticed."

"Yeah, sorry. For the mad, not the kiss." She laughed at herself. "I'm wrecking this. The kiss was nice. More than nice," she continued. "I wanted to be mad at myself for the lousy timing. Isn't it called Nightingale syndrome or something when a patient's attracted to the caregiver?"

He jerked his mind away from her use of *attracted* and addressed the question. "No. Nightingale effect is the opposite situation, when a caregiver falls for a patient." Was she trying to imply that's what was happening? If so, she needed to get clear in a hurry. His brain was mush because all his blood had run south.

"You're not making this easy." Her gaze flitted everywhere but wouldn't light on him.

"I'm not trying to," he said. "If you want to stay at a hotel, we'll stay at a hotel. I think staying here is more convenient and comfortable. Either way, the last few days are proof enough that trouble is likely to catch up wherever we go."

"And the kiss?"

She was killing him. "House or hotel, I'll kiss you whenever you ask me to." He gave in and reached for her, sweeping the heavy fall of her hair back from her eyes. "You've had a tough day on top of a series of tough days. Let's take this inside."

"Kiss me." She scooted across the bench seat, crowding his side of the cab. "Please."

She couldn't mean it. It was his imagination that added the pleading note of need to her voice. "Lissa."

"You just said you would."

He caught her chin and brushed his thumb over those luscious, smiling lips. Slowly, savoring the anticipation, he touched his mouth to hers again. The plan was to keep it easy and simple. Anything else and he'd want to dive in, to give pleasure and take more, but they were in the garage and it was hardly the place for seduction.

His wants spiraled out of control, eclipsed by her soft moan as she tugged him closer. Her long fingers were in his hair, then tracing the shell of his ear, and she angled her mouth to give him better access.

Carson didn't need an engraved invitation. With lips tasting and teasing, both of them tossing away any notion of distance, he maneuvered them on the seat until she was sitting across his lap. His hands were full of her hips. Her skirt parted, granting him access to the smooth, hot skin of her supple thighs bracketing his legs.

He told himself he could stop, that he would stop in just a minute. He kept right on going, his mouth mating with hers while his pulse raced at odd intervals. He ran his hands up her spine, into her hair and back down, over and over.

The dark citrus-scented silk cascaded around them and she arched into his touch. It brought the long column of her throat close enough to nibble and tease. She laughed, her breasts firm against his chest, making him harder still. When she reached down between them and stroked his arousal through his slacks, his hips bucked.

"Lissa, hang on."

"That's the plan." Her sultry laugh lit fires inside his blood, her tongue and teeth exploring his ear, raising goose bumps all over his body.

"Wait a second."

She braced her hands on the back of the seat, bracketing his head. "We're both single, healthy, needy," she drew out the last word.

"We're also in a truck."

Her gaze narrowed. "If you make me walk across the yard in broad daylight, drooling after you…" She rocked her hips over his erection. "Can you even walk in this condition?"

He'd manage. "Think it through."

She leaned in and caught his lip in her teeth, gave it a little tug. "You've been telling me not to think."

"What? Oh, yeah, the amnesia." He groaned, rapidly losing this battle.

"I need this. You. Carson." His name was a soft flutter of sound and seduction over his sensitive skin at the base of his throat. "I left the apartment prepared." She pulled a condom out of her pocket as she ground her hips gently over him.

He gave in, brought her face close and kissed her. It was sex. Nothing more or less. It was no hardship to deal with hot, life-affirming sex between two consenting adults to counter the overwhelming stress and grief and loss. He was convenient for her. That was all. In fact, he was pretty damn happy to be of service. Better him than anyone else who wouldn't understand the limits.

He tore her panties out of the way, reveling in her laughter as she freed him from his slacks and rolled the condom over him with those delicate fingers. He hadn't felt anything so erotic in ages, until she sank over him, enveloping him in mind-blowing heat while her mouth feasted on his.

He gripped her hips and held on as she set the pace. She was every sensual fantasy in his hands. Her body gripping his, moving and taking what she needed. Working open the tiny buttons on her shirt, he spread the panels and groaned at the sexy black lace of her bra. He brought her close, kissing her breasts and suckling the stiff peaks through the lace cups.

He was being used, but he couldn't see the downside, not with her rushing toward a climax that dragged him right over that edge of bliss with her.

Lissa had only herself to blame as her breath sawed in and out of her lungs. Carson had one hand wrapped around her backside, the other stroking her hair, while she mustered enough strength to lift her head from his shoulder. She didn't want to consider the ramifications, not while her body was still humming from that orgasm and Carson's masculine scent surrounded her.

At least with her memories mostly intact, she knew she didn't typically throw herself at the nearest available man. "Wow," she said. It was the best she could manage.

"That covers it," he agreed.

She could hear the smile in his voice, and why wouldn't he be smiling? It made her brave enough to peek at him. "I'd say thank you, but somehow that ruins the moment."

He laughed, the sound starting as a deep rumble in his chest, shivering through her and out to float around them. The most perfect response she could have asked for. Until he turned his face and kissed her with such slow, sweet tenderness that she wanted to cry.

However fate had crossed their paths, she was thankful for a man who understood exactly what she'd needed without rendering any judgment.

With a minimum of awkwardness, they both straightened up their clothing. Her cheeks blazed with belated embarrassment as she stuffed her torn panties deep into the tote she'd used for her toiletries.

"Carson?"

He leaned across the seat and bussed her lips with a fast kiss. "You don't get to ask me anything else until we're both safely inside the house."

He couldn't mean the trouble had followed them so closely. "Safe from what?"

"Each other." He winked at her and opened the door. "This is a family neighborhood." At the truck bed, he pulled out her backpack and then held open the garage door for her.

As they entered the house through the kitchen door, she couldn't help but contrast this moment to the first time she'd seen it. She'd been lost, trapped in a haze that held her very identity out of her reach. Now she didn't recognize herself for other reasons.

She'd thrown herself at him.

And he caught you quite well, said a snarky, thoroughly sated voice in her head. Satisfaction wasn't the point. She accepted the bottle of water he offered, needing to cool her parched throat. She should say something. *Thank you* would definitely ruin everything, although she was plenty grateful he was taking it all in stride. They couldn't do that again, despite the thrumming in her bloodstream that vehemently protested the idea of a one-and-done situation.

She opened her mouth, hoping the right words would

tumble out of their own volition, but his voice filled the room. "I'm going up to grab a shower. If you can't find anything you want to wear here, we have plenty of time to go shopping."

Her mind had locked onto the image of him in the shower, water running all over that hard body. "A shower sounds like a great idea." She caught the husky timbre of her voice and felt another blush climb up her neck.

He raised his eyebrows, the invitation clear.

"Separately." She took another quick sip of water. "I've taken enough advantage of you already." She capped the water bottle and hefted her tote over her shoulder, moving toward the front stairs.

Suddenly he was in her path, filling the doorway, his presence far bigger than his lean frame would suggest. Her pulse skipped in happy anticipation.

"Is that what you think?" His voice was low, packed with warning.

She folded her arms, ignoring the tight sensation in her breasts. "I'm trying to think and be rational rather than simply react the way I did in the garage." She tipped her head in that direction. "You were—"

"Don't say it." He cut her off, his hazel eyes inscrutable. "Just stop talking."

"Shouldn't we—" At his hard glare, she clamped her lips together.

"If the rest of that sentence is 'talk about it' or some other way to define and contain what we both enjoyed immensely, stop."

He took a step closer, close enough that she could smell her perfume on his skin. Good grief, she'd even managed to smear lipstick on his collar in the ultimate cliché. He tipped up her chin, held her gaze for a long moment. "I'm a big boy," he told her in the calm, quiet tone she'd trusted from that first moment behind the club. "I could have said no."

She wasn't sure she'd given him enough time to utter even that single-syllable denial. His eyes cruised over her face, landed on her lips. Deep inside, her body quivered, eager for another kiss. "Why didn't you?"

His mouth tipped up at the corner. "You're irresistible," he replied. He started to say something and changed his mind. "Sex happens." He shrugged. "We're consenting adults with a mutual attraction. You have enough on your plate without overthinking an amazing moment."

He was giving her far more credit and showing more maturity than she deserved. He kissed her cheek, then eased back with a casual smile. "I'm going to take a shower. A cold one, unless you decide to join me. No wrong answers here. It's up to you."

She stood there dumbfounded as he walked backward several paces. When she didn't move, he flashed an unrepentant grin and disappeared up the stairs.

She couldn't join him. She absolutely should *not* join him. Need scorched her blood, pushed her forward and out of the kitchen at last. Upstairs she had another internal fight. He'd called her irresistible, and she thought he might have meant it. It was a compliment she'd carry with her when this was all behind her.

He'd left his bedroom door cracked, and she could hear the water running in his cold shower. *Unless I join him.* If she joined him, it wouldn't be the spontaneous combustion they'd shared in the truck. No, it would be premeditated and amazing and brilliantly satisfying. But she wouldn't be able to rationalize her decision as a lapse in judgment. It would be a definitive step in a direction she suddenly didn't feel prepared to take.

Frustrated with her confusion in the face of his easygoing acceptance, she went into the hall bathroom, closed and locked the door. Not to keep him out. To keep herself in.

Running the tap on cold, she stripped away the black clothing and stepped under the biting spray.

Chapter 8

By the time she'd chosen a cobalt blue dress with a flared skirt from the wardrobe Carson's sisters had stashed in the guest room closet, she'd finally come to terms with what had happened in the truck. Simply stated, they were new friends with amazing sexual chemistry. That was the easy, no-muss, no-fuss explanation. A lack of history was a benefit, she decided, as it left them with less baggage to cart around in the aftermath. The deep connection she'd felt with him amid the urgency of the moment was merely a by-product of coping with a sudden death, exacerbated by the fact that Noelle had been both her age and her best friend.

All of her sensible rationalizations evaporated under the flat-out hot gaze Carson leveled on her as soon as she walked into the kitchen.

"You look great," he said, leaning back against the counter. "Maybe I should change."

"No, don't," she replied too quickly. "You look great, too." The deep green button-down shirt open over a gray T-shirt brought out the green in his hazel eyes. His jeans were faded and molded to his lower body in all the right places. Her mouth watered a little, and she blamed the spicy herbs of leftover lasagna filling the air.

They settled into a comfortable conversation over the meal, discussing topics only slightly more exciting than the weather. New friends, she reminded herself, stuffing another bite of food into her mouth every time she was inclined to ask him to kiss her. It was a great solution until she was too full. Still, Grant was expecting them, and she wanted to thank him personally that his team had saved her apartment and probably the entire house, as well.

Riding in the truck had her blushing at the memories for the duration of trip to the pier, and she was grateful it was dark outside. Carson drove right up to the club, once more parking near the back door. The club was packed, and a heavy rock beat poured from the refurbished warehouse into the night.

"Why don't you ever use one of the parking lots?" she asked.

"I'm not inclined to take chances with you after today."

"Because we had sex?" He didn't strike her as the clingy type, but again, what did she know about him? *Too little, too late on those questions*, she thought, scolding herself.

He rolled his eyes and laughed a little. "I was thinking about the break-in and fire, but I like that you're stuck on that particular encounter."

"Ha." She barely resisted the urge to fan herself, struggling to handle this with the same ease he demonstrated. "I might be irresistible, but *you* are irrepressible."

"Found out so soon? This relationship is doomed for sure."

Relationship? No. No. She didn't know how to do those. Girlfriends, sure, but even in those cases her track record proved she was often more reserved and aloof than her peers. There had been dates, and Carson wasn't her first sexual experience, but *relationships* required a commitment skill set she didn't have.

Her car door opened and she jumped, startled.

"You okay?" he asked with that immediate concern that wrapped around her like a cozy blanket.

"Just distracted." Her gaze involuntarily drifted upriver, where the detective said Noelle's body had been found. "I want to remember," she murmured as he held open the back door for her.

Alone in the back hallway, he pulled her into his arms. "I know. We'll get you through, Lissa. I promise."

With his heart beating under her palm, she believed him. "I want them to catch her killer."

"I understand."

She stepped back, her hands lingering on his trim waist. He did understand every piece of her misery, even coming clean about envying her amnesia. "It helps knowing you do."

Escape Club staff bustled back and forth, greeting them both with open, friendly smiles as they worked. Finding Grant's office empty, they went into the club and found him sitting in as guest drummer. He was having a grand time, not just with the music, but giving a true performance for the enthusiastic audience.

"Grant's made this a special place," she said at Carson's ear as they watched.

"More than a few of us wouldn't have made it without him." Carson bumped her shoulder with his and grinned. "I'm full of energy," he said with a meaningful wink. "I'm going to see what I can do to help. Hang out here for just a few minutes."

He was gone before she could protest or offer to pitch in, as well.

"Left you stranded?" the bartender asked with a wide smile. "Don't worry. He won't be gone long." The bartender stuck out his hand. "I'm Mitch Galway."

She shook his hand. "Nice to meet you, Mitch." She gave her name and saw his eyebrows arch. "I guess you've heard about my situation?"

"Don't let it bug you." He worked on orders while he talked. "Grant brought us all up to speed since your case was more public than most. Even if he hadn't, your face has been plastered all over the news and my fiancée—Julia, the attorney—has kept up with the developing case. I'd have to be blind not to recognize you."

She laughed as her awkwardness faded.

"How are you feeling?"

She wagged a hand side to side. "According to Carson, I'm doing better than expected, and I should be patient."

"Carson would know," Mitch replied as he mixed another drink. "He should've been a doctor. Rest easy. Grant is working his tail off to unravel your trouble." Mitch slid the finished cosmopolitan in front of her, complete with the curl of orange peel. "A Cosmo Escape," he said. "On the house."

"Nice presentation," she said turning the glass back and forth and catching the scent of orange essence.

Mitch held up his hands, surrendering. "Everyone watches too many food shows these days. Enjoy it," he said, moving down the long bar to serve more customers.

She took a sip, and the flavors blended into the perfect burst of happiness on her tongue. When Mitch looked back to check her reaction, she raised the glass in an appreciative salute. Carson returned as the last notes of the song faded away, propping his elbows on the bar top beside her. His hair curled at his temples, damp from sweat.

"Feel better?" she asked.

"Yes." Under the bar, he bumped her thigh with his. "I helped them catch up on glassware for the bar and burned off some extra energy."

If he kept saying things like that, her resolve wouldn't last, and she'd be asking for another kiss within the hour. He turned, leaning back against the bar to watch the band as they dialed up the volume on the next song. She decided the drink was stronger than she'd thought when Carson convinced her to dance with him.

It was a great feeling to cut loose and let her body move with the rhythm. The band was excellent and although the dance floor was crowded, the soaring ceiling and wide space was designed so it didn't feel that way at all.

Dancing had been Noelle's thing, and she'd made an impression on local clubs and DJs starting their freshman year of college. Lissa thought back to how she'd dressed on Friday, comparing it to tonight. They must have been headed somewhere. She rarely wore dresses or skirts to work, since it was impossible to know what she might be called to do on any given day. Slacks or jeans were always the better bets.

When the music changed to something slower, Carson took her hand and twirled her until her hips were close to his, her hand resting on his shoulder. A perfect distraction. He smiled down at her, kissed the tip of her nose, and she laughed. They swayed to the music, letting it pulse around them, through them. The crowd drifted into the margins of her vision, until her world included only Carson and the music. His arms banded around her, sheltering her, his soft denim jeans brushing against her skirt and her skin as fabric swayed and moved.

Something broke loose inside her, floating free and spiraling up and out. Pure happiness and sheer delight, she realized. Had she ever felt anything like it? He gave her another twirl, pulling her tight to his chest as the last notes of the song faded into the rafters overhead.

Feeling light-headed and wary of the emotions surging through her, she excused herself to the restroom, amazed her knees didn't buckle under the weight of her nerves.

The familiar bustle of bodies and female camaraderie settled her, and when she reached the sinks she used a damp paper towel to cool the heat pooling at the back of her neck, and above her heart.

She couldn't be having these wild feelings for Carson. Oh, sex screwed up everything. She never should've crossed that line. He'd been *assigned* to her when she'd been in trouble, and kindness was simply part of his nature.

Forced proximity, simple laws of attraction, she reminded herself. None of her rationales held up this time, and she redefined her part of the equation as a crush.

She could get over a crush. Anything more than that, well…she wasn't willing to take the risk of getting hurt or hurting him.

She turned for the door and caught the whiff of a sweet and slightly familiar odor that flickered at the edges of her memory. Lissa hurried out of the bathroom and away from the unpleasant scent. In the hallway clogged with men and women, she forced her way through, ignoring the curses in her wake.

She needed clean air. She needed Carson. Preferably both. Pulling her cell phone from her pocket, she fumbled with the screen, trying to send a text to Carson that she was headed for the back door rather than the bar.

A hand came out of nowhere and slapped the phone away, grabbing her wrist in a bruising grip. A familiar grip. Panic seized her when she recognized the man she'd bumped into at the museum on Monday. She clawed at him with her free hand and pulled back with all her strength. He was dragging her to the emergency exit, away from the people in the bar and the kitchen who could help her. She screamed Carson's name.

"Shut up, bitch!"

A woman's voice behind her and the feel of a hard hand on her back snapped all the jumbled pieces of her memory into place. The woman had been with the men on Friday. They worked as a team when they'd attacked her and Noelle, drugging them both outside the hospital. Sensing what was about to come next, Lissa dropped low, and saw the syringe meant for her neck land in the arm of the man trying to drag her out of the club's emergency exit. She scrambled back toward the center of the club on her hands and knees.

The tenor of the voices overhead changed. Shouts

and orders flew, and then a blast of river air flooded the corridor a moment before the alarm on the emergency exit door sounded.

Lissa was struggling to her feet, shouting for Carson when more hands grabbed her, hauled her up. She screamed and fought, kicking out and throwing elbows until she heard Carson's voice through the din.

"Lissa, it's me!" He held her shoulders in that firm grip. "Come on, you're safe. I've got you."

She opened her eyes and tried to explain. "They were—that was them." She gave up and buried her face in his shirt as the panic and the near miss kidnapping shocked her system in waves.

Still soothing, he gathered her into his arms, carried her out of the crowd. "You're safe. I promise."

"Don't l-let go." She repeated it over and over as the memories came back in a flood of misery and haunting pain. "Where are we going?"

"Grant's office. Take it easy," he added when the tremors started.

"I remember it, Carson. All of it. Just like you said I would."

He sidestepped through the doorway and set her gently on her feet, not letting go until he was sure she had her balance. "Sit down," he suggested.

She sank into one of the chairs in front of Grant's desk, accepting the jacket someone had delivered and a bottle of water. "Can I have something st-stronger, please?"

"Grant keeps a bottle of good whiskey in his desk," Carson said.

Perfect.

She heard the liquid splash into a glass, caught a whiff

of robust spice and toffee when he wrapped her hands around the heavy, squat glass. She tossed it back in one gulp, letting the bite of the alcohol burn away the remnants of her fright.

"You found me. Saved me." She gazed into his patient hazel eyes.

"You were saving yourself when we caught up with you." His hands ran through her hair and he kissed the top of her head. "I was watching for you and saw the way they culled you out of the crowd."

"It was the man from the museum." She rolled the glass between her palms, wondering if she should have another drink.

"Yes," Carson agreed. "Grant called Werner. Patrols are already searching for them."

"He tortured Noelle." There. She'd said it, maybe just to Carson, but she'd said it. Tears filled her eyes again, but the memories marched with dreadful clarity through her mind. "You were right," she whispered. "Amnesia is a blessing."

"You're strong enough now," he assured her in that steady voice. "You can do this."

Was she? She felt as weak as a kitten, knowing the dreadful events she would soon be telling the detective. Not just about the team who'd set all this in motion, but the way Noelle was connected to the whole damn mess. Her stomach lurched at the flashes of the torture, the shocking truth and Lissa's narrow escape.

"They left me for dead," she whispered. "Noelle made sure of that."

It was the last gift her friend had offered, and now, to save herself, to see justice done, she'd have to destroy her friend's reputation posthumously. Dr. and Mrs.

Anson would soon learn terrible truths about their beloved daughter. Lissa hated adding to their grief, even if it meant getting a killer off the streets. She would lose them, the people who'd shown her how love, acceptance and stability could enrich a family. Curling into herself, she gave in to a fresh wave of tears.

Carson sat in the chair next to Lissa's, quietly willing it to be over, though they weren't even close. Grant stayed, as well, at her request, and that gave Carson an anchor of his own.

With more patience than he'd previously shown, Detective Werner asked question after question, taking careful notes. Carson shifted his evaluation of the man as the detective handled Lissa's answers with a clinical reserve that only a man who'd seen worse could muster.

Even in Carson's ambulance experience it was hard to imagine a scene worse than Lissa had survived. She and Noelle had planned to go out on Friday night, but Noelle had changed the plan to work a double shift. Lissa had stopped by to chat during Noelle's meal break, and they'd gone up to the parking garage because Noelle needed the walk and claimed she had something for Lissa in the car.

"Three men approached us from the other end of the row where Noelle was parked." Lissa explained. "Two men and a woman," she corrected herself. "I didn't realize one of them was a woman until they were closer."

Lissa gave Werner full descriptions, and Carson made preliminary sketches as he listened. "We have the two who attacked her tonight on camera," Grant reminded him. "And the license plate Carson and Lissa noted when they spotted him at the service this morning. My team is getting that video ready for you now."

Carson pushed a hand through his hair. Had the funeral been only this morning? It felt as if they'd packed a lifetime into the last exhausting twelve hours.

"The man and woman tonight were the same as Friday," Lissa said. "Where was the second man?" she wondered aloud, her gaze darting between Grant and the detective.

"He was probably the one waiting outside in the car," Grant told her.

She nodded absently. "The woman took cues from the man," Lissa said as Werner took her through the events of Friday night for a second time. "She had a vicious streak as she confronted Noelle about a supply delivery."

While Lissa had been dumbfounded by the accusations, it wasn't Carson's first experience with the street trafficking of controlled substances. Thugs working for dealers had killed Sarah, as well. To Lissa's credit, it was obvious she tried to intervene for her friend. And in her eyes he could see she wanted to believe the best of Noelle, despite the evidence to the contrary.

Lissa had been drugged and roused and beaten as part of Noelle's torture. She remembered a stale industrial space with tools and lifts, and the smells of oil and the river, but she'd woken in a public bathroom near the Penn Campus and Noelle had been found in the river. With the sedative cocktail in her bloodstream and the terrible revelations about her friend in addition to the excessive violence, it was no wonder Lissa's mind had blocked everything.

To save Lissa, Noelle had caved, claiming she'd shorted the dealers and planned to go to the police.

She'd wanted out and told their attackers she had hidden money and product from the dealers.

"They hurt her," Lissa said. "She was bleeding badly and trying to tell me something. An apology and something more, but I couldn't make out the words. It's not that I forgot. I couldn't hear her."

"This is what we needed," Werner assured her. "We can build a real case now."

Everyone in the room went silent for a time. Carson couldn't speak for the other men, but he was overwhelmed by Lissa's fortitude and all too aware that this wouldn't be the last time she told the story.

"Where was my purse?" she asked.

"In the trunk of Noelle's car," he replied. "The evidence suggests you were locked in there at some point, as well."

"Noelle's parents will hate me," she whispered. "Who wants to hear their daughter was a criminal?"

Carson ached for her as another wave of grief swept across her face.

"They'll be relieved when we put her killer behind bars," Werner said. "I'll make arrangements to move you to a safe house tonight."

"No." Carson sat up. She'd moved around enough in the past few days. Safe or not, uprooting her again wouldn't help at all. "She can stay with me until you have the crew in custody."

"You're hardly qualified to protect her," Werner pointed out.

"So keep a protective detail on your star witness," he shot back.

Lissa's gaze, filled with gratitude, locked with his. "If

I have a vote, I'd rather stay with Carson and attempt to get back to some semblance of my routine."

Although Werner and Grant exchanged a long look, neither argued the point further.

"You've been a tremendous help, Miss Baxter." The detective stood up and slipped his notebook into a pocket.

She twisted her thumb ring. "When will you tell the Ansons?"

"It may be a few days yet."

"They're burying her tomorrow in Allentown."

"I know," Werner replied. "We'll be respectful."

Grant stood up and followed the detective out of the office, leaving Carson and Lissa alone.

He crossed the room and pulled her into his arms, wishing he could whisk her away from all of this. But that would never suit her. Despite her slender build, she was so strong and capable. Still, when he closed his eyes, he saw how close that needle had come to her flesh. "What do you need?" he asked.

"I don't know," she admitted. "I can't believe Noelle hid so much from me."

"You never suspected anything?"

"No," Lissa said, her voice flat. "You must think I'm an idiot."

"Not even close." He was thinking other things, comparing her description of the violence to his own memories of Sarah's murder. Signature bullets or not, he couldn't make the descriptions line up. It seemed only one of them would have justice.

"There were moments when she was stressed out," Lissa said, "but that was her job. I wish I'd heard those final words."

"She loved you," he said.

"Thanks for that." She leaned into him. "You didn't have to stay."

"Leave you? Not a chance." He remembered the sharp loneliness of giving a statement without his best friend nearby for moral support. "Let's get out of here."

"Are you sure you want to stay on duty with me?"

He caught her face in his hands, waited for her eyes to focus on him. "You're no burden to me, and the threat, if not contained yet, will be shortly."

He kissed her, harder than he intended, but he'd come so close to losing her tonight. "Do you understand?"

"No," she admitted. "Can you explain it to me in the morning?"

"Absolutely."

He returned her cell phone and confirmed Grant would keep his team close, despite Werner's promise of protection. Then he ushered Lissa outside to his truck. On the ride back to his place, she rested her head against the window and watched the city go by. He knew she was thinking of their first trip together along this route.

This time last week, he'd been sulking, no other word for it. He'd been puttering through his days, furious at the world over his losses. Lissa's startling arrival had upended everything and given him a new clarity all at once.

He could practically hear Sarah cackling at the curveball life had thrown him. "Sarah would've liked you," he said. She would definitely have approved of the way Lissa turned him inside out.

"Noelle would've liked you." Her soft smile faded. "That might not be a compliment, based on her criminal associates."

"No one's perfect," he reminded her. "Whatever happened to tie her to the drug ring, she was your friend first. That's what you should focus on."

"I'm glad we met, even if your first impression of me sucked."

The statement surprised a bark of laughter out of him. "Me, too." He brought her hand to his lips and then just hung on until they were back to his house.

They held hands as they walked across the yard. "You never mentioned how you got the Escape Club matchbook."

"It was just there," she said. "I'd borrowed Noelle's jacket for the night." In the dim light, he caught her pensive frown. "Why do you ask?"

"It doesn't matter."

Her cool fingertips cruised over his jaw. "I think it does."

"You're chilled, and we've spent enough time on those bastards for tonight." He unlocked and opened the back door for her, locking it behind them. He left the lights off, wanting to get her upstairs where she could rest.

"Talk to me, Carson. I can see something brewing in there." She circled a finger in the air, gesturing to his face.

"There's too much brewing," he confessed. Hands on her hips, he guided her toward the stairs. There were more than a few theories running through his head, and all of them could wait until morning.

The drug dealers knew too much about her for his comfort. They'd lured her out of her office at the museum, attacked her home twice, and nearly succeeded in dragging her out of the club. He wasn't a cop, but his instincts were humming. What had Noelle told the dealers while Lissa was unconscious?

At the top of the stairs, he paused. "Pick a room and we'll share it."

"Is this your answer to me jumping you earlier?" Her eyes darted to the side as if she could see his truck through the walls and the dark.

Yes. "No," he lied. "There's a better way, better words to handle this, but I'm tired." He gestured to the security-system panel on the wall near the door. The lights showed the system was armed. "Windows and doors are wired into the system, but I'm not taking any chances. We're sleeping in the same room tonight. Your choice if we're in the same bed."

For a moment, she stared at him, her lips slightly parted. Then she just stepped close and wrapped her arms tight around his waist, her hands splayed over his back.

Her response made him feel as if he'd conquered world hunger or something equally impressive. He held her close, his hand running up and down her spine, wishing a simple touch would alleviate all her pain.

"Your room," she said.

He wanted to cheer that the first part of discussion was over and they could rest. As much as he wanted her again, they were both wiped out from the ridiculously long day. He told himself sleeping beside her would be enough as they moved down the hall to his bedroom. At the hall bathroom, she retrieved her tote.

Seeing it, he couldn't help smiling that she'd packed condoms. He saw the color come into her cheeks when she caught him grinning. "Stop it," she scolded.

It was a challenge, but he managed not to tease her, or torment himself over the last man she'd chosen to stock condoms for.

He shrugged out of his button-down shirt, peeled the T-shirt off over his head and stepped into the bathroom. When he returned, wearing only his boxers, she was perched on the side of the bed in the sweet camisole and shorts she'd slept in at her place.

"Am I on the bed or the floor?" he asked.

With a slow smile, she pulled back the covers and invited him to bed.

Chapter 9

Lissa blinked against the morning light slipping through the blinds on the window. It took her a moment to realize she wasn't at home in her bed and that her legs weren't tangled in sheets, but with Carson's long limbs.

Who knew it could feel this nice to share a bed? His arm was a warm weight across her midriff, holding her back snug against his chest. She could feel the rise and fall of his even breathing and had never felt safer.

The man was a paradox. Able to be steady in her crisis, though it was clear he was fighting his own demons. Carson demonstrated vast knowledge as well as a wealth of kindness. She knew those two traits didn't always go together.

She'd seen him rattled only once, when the bullets had shredded a beautiful day. Though he counted it a weakness, his panic hadn't set in until the worst of the danger had passed. He didn't seem to have a grasp on how valuable he was to his community or to her.

If she could give him anything in the world, she'd give him that perspective, that confidence that he'd done everything right for his partner. She caressed his arm, smiled as he nestled her closer still. When he relaxed again, she slipped from the bed to get ready for work. Trouble or not, she couldn't leave her team carrying the extra load when she was perfectly safe behind the museum walls.

He shifted as she tucked the covers close to him. That square jaw, talented mouth and sleep-rumpled hair tempted her to climb back into the bed and wake him with a kiss. To let that kiss lead to more. She decided to wait until she understood where they were on the sex issue. Although he didn't seem to mind the way she'd used him yesterday, she was less and less okay with it.

Less than an hour later, in the kitchen over breakfast, they had a short, heated debate about her decision to go into work. Finally Carson relented. Filling a travel mug with coffee, he escorted her to his truck. She soaked up the sunlight, hoping to carry the happy glow with her today, to let today be a fresh start.

"I won't be done until close to six," she said as they neared the museum. "I want to put in some extra time and effort."

"Okay. You call me when you're ready, and I'll park and come meet you at the door."

"That makes you a target," she said.

"No one is trying to snatch me," he countered. "I'm not going to give these thugs an inch of space."

His statement put a crazy flutter in her pulse that she tried to rein in while he found a parking space. She gathered her wits and her purse and let him walk her to the door. He gave her a chaste kiss on the lips and told her to have a good day.

It was so perfectly normal, she wanted to skip like a little girl into the lobby. She managed to maintain her dignity, standing quietly while she made sure he got back to his truck without any trouble. No matter which of them wore the target, they were in this together, and she was entitled to watch out for him, too.

Carson gulped his coffee while he waited for a traffic light to change. His phone rang and his heart skipped until his Bluetooth announced a call from PFD. He clicked the button on the steering wheel to answer and heard Evelyn's voice asking him to fill a swing shift tonight.

"Sorry, Evelyn," he replied. "I'm committed to another project tonight." Carson would not trust Lissa's safety to people on the periphery. The team last night had come far too close to succeeding.

"We need you, Carson. You're one of the best paramedics in the city."

"Come on, Evelyn. It's me. The flattery isn't necessary."

"I want you back full-time." The statement was followed by silence. The woman had mastered the art of the pregnant pause.

He wasn't about to make a commitment to Evelyn or any partner she had in mind for him on a rig. "Thank you," he said into the silence. "I am thinking about it." He just wasn't leaning toward a decision that would make Evelyn happy.

"I need a decision soon. Make some time to come by the office."

"Evelyn, you know—"

"Make the time, Carson." The line went dead before he could argue or explain that there wasn't room in his schedule for a visit to PFD headquarters right now. Unless he took Lissa with him, and he wasn't ready to invite her across that line.

What *was* he ready to do?

The question niggled at the back of his head all day as he worked on Daniel's latest flip in progress. He was halfway through the hardwood flooring install in the master bedroom when Daniel appeared in the doorway. With his height, black hair and startling blue eyes, the man made a lasting impression whether he was in turn-out gear or work clothes on a construction site.

"Hey," he said to Carson. "Is your phone off?"

Panic for Lissa shot through him as he reached for the device tucked into his back pocket. No calls from her, but there were three from Grant and one more from Evelyn. "Wow. Sorry. I must have bumped it to Silent."

"Not like you would've heard it anyway up here." He waved Carson over. "Grant got impatient and tracked you down. Doesn't look good, man."

Carson hustled down the stairs, mindful of the lack of walls or rails on either side. Dodging workmen, he maneuvered to where Grant waited near the front door.

"Looks like the knee's improved," Grant said, giving him a pleased nod.

Carson hadn't thought about his knee since… Well, he didn't remember when he'd stopped thinking about it. At Lissa's house, he realized. Not once had he felt so much as an unfavorable twinge going up and down her stairs. He wasn't sure what to make of it, but the analysis would have to wait. "Guess I am feeling good."

"Time heals all wounds." Grant delivered the line with the irreverence of a man who knew he was spouting crap. "Jennings tells me you're an asset out here." He cleared his throat. "I wanted to come by personally. You, ah, deserve a heads-up on this." Grant paced away from the house, giving Carson time to follow.

"On what?" The good sweat he'd worked up while laying the floor went cold on his skin.

"Werner called. He found a connection between Sarah and Noelle."

"Sarah and I transported several patients to the hospital where Noelle worked."

"But you didn't know Noelle," Grant pointed out. "Not by name or by face when Werner showed you the pictures at the police station."

"Well, that hardly signifies." Carson stopped himself before he blathered on defending Sarah when no defense was needed. "How does the detective think they know each other?"

Grant looked out over the street, up at the house, and sighed. "He tells me he's looking into them both as suppliers."

"No." Carson reared back as if Grant had thrown a punch at him. "That's not Sarah. No," he repeated.

"It explains the attack on your rig," Grant began.

"So does the truth. That was a crime of opportunity." He swiped at the sweat gathering on his forehead. "That's what they said, officially. Crime of opportunity."

"I'm just telling you how it's shaping up for the investigation."

"He'd better keep right on looking until he finds the

criminals responsible. You knew Sarah. Her worst offense was sarcasm."

"I know this isn't welcome news." Grant pitched his voice low. "You know how these things go. Cop work is all about pulling strings and following them, one after another."

"He can damn well pull another string." Carson's hands fisted at his sides. "Sarah wasn't working with any drug dealer." He choked back the indignation and temper clawing for an outlet. "Noelle and Lissa were best friends. If Sarah had been connected to Noelle, Lissa would've known her or heard the name, something."

Grant's gaze sharpened. "You've told Lissa about Sarah?"

"A little," Carson said, not liking the look on Grant's face. The expression, a mixture of wonder and hope, made him uncomfortable. He wasn't ready to analyze whatever was happening on a personal level with Lissa. "She dug up the obituary and news articles. The point is, this is a wild-goose chase."

"Noelle protected Lissa from her unsavory side work," Grant interjected. "Unless she's remembered something else you haven't had a chance to mention."

Carson shook his head, folding his arms over his chest and daring Grant to push him further. "Sarah was not dealing drugs."

"I understand." The older man turned to face the house. His salt-and-pepper hair, close-cropped, didn't shift as Carson's did in the morning breeze. "Werner is one of the good guys," he said.

"So was Sarah." He told himself her memory, her honor were worth every ounce of his belligerence. "I'll cooperate if the detective has valid questions."

"That's all any of us can do."

"Is he doing anything to find the crew that tried to kidnap Lissa?"

"It's all part and parcel," Grant said.

When Grant didn't elaborate, Carson shifted his feet. He didn't need more pregnant pauses today. "This connection between Noelle and Sarah is why Evelyn wants me to come in to headquarters?"

"Can't say. The woman is determined to get you back full-time."

"I'm not ready," Carson said, feeling like he was chewing rocks. Caught without the excuse of a pained knee, he knew he'd just given Grant more information than he planned on. Better Grant think him smitten and distracted with Lissa than a coward who couldn't overcome a tragedy on the job. Everyone had to deal with challenges along the way. It came with a career in public service.

Grant shoved his hands into his pockets. "I won't keep you any longer."

Carson felt like a jerk, snapping at the one person who'd been more help than anyone since Sarah's murder. "Thanks for the heads-up."

"You're welcome."

Frustrated, Carson checked the time on his phone and stalked back into the house. He'd finish the master-bedroom floor and then make time to stop by Evelyn's office. The sooner he cleared up whatever had them looking at Sarah as an accomplice or whatever, the sooner Werner would get back on the right trail.

Lissa was in the midst of a highly productive day when a summons from security interrupted her as she was wrapping up her afternoon break. It seemed Detective Werner needed a word.

Elaine, along with everyone else on the team, was curious as Lissa met him at the elevator and led him to the conference room, where they could speak privately.

"How are you feeling today?" There was a concern in his eyes that she hadn't seen before, and strangely enough, it put her on edge.

"I'm well, thank you. It helps knowing you have someone close by watching out for me."

"There were a couple of details in your statement I've been trying to confirm," he said.

"Okay." She didn't have anything to hide, but she wasn't sure what she could add.

"The cab driver picked you up on the Penn campus."

"Right," she agreed. "I woke up in the parking garage bathroom near the hospital and stumbled out into the street. It's a little blurry, but when a cab pulled over, I showed the driver the Escape Club matchbook. What are you getting at?"

"I'm concerned about the order of events. You were drugged and beaten. Aware of what they were doing to Noelle."

"Yes," she agreed. "I guess they thought they gave me a lethal dose and dumped me in the bathroom."

"Why didn't they kill you with Noelle when they had the chance to tie up loose ends?"

A question she'd been wrestling with, as well. "Isn't it your job to figure that out? Have you found the man and woman who attacked me?"

"I've got a team on that, but the crew has crawled under a very quiet rock," Werner said.

Lissa discovered she was burned out on tears and

fearfulness. She didn't feel courageous, but she would not cower or hide until it was over. "Is there anything else?"

"I'll go speak with the Ansons by the end of the week." The detective drummed his fingers lightly on his notebook. "Contrary to popular belief, I'm not eager to dump bad news on grieving families."

"You have a difficult job," Lissa said.

He snorted. "Do you recall Noelle ever mentioning Sarah Neely's name?"

Lissa was tempted to give him a quick answer and forced herself to take her time. "No. I've heard the name only from Carson and you, after someone shot at us on the roof."

Sarah's face was burned into her memory after she'd gone looking for information on Monday, but she didn't recall any connection to Noelle. "What are you getting at?"

"I'm still following leads, making connections." He stood up, handed her another business card. "If you think of anything else, let me know."

She didn't know how to convince him she wasn't hiding anything. "The break-in and fire must be connected to Noelle," she said.

"I believe so," he agreed.

"And they came after me because Noelle told them she left something there."

"That's not a bad bet." He sighed. "It only makes sense to come after you for information or to silence you," he admitted.

"I've told you everything." She met his gaze, willing him to understand. "Noelle hid this part of her life from me. I can't figure out how anyone convinced her to do this."

"Unfortunately, that makes two of us."

He walked out, leaving Lissa at the elevator, wondering if they'd ever get to the bottom of this. If they didn't, would she ever be safe? With the skills and education to follow in the footsteps of her parents, she could leave Philly behind and keep moving. A local drug dealer couldn't possibly have the resources or inclination to follow her, but was that choice worth the price?

It was hard to argue against a solution that kept her alive.

Bad people thought she knew something or had something they wanted. That was probably the only reason she was alive. Noelle had sheltered her from this side of her life, right up until they were attacked. Her friend would never have willingly led her into trouble. She knew that deep in her heart.

Returning to her desk, Lissa opened a notebook and spent the next fifteen minutes making notes of everything she could remember about the last week of Noelle's life. She turned the page and made a list of questions. Then she shoved the notebook into her purse and focused on the job she loved for the rest of the day.

She was not going to run away from Noelle's trouble, and she wasn't going to sacrifice a career and lifestyle she loved because she was too afraid to stick it out.

She'd planted roots, damn it, and she intended to sink them deep.

Carson was cooling his heels in the hallway outside Evelyn's office. He'd gone back home and cleaned up, deliberately choosing business casual attire with a dress shirt, khakis and polished loafers over the PFD paramedic uniform.

Her door opened and a blond man walked out, face red with temper under a fierce scowl shading his brown eyes. Both he and Carson did a quick double take. "Yardley?" Carson stood up and extended a hand, clasped his old friend's hand.

He and Brett Yardley had gone through training together, and both of them had counted Sarah a close friend. Sarah had crushed on Brett for a while, spending many a call discussing the pros and cons of crossing that line. As far as Carson knew, she never had.

Yardley jerked his head toward the end of the hallway and lowered his voice. "She called you, too?" he asked, watching the hallway behind Carson.

The bottom dropped out of Carson's stomach, fearing the worst. "What the hell is going on?"

"Hell if I know." Yardley threw up his hands. "I hadn't seen Sarah for over a month when you two were attacked." He shoved his hands in his pockets. "Now Evelyn drags me away from a shift for a damn witch hunt."

Great. Carson wrapped one hand around the other fist, massaging at the building tension. No way was this meeting solely about convincing Carson to return to fulltime, active status.

"Just because the cops can't find her killer doesn't mean she was dirty," Yardley continued, taking a step back toward the office. "Come on. The two of us can talk some sense into her."

Carson stepped in front of him. "Evelyn knew Sarah and respected her like we did. Whoever she calls in will say the same." He sighed.

Yardley muttered a curse. "Rumors and red tape. As

if we don't have enough of a challenge out there already. Good luck," he said and stalked away.

Uncertainty dogging his steps, Carson returned to Evelyn's office and rapped on the door.

"Come in," she called.

He did, and closed the door behind him. Hovering somewhere shy of fifty, Evelyn wore her decades of experience with the PFD and paramedic services well. She led her department by example in everything from physical fitness to continuing education, and it showed in her tanned skin, sleek runner's body and bright mind. Though they were night and day in appearance, Evelyn reminded him of what Sarah might have become.

Her head down, short cap of blond hair gleaming under the overhead light, she continued making notes by hand in a file. "Take a seat," she added without looking up. "Just need to finish my thought."

Carson waited until she looked up. "I made time."

"Thank you." She smiled, but it wasn't the bright, near-cocky expression he was used to. No, this smile was fatigued, until she glanced at her notes and it faded entirely. "I need to ask you some tough questions." She rolled her pen between her thumb and fingers. "The police believe they have a link between a recent murder victim and Sarah."

He bit back a spontaneous defense of his partner. It wasn't as if he'd been blind to Sarah's faults. Since Grant's warning, he'd run through several potential versions of this conversation. "You're referring to the Noelle Anson case?"

Her pale eyebrows climbed high on her forehead. "You knew Noelle?"

"No," Carson replied immediately. "I know her best

friend, Melissa Baxter." He decided to keep it clinical. "Miss Baxter showed up at the club on Friday night, disoriented and battered. Grant Sullivan and I gave her assistance."

Evelyn pursed her lips. "You're still helping her, according to Detective Werner, who ruined my schedule first thing this morning."

Carson waited her out this time.

"He's convinced Sarah knew Noelle." Evelyn closed her eyes and rubbed the pressure point between her eyebrows with her thumb. "Can you shed any light on that for me?"

"No. I never saw them together."

Evelyn reviewed specific incidents and reports until her questions eventually veered toward the protocols on the ambulance. *Definitely a witch hunt.* Carson told her in several different ways that he couldn't recall a single instance in which Sarah had acted inappropriately during a call or they'd found errors in the ambulance inventory.

"You never saw her speaking to anyone near the rig who had no reason to be there?" Evelyn pressed.

"No." Carson gripped the arms of the chair, prepared to stand. "Are we done?"

Evelyn's lips pursed again. "Not yet."

He remained at the edge of the seat. "What else can I tell you? Sarah wasn't a perfect person, but she was clean."

Evelyn continued to roll the pen between thumb and fingers, back and forth. "Walk me through your routine after patients were transferred to ER care."

"What?"

"I believe you understand the question, Carson. Did

Sarah stay with you, take a minute to chat with friends, grab a soda?" She leaned forward. "Walk me through it."

It had been over eight months since he'd handled a routine patient transfer with Sarah, but that was no excuse. "Sarah believed in helping people. She was direct to a fault, but honest. You *know* that."

"Answer the question, please."

In his head he spewed an ugly curse. "All right," he replied with far more calm than he felt as his gut churned. "Neither of us made a habit of wasting time with socializing after a transfer, although both of us often exchanged words with individuals we knew. We took our bathroom breaks separately. Typically we were together for the paperwork, the cleaning and restocking. You remember how that goes. We weren't glued at the hip every hour, but she didn't disappear frequently, either."

"No phone calls she didn't want to explain?"

"No." Toward the end there had been days when she texted like crazy. Carson shoved the thought aside. They were making him paranoid, forcing him to second-guess every action his best friend had ever made. No one held up to that kind of scrutiny if the end goal was perfection. "You realize it's professional coincidence that as health care experts, Noelle and Sarah were in similar places at similar times."

"Carson, I should warn you, the detective has more than that to support his claim. If you're hiding something to protect Sarah or Melissa, now's the time to come clean."

He understood why Yardley had left the meeting in a temper. "I've got nothing to add. Whatever they think they have on Sarah, I never saw her do anything remotely illegal. Not even borderline. She was a fine paramedic, and she pushed me to give my best every day. I'm glad I worked with her."

He pushed up and out of the chair, not waiting to be excused this time.

"Carson."

He stopped, barely, one hand on the doorknob.

"You gave your best every day, every shift," Evelyn said. "The two of you were an excellent team."

He glanced over his shoulder. "We can agree on that."

"No one in this department blamed you when she died," she added. "If the incident had happened to any other paramedics, you would have pointed out everything they'd done right, yet you won't consider giving yourself the same grace."

Incident. The word was too clean for the nasty attack. "Don't try to tell me it was her fault."

"I'm not." Evelyn sighed and leaned back in her chair. "Like you, I can't find a single cause for concern in her record, and yet the police are sure they are on the right track."

He strode back to the guest chair, bracing his hand on the backrest. "They can't be, Evelyn."

"Your rig was robbed, your partner shot. If it wasn't a random criminal act, if there is a bigger threat at work here, you know I'll do everything in my power to protect this department."

"That I understand," he admitted. "But it's been eight months." He stopped short, working to recall the exact number of days. "If there was something bigger going on, wouldn't you have your hands full with other attacks on ambulances?"

"I'd think so. The police aren't so sure." She swiveled

from side to side in her chair. "I appreciate you coming in. This wasn't easy for either of us."

He didn't envy her position. "Have a good day, Evelyn."

"One last thing. When are you coming back on full-time?"

"I'm not ready." Her gaze narrowed, and he realized the habitual answer wasn't going to cut it, not while he was standing in front of her.

"I can't commit to anything while Lissa—Miss Baxter—is still at risk."

Her gaze narrowed at his slip. "You're aware that reply raises concerns for me?"

"Other than covering shifts, I don't see a problem. Lissa didn't know Sarah any more than I knew her friend Noelle."

"I hope that's true, Carson. I want an answer from you about the job by Monday, regardless of Miss Baxter's situation. I need to get back to full staff, and this department needs *you*." She punctuated the last words with her pen aimed at his chest.

"Yes, ma'am."

The conversation circled through his head as he drove over to the museum. Too distracted to be helpful at the house, he decided to wait in the parking lot or walk the grounds for an hour or two rather than be anywhere else right now.

He noted the increased police presence along with an extra security guard patrolling the grounds on foot. Thick walls and layers of protocols stood between her and any drug dealers out here. So why was he avoiding the obvious decision to go back full-time? Evelyn would keep him on days for a while if he asked nicely.

Being a paramedic had always felt like the best combination of all his interests. Boring shifts were rare, he faced new challenges each week, and he could use his skills to help others.

Sarah had been all about helping people. One more reason he couldn't see her running drugs. When they were on a call, she was dialed in to doing what was best for the patient. No way in hell that equaled dealing drugs.

Increasingly frustrated with the mental gerbil wheel and with more than an hour before Lissa was done for the day, Carson walked around to the front entrance of the museum and bought a ticket. He hadn't been here as a visitor in ages. His last visit, with Sarah, was to answer a call on a suspected cardiac arrest. That was just over a year ago, he recalled, as he took the central stairs up to the Arms and Armor gallery, as he remembered doing on that call. They'd just dropped off a patient and had been heading back to the firehouse when dispatch sent them over. Museum security had used the mobile defibrillator to keep the guy going, and Carson and Sarah had taken over from there. It was a good day with a happy ending, and both the victim's family and the museum had written thank-you notes to the PFD.

His phone gave off the double-vibration signal of an incoming text message, and he pulled the device from his pocket to check. He felt the smile on his face as he read the note from Lissa telling him she could leave anytime.

He sent a reply, letting her know where he was, and she responded that she would come up to meet him. Maybe she'd show him some piece she'd worked on. Or maybe he should take it down a notch. He wasn't in the market for a relationship, no matter how pleasant it was to spend time with Lissa. And she had enough on her plate without his particular brand of brokenness clogging up her situation.

Still, he discovered he was as eager as a kid looking into a candy store window while he waited for her. Something about the woman made him wish for the elusive happy ending his parents and sister Renee had found. It didn't help that Lissa made him want to flirt and linger over the smallest kisses, or share small talk and simple meals.

Scrubbing a hand over his face, he pulled back from that slippery slope. He was reading way too much into a random moment when he'd been the safe outlet she needed. He knew from experience that grief sex and a few kisses didn't make a relationship. He blotted the *r* word from his vocabulary. She needed support through the crisis, not a clingy guy who had yet to reclaim control of his own life.

Watching for her, he enjoyed the view as she walked across the gallery, her long hair pulled back from her face, her smile wide when she spotted him. In her tailored navy slacks and a pale green sweater set, she was a vision.

"You look handsome." She pushed up onto her toes and kissed his cheek. Her hand slid into his as naturally as breathing, but her gaze turned wary. "Are we going somewhere?"

"Yes," he decided on the spot. He didn't want to share why he'd really cleaned up, didn't want to dwell on the baseless accusations against Sarah. Quickly he did a rundown of restaurants nearby and decided on a place he'd missed recently and trusted completely. On a Wednesday they shouldn't have trouble making a short-notice reservation, and if they did, he'd come up with an alternate plan. "Do you like sushi?"

"Yes!" Her dark eyes sparkled.

"Great." He pulled out his phone again. "I'll make sure they have a table ready for us after you show me your favorite gallery."

She squeezed his hand. "Sounds a bit like a date."

Glancing down, he saw she was teasing and replied in kind. "Is it standard practice to bring dates to work?"

"No. I prefer to scope out the galleries for single men and circle like a shark until it's time to close in."

He laughed, trying to imagine Lissa as a maneater. "Does that make me the bait or the catch today?"

A big laugh burst out of her, and she smothered it against his shoulder when other visitors turned and stared at them.

"You're setting a bad example for museum goers."

"Oh, you have no idea the trouble I'm capable of." Her lips curved in a sly smile. Then her cheeks went red. "Well, maybe you do."

He liked this side of her, the woman she was without the pressure of unpleasant circumstances.

"Why is this one your favorite?" he asked as they entered one of the European art galleries. When she didn't answer, he wondered if he'd finally hit the too-personal mark, though he couldn't imagine it after recent events.

She wandered by a few more paintings. "For the longest time, I dreamed of becoming a writer or an athlete or a secretary. Anything as far removed from my parents' absorption with history and artifacts as I could get. Don't let me mislead you. They are wonderful people. They're just completely engrossed with their purpose in life. I envied that focus, especially when I came to the conclusion there wasn't room for me within that tight sphere."

Her struggle to be noticed and accepted by the people who shouldn't have ignored her astounded him. His parents weren't perfect, and there were times when he would've preferred going *unnoticed*, but he'd always known he was valued for his own skills.

"So I rebelled in my way, searching for who I was, where I could fit in." Her lips tugged to the side as she shook her head. "Imagine my surprise when I got to college and discovered I didn't want to stray too far from the way I was raised. Preserving the past, seeking to uncover the secrets of master artists." She sighed, pausing in front of a painting of a boulevard at night labeled as a Pissarro. "As much as I'd like to avoid the phrase, it's in my bones."

He reached out and twirled a lock of her hair around his finger, much the way he felt utterly twisted around hers. "But as you said, you found a way to put down roots."

"Yes." She tipped her head to the side. "You have no idea how good it feels to wake up in the same place month after month. Traveling is exciting, but to have a routine and see familiar faces? No contest."

They walked the gallery, chatting about how she and the team of conservators kept various displays in ideal condition for visitors and history. It was the respite they both needed, he realized as they worked their way back toward the west entrance. "As a kid on field trips, we'd come here and be awed by it all, but aside from Indiana Jones, I never gave a thought to how it got here."

"Good," she said.

"Good?"

She grinned up at him. "If we're doing our jobs right, the focus should be on the beauty of the exhibit, not the preservation."

They passed through security, his patience tested while she exchanged a few words with everyone on duty, until at last they were outside. His nerves gave a kick during the short walk to the truck despite the awareness that Grant's team and others from the police department were out here keeping an eye on them.

Nothing untoward occurred on the short drive to the restaurant, and walking in, they were greeted with a bright exuberance and led to a table that gave them an excellent view of the sushi chef.

Accepting steaming towels, she and Carson wiped their hands as the waiter brought sake and poured for both of them. "You're popular here," Lissa said.

"Sarah and I were regular customers." He lowered his voice to add, "And we've answered a kitchen emergency call once or twice."

"The detective came by the museum today, asking about Sarah and Noelle." She picked up her menu. "We don't have to talk about it right now."

"Now's fine." He gestured for her to spill the details. As she filled him in, he wanted to swear. Werner was worse than a dog with a bone, determined to find the link between the two women.

When they'd placed their orders, he refilled her sake cup, then his. "I'd like to know what he thinks he has. As close as we were to our friends, as much time as we spent with them, I find it strange neither of them ever crossed paths with either of us."

She ran a fingertip around the edge of her cup. "I've

been mulling over that same thing off and on all day. I'm convinced he's on the wrong track."

He thought they were the only two people in the city who agreed on that score. "Why?"

"Because Noelle shared everything with me. Well, everything except the drug situation, I mean. I just can't make what I heard that night fit with who she was."

"Two things bug me," he admitted. "The matchbook and what feels like excessive interest in you and your apartment."

Her eyes went wide. "I know!" She leaned closer. "I can see them trying to silence me as a witness." She shivered. "But why tear up my apartment or try to kidnap me?"

They tabled the conversation as the waiter delivered a savory tuna *tataki* appetizer, courtesy of the chef.

"Why are you hung up on the matchbook?" she asked when the waiter walked off.

"Once word got around that Grant was using the club to help out people in a jam, civilians or first responders, Sarah started carrying matchbooks in the rig. She'd leave them with victims sometimes to let them know help was out there."

The conversation drifted away from Sarah and into other, more pleasant areas while they ate and watched the chef conduct his own brand of artistry.

"Have you ever been called out to treat a knife injury?" she murmured at Carson's ear, watching the chef slice and plate another beautiful order.

Carson smirked. "Privacy laws mean I'm not allowed to disclose that kind of thing," he teased in a whisper.

Her entire face glowed with suppressed laughter, and the intimacy landed like a punch in his gut. He hadn't been so open with anyone other than Sarah. It felt good. Right. While the first meeting hadn't been ideal, he marveled with more than a little gratitude that his path had crossed with Lissa's.

Lissa thoroughly enjoyed both the food and the company, despite their occasional conversational forays into the mystery of Noelle's murder. Maybe Noelle had simply found the matchbook or picked it up when she'd been out with other friends. Or maybe there was a lot more to it.

Either way, she didn't recall Noelle urging her to find the Escape Club that night, just her best friend's pleas to let Lissa live. "She bargained for my life," Lissa said quietly as they walked out of the restaurant. "I'll never forget the sound of her voice, begging for my life."

"She loved you."

He'd said that before, and she thought she might need the reminder frequently for some time to come. "Because I expected her to be around forever, I took my time with her for granted." She snuggled into the warmth of his arm as it came across her shoulders. "I wasn't ready to lose her, and contrary to the evidence, I can't make myself think the worst of her."

"No one is asking that," he said.

"Aren't they? It's pretty obvious Noelle was in up to her eyeballs with those people. There had to be a reason— an excellent reason—she was associating with criminals."

He pulled her close. "The cops will figure it out."

"Before or after you get tired of babysitting me?"

"Long before," he replied. "You can count on that."

His certainty simultaneously comforted her and worried her. At the corner, waiting for the walk signal, she felt his gaze on her. She couldn't make herself look at him with this odd combination of vulnerability and anticipation sliding through her.

He cleared his throat and his lips parted. "Lissa—"

His words were cut off when someone rammed him from behind, pushing him into the street in front of oncoming traffic.

Lissa screamed as Carson stumbled and curled away from the first vehicle, got jostled by the fender, and slid over the hood of a compact sedan, disappearing behind a passing truck. Brakes squealed, car horns blew and flashes went off as bystanders snapped pictures with cell phones.

Helpless and horrified, she surged after him, only to get caught when someone grabbed her, one unyielding hand on her shoulder, the other on her elbow and propelling her forward. Damn it, not again. She twisted, following the movement with a balled fist, and connected with her captor's rib cage. The strike made her bones sing, but she tried again. The thugs would not take her, not now, and definitely not when Carson needed her help. She lifted her foot, planning to stomp her captor's foot, and was blocked.

"On your side." The woman holding her jerked her around, revealed a silver badge hidden under a long sweatshirt, and then rushed her across the street. "Hurry up."

Lissa's mind reeled with the new information, and she tried to get a better look at the woman behind her, but couldn't. She forgot about the woman when she spotted Carson. He'd been pulled out of the street by a man she'd never seen before, who had propped him against a building, his long legs stretched out toward the sidewalk. "Are you okay?" She knelt at his side, her hands running lightly over his face, down his arms while she asked him where it hurt. "Do you know these people?"

"Not directly," he said.

"We'll get acquainted," the woman said. "Can you walk?" she asked Carson.

"Sure. Nothing feels broken."

Lissa worried over every wince and sigh as they helped him to his feet. "What the hell is going on?"

"Thanks for going out tonight," the woman addressed Carson again. "Smart move."

Lissa studied him, saw his face pale at what was probably meant as a compliment. She couldn't believe he'd used them as bait, yet she saw the flicker of guilt in his eyes.

"We'll walk you to your truck and follow you to the house," the man said.

"Great. Thanks." Carson wheezed.

Lissa tucked her body close to Carson's and leveled a hard stare at the woman. "We're not going anywhere until I see full identification and hear an explanation."

The woman, her pale hair reflecting the various lights around them, hitched a shoulder. "Nothing to explain. We're just a couple of good people helping out a guy who had a little bad luck," she said.

"It's okay, Lissa," Carson said. "Let's hear them out."

"I get the feeling we don't have a choice," she muttered. "Do you want a hospital?" Her heart had yet to settle back to its normal position or slow to a reasonable rate.

"Not now. I'll let you know," he replied as they walked up the block.

She could hardly force the issue after she'd put up

such resistance to medical care. Still, she had to try. "It's one thing when you have an expert to keep an eye on you. But I don't know what signs of trouble to look for."

"I'm fine," he assured her. "Better if you drive."

She took the keys when they reached the truck and, like a mother hen, watched his every move as he settled into the passenger seat and fastened his seat belt. She closed his door and turned to where the man and woman who'd helped them lingered at the tailgate. "Who are you two?"

"Friends," the woman assured her. "Werner has had me tailing you, and this is Adam. He's here doing a favor for an old friend."

"Grant Sullivan," Lissa said, and the big man inclined his head.

"Drive straight to the house and stay put," the woman said. "We'll let Werner know what happened."

"Thanks for your help," she said, hoping it came out more sincere than grudging.

Neither of them spoke on the way to Carson's place, though she suspected they had differing reasons. Adrenaline pumped through both of them. She could practically see it flashing in the air.

She bit back the questions tumbling through her head. All of them sounded more like accusations he didn't deserve. He hadn't taken her out specifically as bait. He'd taken her out for dinner. The critical factor was that being with her had put *him* in danger. When they turned down his street, she opened her mouth and heard his voice.

"Don't say it."

She shot him a long look. "I beg your pardon?"

"You're either going to ask if I planned it or tell me

you're staying elsewhere tonight with some dumb excuse that I'm at risk."

She drummed her fingers on the steering wheel, wishing the garage door would open faster. "I don't want to talk about it out here," she said, pulling into the garage. She cut the engine and handed him the keys, but he caught her hand instead.

"Good. I don't want to talk at all." He punched the button to lower the garage door and yanked her across the seat, all but devouring her mouth with a searing kiss.

She gave herself up to his sensual demands, too wired and weary of death to deny herself a moment's joy.

"Not here," he said against her cheek, his hand cupping her head. "In a bed this time."

She fisted her hands in his shirt, searching for the warm, sexy scent of him under the layers of fear and the harsh smells of traffic. "One condition."

"Anything."

She sympathized with the hint of desperation in his voice. Her body was aching to be with him again. "You didn't take me to dinner to give some bad guy an opening?" Damn it. Her voice quivered on the question and not because of where his lips had been.

"No. Dinner was for us." He cupped her and held her gaze captive. "For me. I want you, Lissa. How we met, whatever danger is out there doesn't factor into it."

"I want you, too." She bolted from the car and, taking his hand, practically raced across the yard and into the house.

Their progress was slowed by kisses and caresses that threatened to buckle her knees. When they reached the bedroom it seemed to take an eternity to get him out of his clothing, to see his chiseled body in the soft light of the bedside lamp. "You don't look too injured," she whispered. She felt suddenly shy, and her worry for him returned as she outlined a few scrapes and areas of swelling along his side. "You'll have bruises by morning."

"We have arnica oil," he said with a wink. "I'm not really hurt, I promise."

"It terrified me to see you bouncing like a pinball out there." She examined him from head to toe, walking in a tight circle around him.

"I'll jump out in traffic every day if you'll keep looking at me like that."

"Like what?" She licked her lips, raised her eyes to his.

He groaned and pulled her close, wrapped around her as he fell with her to the bed. Her head swam and her body soared as they explored each other in alternating waves of excitement and tenderness. He came over her slowly, drove deep into her body, and she matched his passionate pace. When her climax hit, she clung to him, hanging on until he found his release.

Breathless, she curled into the shelter of his body and lulled herself with the sound of his heart beating under her cheek. That was Carson, rock steady. How lucky was she to have found such a remarkable man? A man who seemed to find her both interesting and enticing.

She trailed her fingers over his torso, hoping they hadn't made any bumps and bruises worse. "Did you bump your head? Should I wake you every hour?" she asked, kissing the velvet skin on his chest.

"Not to ask me the date or time," he said, snuggling her closer and pulling the sheet over their cooling bodies. "But if you have something more active in mind, I'm all yours."

She smothered a laugh. "I'm allowed to worry after seeing you shoved into traffic."

He shifted so they were nose to nose. "It wasn't as bad as it looked."

"You weren't the one looking," she said with a shiver. For a moment the scene crowded out the pleasantness here beside him. "I thought the worst."

He kissed her with feathery touches that soothed and seduced. "So did I, for a second," he admitted. "And I'm glad for the backup Grant sent along. Otherwise—" he kissed her again "—I would've missed this."

"I'm glad we didn't miss this." Her body was primed for another round, but she thought it smarter to proceed with caution. He was so special and didn't seem to realize it.

"Lissa, I was trying to say something important on that corner." He played with her hair again, not meeting her gaze. "You implied I'll get tired of babysitting. That's not how I see it."

"That's how it started," she pointed out, studiously avoiding eye contact.

Her heart would have been flopping about on her sleeve had she been wearing any clothing, and she didn't want to endure another conversation about how functional sex was okay and acceptable. Yes, she'd started it, but somewhere along the way she'd discovered that's not how she wanted it to finish.

"A woman in trouble walked into a bar," he began.

She heard the smile in his voice, couldn't resist him. "Or was carried." Her pulse fluttered at the memory of him simply taking over, taking care.

"However it started," he continued, "you've shifted something inside me." He brought her hand to his lips, then laid it over his heart. "We might be moving a little fast here, but do you think we might…"

His voice trailed off, and she gathered her courage to meet his gaze. "…might keep dating?" she finished.

"That's a good start," he agreed. There was a smile on his lips and a deep seriousness in his eyes that just melted her.

Then his expression brightened. "Maybe one of these days, we'll have a date that doesn't end in some attempt to kill one or both of us."

She rolled him to his back and covered his face in soft kisses. "The rooftop wasn't a date."

"I think you were making a play there," he teased.

"Uh-uh. You'll know when I'm making a play." She brushed her lips over the hard ridges of his chest, down the slope of his abs.

"Promise?" he asked, but she was done talking for tonight.

Chapter 10

Morning came far too soon for Carson when his cell phone sounded long before the alarm. Half asleep and wanting to stay that way, he slapped at the nightstand but couldn't put his hand on the phone.

Where was it?

His foot bumped a feminine leg, and he heard Lissa mumbling about alarm clocks. Praise God she was still here. The impromptu date had ended with incredible sex—with a side trip into traffic, his body reminded him with a few complaints as he scrambled for his jeans and the pocket where he'd last seen his phone.

He found it, swiped to answer when he saw Grant's face on the display. "We're fine," he said immediately. "Didn't your guy call?" He leaned against the side of the bed and scooped his hair out of his eyes. He listened as Grant ran down the facts he had.

"That covers it," Carson said. "It was a pretty lame effort to hurt me," he said. "There was no reason for it," he added.

"Carson?" Lissa queried from the bed.

"Down here. It's Grant."

Through the phone, he heard his boss smother a laugh. "How did the meeting with Evelyn go?" Grant asked diplomatically.

"I'd like to discuss it with you," Carson replied. "Can I swing by the club after I drop off Lissa at the museum this morning?"

"I'll look forward to it." Grant ended the call on a cough or a laugh. Carson decided it didn't matter when Lissa's hands raked through his hair, down to his shoulders. He didn't need an engraved invitation.

When her alarm went off a half hour later, he plucked her lithe body from the bed and carried her to the shower.

He could get used to this. Even breakfast on the run was worth it for a few extra minutes kissing Lissa. Life was urgent and he was done wasting time. At the museum entrance, he gave her a goodbye kiss that jacked up his heart rate and with luck, hers, too, to tide them over through the day.

He still struggled with the idea of leaving her alone and then called himself an idiot. He thought of picking up coffee and finally recognized the procrastination hitting him square in the face. Grant always had coffee brewing at the club, strong enough to melt chest hair.

He drove straight to the club and found Grant outside, staring at the river that separated Pennsylvania and New Jersey. By way of greeting, Grant handed Carson a to-go cup filled with coffee.

"Thanks."

"Last night bothers me."

Carson had figured that, too. "Which part?" he asked, knowing Grant's mind, sharpened by his years on the police force, often delved deeper than surface details at a swift pace.

"I gave you all night to call me," Grant said, leveling that steely stare at Carson.

"Your man told me he had it covered."

"Not the same thing." Grant rolled his shoulders. "When I took on this place, I just wanted it to be a club. Good music, good people having a great time."

Carson thought he'd nailed it.

"Then it changed, just a little, under the surface." He chugged more coffee. "Maybe it was always supposed to be more."

"You've never stopped being what made you a cop," Carson observed.

"It hooks you deep and keeps you," Grant agreed. "Same for most of us in public service."

So this was destined to be another "get back on the horse" pep talk. "Evelyn gave me until Monday to decide about going back full-time."

"Gracious of her."

"I suppose. She's been more than patient." Carson took another cautious sip of the hot, strong brew in his cup. "I hesitate to leave Lissa alone."

"She's got two teams of good guys tailing her," Grant pointed out.

"And still the bad guys pushed me into traffic." Carson realized why and swore. "They were checking who would help her out."

"Calculated risk. The woman who jumped in is from

Narcotics. She's temporarily off the rotation until they know if her cover is completely blown."

"They played it like Good Samaritans," Carson assured him. "But anyone watching Lissa has more information now."

"She means something to you." Grant stated the truth in his direct way.

"Yes." The admission was out there and impossible to take back. "I know it sounds strange and probably dumb."

Grant winced and held up a hand, stopping him. "Please don't explain it." Rubbing the stubble of whiskers on his chin, he pondered a tour boat moving up the river. "I just wanted it to be a club."

They were quiet for long minutes and the persistent restlessness Carson had been fighting since Sarah's death eased. "Why is *Alexander* the code name?" he asked at last.

"Definition of the name is *defender*. It's also Katie's maiden name, and she was sort of the first client." Every time he mentioned his wife, he smiled. "Plus, no one on the staff went by the name when the Escape Club opened."

"Why start that protocol, anyway?" He was still sorting out the matchbook and Sarah's possible connection to Noelle.

"You've been here for months, Carson. Has the club been any help to you?" He sipped his coffee, waiting for the expected confirmation.

"Of course, the club's been a big help. Being here kept me going through some hard days."

"There's a vibe," Grant agreed. "One I should've expected, considering who I hire. I created the Escape Club for me, my interests, and soon discovered I couldn't turn away others in tight places, civilian or civil servant."

"You've given the community an anchor, especially on this side of town."

"Right." Grant turned to face him. "You were strong enough to go back to work months ago. You just couldn't see it. I've been through those dark days myself."

Carson swallowed the hollow protest.

"It's impossible to know how long it will take to drop a net over the people chasing Lissa," Grant continued. "You can't keep your life on hold. Evelyn, you—hell, the community at large—needs you to make a decision."

Carson snorted at the idea of the community waiting for him to do anything. He was one man assigned to an ambulance. The fear of commitment and failure twisted in his gut. What if—

"What if nothing." Grant glared at him, and only then did Carson realize he'd voiced the partial question. "You're one of the best. Not just good. One of the best."

As pep talks went, the words were familiar, but not the hard tone.

"Listen to me. I didn't have a choice. You do. You went through hell with Sarah. Do you think we don't understand that? You grieved. News flash, pal. You always will. Whether it gets better with time depends on you and what you choose to focus on."

"I panicked on the rooftop when someone shot at us at Lissa's place," he confessed. "She covered for me and pulled me out of it. We both know if that happens on a call, my partner's in jeopardy." That useless sensation weighed him down.

"Now we're getting somewhere." Grant studied him, and Carson feared he saw too much.

"No, we're not." He had to make his point and get out of here. "It's the same damn cycle. I choked out there with Sarah, I choked on the roof and I could choke again. That's not good for a partner, the department or the community at large." He was shouting by the time he finished, his breath sawing in and out of his lungs. He doubled over, hoping this time the anguish tearing at him would be purged for good.

Grant crouched beside him. "It's hard work being a hero, harder still to deny it. You're a paramedic, Carson. You know you can't save everyone."

"Sarah..." He couldn't say more than her name.

"Come on." With a groan, Grant pulled them both upright. "My partner died the night I was injured. Guilt is a brutal mistress, and you've got to cut her out if you want to make room for a life worth living."

Carson didn't reply. Logic and emotions were still wrestling for dominance.

"Have you visited with the people who are alive because you kept Sarah going long enough to donate her organs?"

He shook his head.

"I have some experience with survivor guilt," Grant said. "I know how our minds can blow things out of proportion. You need to give yourself some grace."

"Everyone says that to me," he snapped. "I'm just..." Did he dare admit it? "I'm furious." He tapped his sternum with his closed fist. "I'm furious with me. I should have protected her somehow. Taken the bullet. Something! I'm furious with the bastards who killed her and with the cops who can't find them and close her case." The only time that fury had eased was when Lissa entered his life and things got personal. Still, he worried that if he wasn't careful, he'd let her down, too.

"Always the quiet ones," Grant said with an amused snort. "The first step is admitting it. Good job."

"And the second step?"

"Justice for Sarah wouldn't hurt. Failing that, you need a safe outlet." Grant rocked back on his heels. "You must be pissed all over again with Werner's insinuations that Sarah was playing for the wrong side."

"Damn right I am. She wasn't dirty. You don't know her past like I do."

"I looked into it," Grant said.

That caught Carson off guard. "Why?"

"She got wind that I did more than offer temp positions to cops and firefighters here. She came to me, looking for a way to help out beyond stabilizing and transporting patients."

Carson could see that perfectly. Sarah would rant, feeling particularly helpless when they were dispatched time and again to the same domestic violence calls. "That's why the matchbooks were in the rig?"

"Yes." Grant nodded slowly. "Once I was satisfied she was trustworthy and absolutely clean, we created a system."

"Then you know after surviving her addict mom and violent dad, she'd never mess with dealing drugs. She barely escaped her neighborhood alive."

"I know." Grant sighed. "I've told Werner and Evelyn the same thing."

"Lissa told me she was wearing Noelle's denim jacket on Friday night and the Escape Club matchbook was in the pocket."

Grant gave that some thought. "If Noelle got that

matchbook from Sarah, it was because Sarah wanted to help her."

"Could it be that what Werner sees as guilt by association was really a rescue attempt?" Carson asked.

"I'll share the theory with him," Grant replied.

Sarah working with Grant threw an entirely different spotlight on the potential connections between her and Noelle. Carson needed some time and space to go back and review those final days and weeks with Sarah in this new context. "She didn't do anything criminal," he said.

"No argument here," Grant said. "You know, if you don't feel like going back on a rig, you might try being a private investigator."

"Nah." Carson felt his lips curve. "The last thing I need is a new career." He was starting to believe the original career might fit again, after all.

Lissa managed to get through the morning almost as if it was a normal day. As if she hadn't shared mind-blowing sex with a man who'd slipped into her heart when she wasn't looking. While part of her floated about three feet off the ground, ready to burst into song and dance, another part of her mind poked at her relationship with Noelle and what it meant to know her friend had been involved with drug dealers.

Her delicious crush on Carson and her work offered only so much distraction from the recent hellish events, and her focus shattered completely when security called down to announce she had visitors in the form of her parents.

No doubt now, the end of the world was imminent. The visit wasn't just a surprise. It was completely out of character. They hadn't even bothered attending her college graduation, mystified by her decision to stay in Philly. She'd been expecting a phone call, but to leave a dig was an extreme gesture and she wasn't sure how to feel.

She crossed to Elaine's office, marveling that she hadn't yet been fired. No, Friday's attack wasn't her fault, yet her work was far from her best this week in light of everything. "Pardon me," she said, hesitating in the open doorway.

Elaine shifted her gaze from her computer and smiled at Lissa. "What do you need?"

"Security says my parents are here. Is it okay to bring them down?"

Elaine was out of her chair in a shot, smoothing her hair and reaching for her jacket. "Of course! What an honor."

Lissa's stomach bottomed out. She knew being the Baxters' daughter hadn't gone unnoticed when she applied for jobs, but it deflated her ego to see the affiliation in action and how much weight her genetics carried.

"For everyone," Lissa said, bitterness creeping into her tone. "They have great respect for this museum." *None for their daughter, but for the museum, definitely.*

"Lissa." Elaine halted halfway between the office and the elevator. "I hired you on your merit alone."

The statement startled Lissa, and she eyed her boss with a wary gratitude. "I know they're rock stars in the field," she began.

Elaine cut her off with a quick head shake. "Meeting them will be a thrill, I admit that. Having *you* on our team here is a point of pride for me. Never doubt it."

Lissa didn't get a chance to reply as the elevator doors parted to reveal her parents.

Drs. Vincent and Joyce Baxter had both gone gray and transitioned to bifocals years ago, but those were the only concessions to their age. They wore crisp khakis and matching black polo shirts with their business logo embroidered on the sleeves. Lissa just barely kept her gaze steady when she wanted to roll her eyes. Always building awareness, her mother would say.

"Hello," she greeted them as they stepped forward. "This is my boss, Elaine—"

Her mother interrupted the introduction, pulling Lissa into a close hug. For a moment, she didn't know what to do. She and her parents had never been particularly good at affection.

Awkwardly she patted her mother's back, uncertain how to proceed. When her mother released her, Lissa tried to make introductions again, only to have her father take his turn with a rib-cracking embrace.

Had they been struck by lightning on the dig? Where were the aloof, distracted parents from her childhood?

Elaine beamed at all of them and introduced herself, extending her hand. "It's a pleasure to meet you both. We are thrilled to have Lissa on board. Would you like a tour of our space?"

"Lissa?" her mother queried, with an elevated eyebrow. "You really shouldn't encourage such a nickname."

Ah, the disapproval and subtle judgment was more familiar, and Lissa smiled. "We're a pretty relaxed team here." She repeated Elaine's offer of a tour.

"That would be intriguing," her mother said. She exchanged a glance with her husband, one that communicated volumes and effectively eliminated anyone else's input or opinion.

Lissa deferred to Elaine, only half listening to the presentation that was similar to the tour used during her internship orientation. Elaine praised Lissa's skills without going overboard, although Lissa knew the admiration mattered little to her parents. Until they knew Elaine better, they wouldn't put much stock in her opinion.

She saw her parents' expressions change along the way and noticed a smidge of grudging respect for the team's work. Wrapping up the tour, Elaine suggested Lissa take her parents to lunch and excused herself. Dr. and Dr. Baxter didn't reply immediately, merely shared another long, speaking glance.

"I'm sure you have other obligations," Lissa said, giving them an easy out. "Thanks for coming by to say hello." A short visit was more than she'd ever expected from them.

"We'd like you to come with us."

To the obligation? "To lunch?" Lissa asked.

"As a start," her father said. He plucked a troll doll from its place of honor near her monitor and turned it back and forth, clearly stumped by the purpose of the spiky neon-green hair. "What is this?"

She and Noelle had won those during one of their weekend jaunts to the Jersey shore. "It's a memento of good times with a friend," she said, returning the doll to its place. She had no expectation that her parents would recall the names she dropped in her occasional emails.

"Not Noelle?" her mother asked, eyes filling with worry.

"Yes, actually." When her mother's lips thinned in disapproval, Lissa's patience snapped. "Why exactly are you here?"

"To help you pack," Joyce said. "We sent an email."

"When?" Lissa dropped into her chair and opened her email program, searching for this supposed notification.

"This morning, before we boarded the plane." Vincent cast a critical eye over her desk. "Come now, is anything here essential?"

Naturally they'd made a decision and didn't feel inclined to discuss it with her. Had they completely missed her transition to adulthood and her striking out on her own despite their delusional expectations?

"All of it is essential right where it is." Lissa bit back the tirade that begged to be unleashed, tamping down her temper. They hadn't helped her move out of college, so disappointed in her when she'd refused to come back to field work with them. It didn't matter that she'd considered fleeing from her current trouble in Philly. This was her place and her life. "I'm not going anywhere."

"You were attacked," her mother said. "We won't let you stay."

"People are attacked every day in cities all over the world." She spread her hands. "You can see for yourself that I'm fine."

"I'll feel better when you're back on the site with us."

Absolutely not. "Where is this coming from? How did you even hear about Noelle?"

"The papers," her father replied with that icy calm. "We do pay attention to current events."

Lissa wasn't buying it. "Dr. Anson called you, didn't he?" Noelle's father meant well by reaching out, but her parents couldn't provide the comfort Lissa needed. This was not the conversation to have in an office. "Why don't we discuss this over lunch?"

Her mother nodded. "We can take sandwiches to your apartment and pack while we catch up."

"Sandwiches at my apartment." Which was still a repair in progress. "We'd have more fun with a picnic in Liberty Bell Park," she countered.

"We aren't here as tourists, Melissa." Her father clasped his hands behind his back. "We've indulged this diversion long enough. You can be more help to us on the dig site, and we can see that you're sufficiently protected."

They could pull and prod all they wanted. She would not budge. "Why now?"

Behind her stylish glasses, Joyce squinted, clearly baffled by Lissa's question. "You're our daughter." Her nose wrinkled as she gazed around the wide room. "This isn't where you belong."

"But it is. It's exactly where I want to be, Mom. I appreciate your concern. I'm sure it was a difficult time for you both to leave the site, but I'm staying."

"Melissa." Her father used the disappointed tone.

"I love you both." She startled all three of them with her sincere declaration. Losing Noelle had brought that urgency of life right to the front of her mind, her heart. "If you have time for lunch, I would enjoy catching up."

Another glance between them ended with a distinctly unenthusiastic agreement. She knew the relocation conversation wasn't over, at least not on their end. They opted for the museum cafeteria rather than a restaurant and took the food outside to have a picnic in a shady spot on the grounds. As they ate, Lissa shared some recent project successes and listened to her parents gloss over the details of their latest dig. It was the communication pattern they all understood.

Finally they circled back to the issue that brought them and confirmed Noelle's parents had notified them of the trouble. "It's a beautiful day," she said. "Why don't we take a walk?" It would buy her some time to present logical arguments for staying.

Her first attempt to point out she was a capable adult fell on deaf ears. On her next attempt, she emphasized her commitment to her work. That one might have been more successful if she hadn't spotted the man who'd tried to drug her at the Escape Club. He was matching their pace on the opposite walkway.

This was the man half of the Philly police department was searching for. She pulled out her phone and sent a group text message to the detective, Carson and Grant, just to cover all her bases. She rejected the urge to panic. She wasn't alone, and there were people nearby watching out for her. She simply had to stall and give authorities and Carson time to arrive. And she had to do it in a way that wouldn't reinforce her parents' notion that Philly was all wrong for her.

Realizing she'd walked a bit further without her parents, she turned back, catching them in a heated, nearly inaudible discussion.

Her father linked his hands behind his back. "We've danced around this long enough, Melissa. You need to tell your boss today is your last day."

Her shoulders sagged and her gaze darted to the man shadowing them. It occurred to her that other than bumping into him outside the museum her first day back, she'd never seen him work alone. Now she searched every face, looking for the woman. "That's ridiculous and hypocritical. I'm well aware you both hold a low opinion of anyone who quits without notice."

"In normal situations, that's true. If you've been honest with Elaine, she will understand you cannot stay in the city another moment," Joyce said. "Dr. and Mrs. Anson assured us you've done all you can for their daughter's case."

Her mother droned on, and Lissa tuned her out. She'd given the detective everything she could remember, but for some reason, the drug crew hadn't given up on her.

"Are you listening?" Vincent demanded, giving her shoulder a shake.

"Yes," she fibbed. The contact had jarred something loose in her memory. Too flimsy to hang onto while her attention was divided, but an important detail. "Were the Ansons worried for me?"

Her mother scowled at her. "They are concerned this isn't a safe place for young single women."

"Did they say why?" she pressed. Maybe Noelle had left them a message of some sort and they didn't recognize what it meant.

"We've wasted enough time. You're leaving with us. Today." Her father took her by the elbow and started marching back to the museum. On the other path, the man followed their movements.

Lissa dug in her heels at a park bench. "Please sit down. I'm staying right here until we come to a reasonable agreement." Her phone buzzed with a message, and she glanced down to see the detective's reply that uniformed officers were on the way.

"You must understand we only want what's best for you," Joyce said calmly.

Lissa laughed. Why was Carson's calm voice reassuring and her mother's so aggravating?

"She's hysterical, Vincent."

"I should be furious," Lissa said, keeping tabs on the

man. "I want you to understand that what's best for me is this job in this city."

"You were raised for more important endeavors," her father said.

Lissa watched a patrol car cruise by on the route that circled the museum as another turned down the street near the river. The man hurried away and, with any luck, into custody.

"You used to approve of my work," she said.

"We approved of your major," her father corrected her. "In fact, we've gone to great lengths to secure a new post for you at the Smithsonian in DC."

"Your father and I have rearranged our schedules so we'll be working there, as well. Two years as adjunct professors. It will give us long-overdue time with our lab research."

Her first thought was how her parents would wither without the sunshine, air and pervasive grit of a dig. Her second thought was how much she'd miss Carson if she followed them to DC. As she'd told him, they loved her. They just had a strange, unsupportive way of expressing it.

"You really shouldn't have made those plans without talking to me about it."

Her father steepled his fingertips and tapped them together repeatedly. It was a dead giveaway he'd lost his patience. "Why not?"

No sense repeating arguments that hadn't worked a few minutes ago. "I love you both," she said instead.

They gawked at her in tandem as if she'd dropped the Rosetta Stone.

"Yes, there's been some trouble. My best friend was murdered," she said quietly. "I was in the wrong place at the wrong time. My injuries were minor, aside from brief amnesia, and I'm recovering.

"My work matters. Not just to me, but to my team. I'm not walking out on that, or on what I've built here." She turned to her mother, hoping her next tactic hit home. "I've fallen in love with a great guy," she said. "And his home is here. I believe if I have any hope of finding the amazing lifelong partnership like you have with Dad, it's here with him."

Behind her someone coughed, sputtered, then said her name. She twisted around, mortified to come face-to-face with Carson. "Hello."

"Hi." He'd obviously overheard everything. Heat rose in her cheeks and ears like a pot ready to boil over, while her fingers and toes went numb. She hadn't really embellished her feelings for him, but she hadn't intended to share them yet, either.

As much as she wanted to blame this on the untimely visit of her parents, she couldn't do it. Since going to college, she'd been making strides to overcome the reactionary remnants of their carelessness and her insecurity.

She greeted him with a quick hug and a kiss on the cheek, noting he'd come straight from a construction site. "What a nice surprise." She'd managed to get the words past the lump in her chest as she sent him a pleading look. *Please don't dump me right here*, she thought, making the introductions.

"My parents heard what happened and came to check on me," she explained.

God bless him for keeping his cool when her stomach kept turning inside out. He didn't give the slightest indication that her declaration of love was news to him, or that trouble had been as close as the sidewalk a moment ago. If that wasn't heroic compassion, she wasn't sure how to define it better.

Chapter 11

Carson followed her lead, greeting her parents, who eyed him as if he was the lowlife the police had just chased out of the area. Lissa behaved with such composure, he might have thought she made a habit of identifying criminals while showing her parents the sights.

They walked back toward the museum while Vincent and Joyce sought his support in moving her out of the city immediately.

There was not a chance in hell he was letting that happen. He couldn't believe their blatant disregard for her thoughts and feelings. She'd just said she was in love with a great guy—with him—and wanted to stay here, and they responded as if she were twelve, incapable of knowing her heart or mind. He had the ironic pleasure of thinking he'd never met two more detached people. No wonder she craved stability and connection.

"Where are you staying?" It was the most polite diversion he could come up with as the three of them quietly argued about Lissa's resignation.

"We're in town only through tomorrow," Vincent replied.

When they were back inside the museum, Joyce nudged Lissa aside for a private word. The tension from both women was unmistakable. Carson took the opportunity to speak with her father. "I know you're concerned for your daughter, Dr. Baxter, but she's recovering well, and she loves Philadelphia."

"How long have you known my daughter, Mr. Lane?"

Carson noticed the emphasis on the mere *Mr.* and smothered a smile. He suddenly realized how long he'd known her paled in comparison to how *well* he knew her. The Baxters didn't understand her at all. "Not long," he admitted. "She's a fighter, isn't she? You must be so proud of her accomplishments."

"Graduating college with top honors was hardly an effort for her." Dr. Baxter flexed his bushy gray eyebrows. "She has so much more to offer than dusting off parchment and assessing lighting conditions."

"You're right about that," Carson said. "Wherever her work takes her, she will excel. You should ask her to take you through the museum galleries. Her knowledge brings it all to life."

"We saw that she had the best education, even out in the field."

Education, sure, but no sign of respect or affection. The Baxters loved their daughter, just as she'd said. They just couldn't seem to separate love from credentials.

Lissa and her mother returned, both of them blushing. He'd ask about that later. He announced, "Lissa is staying with me while her landlord sees to a few repairs at her apartment." He ignored the collective gasp from her parents. "Would you like to join us for dinner tonight?"

He hoped that was amused gratitude flashing in Lissa's dark eyes as he waited for an answer.

Joyce handled it while Vincent's complexion turned a deep crimson. "We'll let you think things over tonight," her mother said to Lissa. "You can give us your decision in the morning."

"What's with the high-pressure questions lately?" he asked as Dr. and Dr. Baxter walked out of the museum.

Lissa blushed and pushed the button for the elevator. "Mom doesn't want to take no for an answer, but since I told her I'm sleeping with you, she's giving me until morning to decide which I want more, a danger-filled life with you or safety with them."

"A sex test?" he whispered at her ear. "Again, no pressure."

She burst out laughing as they stepped into the elevator. "You're the only person, besides Noelle, who has ever made me laugh when my parents are around."

He pulled her close and kissed her before the chime sounded on her level.

"Did they catch the man following me or the other two?" she asked.

"Not yet." He hesitated as she stepped out of the elevator to return to work. "Grant's man followed him for a few blocks before he had to bug out."

"Is that good news?"

Carson nodded. "When you're done for today, we need to have a long talk."

She tugged him into the hallway with her. "About what I said, um, out there?"

"No." Was that disappointment flashing in her dark brown eyes? He didn't mind being her excuse for her parents. Or rather, he wouldn't have minded it so much if he could slow down the effervescent feeling her words had stirred up. "I meant about Sarah and Noelle. I was running down a few theories when I got your text."

"What kind of theories?"

"Later." He hooked his thumbs in his back pockets. "I'm sure our bosses would appreciate it if we put some time in today."

"You're going out on an ambulance?"

She sounded so excited for him, he almost lied. He really should have told her what had happened with Evelyn yesterday, but he kept cycling away from it. "No. I'm due on the construction site." He stepped close and brushed a kiss to her lips. "Call me when you're ready and I'll be here to pick you up."

"Thanks."

Carson waited until he was well away from the museum before he called Grant. "Has anyone found him yet? Should I go back and look around?" The man Grant had assigned to Lissa had fallen off the radar shortly after the drug dealer left the museum grounds.

"No walking alone for you," Grant said. "I've got someone pinging the cell signal now, and we should find him shortly."

"Does Werner still have someone watching Lissa?"

"Yes."

"All right." Carson tried to settle down. "As long as she isn't alone."

"No one plans to leave her alone until we have this case wrapped up," Grant said. "How did you enjoy her parents?"

Carson thought about that. "They were an interesting blend of helicoptering tendencies balanced with benign neglect."

"Well, that paints a picture."

"They mean well," he said. "They want her to move to DC with them, where it's safe."

"When?"

Carson choked on a bitter laugh. "Today." He laughed again when Grant sputtered about crime rates. "She held her own, but they want her decision by tomorrow morning."

Grant coughed. "The victim who showed up here on Friday night might have agreed. Now that she has her memory back, I don't think they stand a chance of budging her."

Somehow Grant's assessment put Carson at ease. He let the entire mess filter through the back of his mind during the remainder of the afternoon. He gave Daniel's task list his full attention on the job until Lissa called. As he'd anticipated, she worked late to make up for the lost hours this week. Either that or she didn't want to spend extra time with him tonight.

He pulled himself back from that idea, thinking of the way she'd blushed when she saw him standing behind her. If she'd meant it about being in love with him…

He rubbed a fist over his sternum when his heart gave another kick at the concept. Was he ready to take that emotional leap after such a short time? Well, if she meant it, he'd do everything in his power to make sure she didn't regret it.

He used the voice-to-text option and sent her a message when he was a block away. He added a second message asking her to have a security guard walk her to the truck. The light was fading, and since they had yet to find Grant's man or anyone from the drug crew, he wasn't inclined to make either of them a target.

She reached the truck without incident and leaned over to kiss him before she buckled her seat belt. It wasn't anywhere close to the most passionate kiss they'd shared, but it gave him the strangest sense of being caught and flying free at the same time.

"Did your parents change their minds about dinner?"

She grinned. "Not a chance. They have two dining extremes, camp food and five-star fare. A normal home-cooked meal isn't typically high on the list." She didn't appear bothered by the snub. "I wanted to do a backflip when you put them on the spot like that."

"I was trying to be nice."

"Oh, I know." She grinned. "I know. That's what made it so perfect."

"Huh. Let's pretend I understand that. Were they here because you told them about Noelle?"

"No," she said, sounding horrified at the concept. "Noelle's parents reached out to them. I have no idea how the Ansons even found them. Half the time I can't reach them when I want to wish them happy birthday or whatever."

"And yet they came all this way."

"They went to 'great lengths,'" she said with air quotes. "They mean well."

There were stories in there and lots of them, he thought. It surprised him how much he wanted to hear them all and soothe the deep aches her parents had left behind. He glanced over at her and saw the glow of satisfaction on her face. "You know something."

"I know a lot of things. Your comment about theories on Sarah and Noelle kept my brain engaged while I waited on some tedious tests to run their course today."

"Did you find or remember another connection?"

"Yes." She bounced a little in her seat. "Noelle had a penchant for bad-boy types, so we always had a deal. She usually gave me names and a picture when she went out on dates."

"The easy escape."

"Exactly. The guy's face has felt familiar, but I couldn't place it. On a hunch, I went through my old text messages from Noelle when I got back to my desk. His name is William Hammond. At least, that's the name he gave Noelle when they went out on a blind date."

"What?" Carson looked for a place to pull over. "We have to get this to Grant or Werner."

"I sent everything I had to both of them already," she said. "Noelle dated him off and on, but I saw him only in the first picture until I caught a glimpse of him when he picked her up at my house just a few weeks ago. He didn't come up, just waited in a convertible on the street." She shook her head. "I can't believe it took me this long to remember his face out of the context of Friday." She went quiet for a moment. "Noelle must have left something in my house, or picked something up that night. We should go search," she suggested.

"Not without backup," Carson said. "Let's slow down and think this through." He was about to say more when the phone rang through the speakers and caller ID gave Grant's name.

"Where are you?" Grant asked the moment Carson answered.

"On the way to my place. Lissa is remembering more about this William guy."

"Go home and stay put," Grant ordered. "And turn on your security system."

He glanced at Lissa and assumed her bewildered expression matched his. "What the hell is going on?"

"Get inside and set the system. Then call me and let me know what Lissa remembers."

Carson didn't have a chance to argue as Grant ended the call.

"What on earth?" Lissa mused.

He had a bad feeling, but he didn't want to speculate on worst case scenarios and upset her for nothing. "Can you call your parents, just to check on them?"

"Do you think they're in danger?"

"I seriously doubt it, but I'd rather be safe than sorry."

She used her phone and made the call as he turned in to his street. He listened as she confirmed her parents were dining at the hotel restaurant. Naturally they were eager to know if she'd already changed her mind about the new post in DC. By the time she'd extricated herself from that sticky web, Carson had parked in the garage.

"What do you think is going on?"

The fear in her voice made him want to soothe her. Although he'd hoped to discuss what he'd overheard today, that had to wait. "We'll find out soon," Carson said. "Grant isn't known for overreacting."

Inside the house, he armed his security system, sharing the code with her so she could turn it off if they tripped it by accident. Her earlier excitement over making some progress about Noelle's case had given way to abject worry. It didn't help matters that Grant didn't pick up when Carson called in as ordered.

"What are the odds we'll find any sign of your theory about Noelle after the break-in and fire?" He pulled out two beers from the refrigerator and opened both, handing one to her.

"Low," she admitted. "Still, I want to try. Our best friends were keeping secrets from us, and now they're dead." She took a long drink of the beer. "I'm strongly opposed to either one of us becoming the next victim."

"We have to be close, or they wouldn't be so persistent."

Carson regretted his words moments later when Grant returned their call and brought them up to speed. "Turns out the man Lissa has identified as Hammond got close to Lissa today because his accomplices intercepted Adam. I had him following you," Grant explained, his voice grave over the speaker. "If you hadn't kept your cool, it's hard to say what might have happened."

Carson watched the color leach from Lissa's face and took her hand, willing her to hang on. "Is Adam okay?"

"He was drugged and left for dead in an alley. We got him to the hospital and they think he will pull through. In his pocket, they'd planted an Escape Club matchbook, and tucked into that was a demand for the missing product."

"That's what they want me for," Lissa said. "They think I know what Noelle did with their drugs."

"That's my guess," Grant agreed. "Stay inside. Don't even order takeout. We have a potential sting going here tonight. With luck, that will bring this bastard out to play, and we can be done already. I'll be in touch."

Carson set the phone aside and gathered her into his arms as tremors shook her body. "It's my fault." She hiccuped. "Someone nearly died because of me."

"Hush." He rocked her a little. "You've been so strong through all of this. So steady. Don't fall apart now."

She shook her head, balling her fists in his shirt and hiding her face.

He took her into the front room and pulled her onto the couch, waiting for the shock to fade. This reaction was an echo of her grief over her friend. He understood that. He rubbed her back, smoothed her hair and handed over tissues until the worst of it passed.

"After Sarah—" he forced himself to say the next word "—died, everything was magnified in my world. There weren't simple emotions. Anything alive was too alive. Anything dying or dead brought it all back. I hated lilies because they reminded me of her funeral. Cats, too."

"Cats?" She lifted her head, and he smiled at the confused frown on her face. "You don't like animals?"

"Actually, I'm a big fan. Sarah had a snarly gray tabby cat who hated me. She left him to my sister Becky. He and I were both so miserable without Sarah that I hated him right back for a while. I begged her to dump the beast at a shelter. Everything was too much to cope with."

She snuggled into him. "Adam nearly died helping me today."

"He survived," he reminded her. "I know him a little from the club, and he loves helping out in any capacity. You've remembered an important name, and we're both looking at our best friends, eyes wide open now. We'll find justice for them. The cops are running every lead, and Grant is working double time. Together we'll figure it out so you can feel safe again."

"I feel safe here, with you." Her low whisper drifted over him, soothing the tattered edges of his soul. "You've been in danger because of me. I couldn't bear losing you, too. Not now."

"Now?" he prompted when he couldn't take the silence anymore. Had she meant what she'd told her parents today?

"You remind me what it's like to have someone who understands *me*."

Not exactly the answer he was looking for. Then again, was either of them ready for something more significant?

"That has to sound weird," she continued. "All things considered, but it's true. I could never go to DC and start making friends all over again. Not after losing Noelle and meeting you. Definitely not with the absurd expectations of my parents hanging over my head."

She'd included him in the reasons to stay. He'd follow his own advice and focus on the positive. "You could do it."

"I don't want to," she insisted. "Some days I wonder if they even notice that I'm an adult. I think they ignored me so often that they missed some important milestones along the way."

"Like what?"

She blotted her eyes and swiped at her nose, balling the tissue into her hand. "I didn't mean to lose it," she said, dodging the question. "Death is so permanent."

He bent his head and kissed her. "And life is precious. He survived. *We* survived." His heart hammered as she angled her body across his to kiss him back.

"I'm the Baxters' daughter. I should be used to life and death and what we leave behind by now, and yet…"

"The *yet* is what makes you Lissa Baxter, CSI for priceless documents and artifacts."

"I made it clear to Elaine that I have no intention of going anywhere, despite the rumors my parents have surely started."

"I'm glad to hear it." Would she make it clear to him, too, now? He could see a life with her so easily. It didn't scare him as much as it excited him to think of dinners at home after shifts, date nights in the city or movie nights here on the couch. She'd be safe inside the museum when he was on duty. His family tree was rooted here, right where she kept saying she wanted to stay firmly planted.

"Elaine said the nicest thing to me today." She stroked her thumb over his cheek, made a study of his face.

"What was that?" he managed to ask as the affectionate touch undid him.

"She said she hired me on my own merit." Lissa smiled, her eyes lit with happiness. "It's how life is supposed to go." She lifted herself off him and retreated to the far end of the couch. "But I rarely knew for sure if it was really my effort or their influence when things went my way."

"Well, neither one of us knew your name when you fell into my care, and I liked you just fine." Her smile blossomed, as he'd hoped it would.

"Obviously that was my luckiest day ever."

"People are allowed to have more than one lucky day," he said, crawling toward her. "If we have to stay in, we should make the most of it."

He kissed her and she sighed. "We should make the most of it and help Grant and Werner sort out how our friends were connected."

She was right, but kissing her was such a lovely distraction. "In a minute."

Chapter 12

The minute Carson suggested turned into an hour of sensual bliss, and Lissa couldn't fault either of them for taking the time to enjoy the moment. Sensing a reflection of her urgency in his caresses only amplified each detail. Content and hungry, they'd made a meal of leftovers and were now searching for the connection points between Sarah and Noelle.

She understood him more, adored him more, with every interaction. Until Sarah had been killed, he'd dealt with life and death every day in the course of his job. And every day since losing his best friend, he'd been dealing only with death, stuck in a loop of despair. She recognized how easy it would be to get mired down by the grief whenever she wanted to share something with Noelle and couldn't. The harsh reality stung.

All of that was compounded for Carson, losing his

best friend and his partner. It was no wonder he wasn't eager to go back full-time on an ambulance. She wished there was something she could do for him, some way to help him feel as strong and empowered as he kept making her feel.

She ached for him when he relayed the conversation and negative implications his boss had made about Sarah. Once he'd explained her background and how much she'd overcome to break the drug and abuse cycles, Lissa agreed with his adamant opinion that Sarah hadn't been working with the dealers.

"Okay," he said as they dissected Sarah's final shifts and personal time. "We did transport two patients to the hospital where Noelle worked the day before the ambush, but I never saw your friend."

Lissa didn't stand a chance of recalling Noelle's schedule from eight months ago, but she tried to think of anything else going on at the time. "Noelle often took short breaks in odd places. The parking garage or the chapel. Sometimes we went to the diner or the park across the street from the hospital. There aren't many ways to get away during a long shift."

He pushed a hand through his hair. "The only time our rig had a discrepancy on drugs was the night we were attacked. They shot her and took everything that wasn't locked down."

"What if someone on the drug crew saw Noelle speaking with Sarah and thought there was an exchange?"

"Where and how could that have happened?"

"That's the big question," she murmured.

Carson's studied the notes he'd been making all day. "It wasn't like we were answering multiple calls to the same address. Not even a significant percentage of our calls were going to Noelle's ER."

Lissa got up from the table and paced the length of the kitchen. Carson had pieces from more than nine months ago. She had only a scattered picture of Noelle's last few days. When and how would someone have spotted them together, and with Sarah dead, why wait so long to attack Noelle?

"The timing bothers me," she said. "We know Sarah wasn't helping drug dealers. Noelle shouldn't have been doing so. I can't pinpoint a single reason she'd get involved with such a scam."

When and how had someone from the crew seen them together?

"Your boss didn't mention why she's so convinced?"

"The only thing that makes sense to me is cell phone records," Carson replied. He propped his cheek on his fist and watched her pace. "Maybe we should table this for tonight."

She caught the flare of desire in his hazel eyes, and her body reacted immediately. Sleeping in his bed, her body twined with his, would be perfect. "Assuming we're free to leave tomorrow, I'd like to go by the hospital first thing. We can take flowers to Grant's friend."

"Flowers?" He arched an eyebrow.

"How about balloons?" she suggested instead.

"You're a special person, Lissa." He walked over and gave her a hug. "I'm glad you stumbled into the Escape Club."

"So you'll take me by the hospital?"

"Definitely." He set his mouth to her neck, just under her ear. "But first I'm taking you to bed."

The next morning they got word they could leave the house. Even though Grant's sting hadn't worked as he'd hoped, he and Werner had a new team in place to protect Carson and Lissa and cops all over the city were on high alert for any sign of Hammond.

The first stop was to visit Adam, and Lissa's knees were knocking when they reached the hospital. This was where Noelle had worked. Her heart hammered in her chest and her palms were clammy as Carson asked for Adam's room number. She had the hysterical wish that the balloons would carry her out of there.

"Are you okay?" Carson murmured as they approached the room.

She gave a tiny shake of her head. More of a twitch. "I don't want to be here, but I'm not leaving." Something deep inside was screaming at her to run as far as possible. She realized just how out of control her fear was when moving to DC with her parents suddenly sounded like a good idea.

"I'm right here." Carson's rock-steady voice calmed her enough that she didn't do an about-face and run for the stairs when they reached the right door.

"Thank you." With her hand tucked into his, he knocked on the cracked door.

Adam invited them in. He looked groggy, and the bruises on his face and arms were colorful. She offered the balloons and he smiled, though it didn't hide the pain.

"I'm sorry you were hurt," she began.

He waved it off, seemed to struggle for a deep breath. "Risk comes with the territory. Happy...to he-help."

Suddenly an alarm went off on the bedside monitor. Screeching alternated with a calm directive, but the words were a blur to Lissa. Carson leaped into action, checking the man's pulse and reading the monitors.

"Call button," he told her, climbing onto the bed.

She pressed the button and then rushed to the hallway, shouting for help. Nurses were already heading her way with the crash cart, a term she'd learned from Noelle. A man in a doctor's coat looked up from the chart he was reading and stared straight at her.

A chill swept over her body as she recognized William Hammond. "You." It was a whisper rather than a shout. Lissa's blood ran cold as he smirked and turned away. He wasn't coming to help Adam. Her fear of hospitals suddenly seemed far less irrational. On instinct she chased him, down the hall, to the corner stairwell.

She shouted for him to stop, fumbled with her purse in an effort to use her phone to call for help. His coat flapped as he rounded another landing, their footfalls reverberating up and down the stairs. A gunshot ricocheted and she ducked back, as close to the wall as she could get. Another shot, and one more, then the slam of a door far below. The sullen silence underscored her sense of defeat. She'd lost him.

"Lissa?" Carson's voice cut through her misery. "Are you in here?"

"Yes." She stood up, kept close to the wall as she started back up the stairs.

He met her halfway in full paramedic mode, searching her for injuries. "What the hell were you thinking?"

"I saw him," she said. "Hammond. He's gone." She trudged to the nearest door with Carson. "How is Adam?"

Carson shook his head. "He didn't make it."

"Hammond killed him."

"That's a big leap," he cautioned.

"You didn't see his face." She shook her head. "I've never been afraid of hospitals, but I didn't want to see a doctor the night you found me. Noelle must have warned me off with good reason."

"Let's get out of here. We'll find a better place to give Werner our statements."

Thank goodness she wasn't expected at the office. Elaine had given her another day off to spend time with her parents. Exhausted and frustrated, in the diner across from the hospital, Lissa gave her account of the facts to Werner, adding a hefty dose of her opinion. "He's a monster. He had something on Noelle. She wouldn't have cooperated with a criminal scheme otherwise."

Werner explained they'd reviewed Noelle's bank and phone records and found no evidence that she was profiting from her cooperation with Hammond. "She was in frequent contact with an unlisted cell phone number we traced to Sarah. Grant told me Sarah had been cautiously guiding victims to the Escape Club for help."

"Okay, we all agree Sarah was clean and Noelle wasn't but should have been," Lissa said. "This doctor had something on my friend," she insisted. "Carson and I were trying to figure out how anyone at the hospital would've seen Noelle and Sarah together. As their best friends, neither of us had any idea they knew each other. This doctor must have caught Noelle confiding in Sarah. He had Sarah killed and eventually turned on Noelle, too."

"We don't have evidence to back that up one way or another," Werner said.

"I know." Lissa groaned. "Can you haul him in for shooting at me?"

"Did you see him pull the trigger?"

"No," she admitted, filled with misery that had no outlet. "No one else was in the stairwell."

"That you know of," Werner said. "We'll follow up."

"Great." Lissa didn't have a lot of confidence it would result in an arrest.

"I want the two of you to be particularly cautious," Werner said. "As you know, the sting we tried last night didn't lure out Hammond or his accomplices. We have more surveillance in place, but this crew has proven they are a resourceful lot. Since you saw him on the floor when Adam died, I can make sure we take a close look at him."

It was a start, she supposed. "Thank you."

Carson worried a little as Lissa's agitation only increased when they were back at his house. She'd turned down food, chocolate and a shot of whiskey. And she'd turned it all down again after another round with her parents over the phone.

When he put a bottle of water in her hands, she just played with it, not drinking.

"What's going through your head?"

"It's a puzzle," she muttered. "What we know doesn't line up or point to what we need to know. I mean, we have confirmation of Sarah's role, but not Noelle's. I have to assume the doctor dragged her into it, that he's the leader of this drug ring, even though the woman called the shots on Friday night."

"Assumptions aren't the best idea here. Give the detective and his resources time to figure it out."

She kept pacing, completely engrossed with the problem. He counted it a small blessing that she wasn't berating herself for Adam's death.

"Why don't we go to the site Daniel is flipping? It would get us out of here."

"You could drop me at the museum."

"No." He didn't want her out of his sight after the incident at the hospital. "We're together until we hear that Hammond is in custody." He wasn't losing anyone else to this mess.

"Fine. What can I do at the site?"

He smiled. "You can be awed by my skills while you keep stewing and pacing for answers."

"I'll need more than that," she said. "I'm not good at being window dressing."

"I figured that already." He urged her up the stairs to the room he was happy to be sharing with her. Hard to believe that he, Mr. Solitude, wanted this woman nearby all the time. Sarah would have laughed her butt off, but he had to admit she'd been right every time she'd told him the right woman wouldn't get in his way or chafe his independence.

Keeping the realization stuffed inside before he dropped to one knee and proposed way too early, he gave her an old T-shirt so she wouldn't trash her good clothes and eyed her jeans. "You're okay if those get ruined or stained?"

She nodded, her mind still working overtime on the trouble Noelle had chosen to face alone. It was the same thing in the truck. He'd say something and she'd mutter about something else. It should have annoyed him, but he found it endearing. He decided his attention was best spent keeping an eye on her while she was distracted.

"I was her best friend," she mumbled when they were walking up to the house in progress. "Why didn't she trust me?"

"My guess is she was protecting you."

"I have to agree with you on that." She sighed. "I don't have to like it." She stopped short and gave the house a critical eye, then shifted her gaze up and down the street, deliberately turning her back on the patrol car that cruised to a stop at the end of the block. "This will be nice when he's done."

"Come on inside so I can really impress you."

Carson made introductions, and although Daniel was on shift at the moment, the job supervisor was pleased to have extra hands. They put her to work cleaning up finished areas until lunch, and they elected her to make the run. At the last second, Carson went with her, unable to trust the rest of the world even that much.

He'd spent his time installing tile, and with the calm rhythm of it, he replayed Adam's final moments in the hospital room. The man had clearly been poisoned. Carson had told Werner his suspicions, but only an autopsy would prove it. And possibly not even that. There were too many options for a doctor who knew how to manipulate meds and symptoms.

Suddenly he swore.

Lissa jumped. "What's wrong?"

"My last patient with Sarah was transported to Noelle's ER."

"So you've said."

"Hammond was there. I don't recall Noelle, but I remember him." He pounded a fist against the steering wheel. "I saw him with Sarah. Good Lord, I can't believe I forgot. We were attacked less than two hours later."

"But she wasn't transported back to that same ER."

"That wouldn't have mattered. She was dead."

"I meant the decision might have saved your life,"

Lissa murmured, laying her hand on his thigh while he drove.

"I can't believe I forgot his face."

"You had no reason to remember it until now. Be nice to yourself."

He tried, as they picked up the food and returned to the construction site. Everyone knocked off long enough to cram in their meals and then went back to work. He was nearly done with the bathroom floor when Lissa wandered in to watch.

"Need something?" he asked.

She sank her teeth into that full lower lip and winked at him. "I'm doing okay for the moment." She fanned her face.

He flexed his biceps as a joke, but when her gaze turned hot, he had to concentrate or he would have screwed up the tile pattern.

"Can we swing by my apartment?" she asked when they were leaving the site. "Mrs. Green says it's ready, and we have backup right behind us."

He checked the mirror and confirmed the patrol car in their wake.

"Is it done?" He tried to keep the disappointment out of his voice. He wasn't eager to return to an empty house again. They never had discussed what she'd said to her parents, and it was starting to feel like the opportunity had slipped away.

If he let her know the way his thoughts were running, if he told her he loved *her*, he couldn't be sure it would end well. They'd both been through so much. Would she blame the emotion on great sex and bad trauma? Sarah would tell him to picture a positive result for a change and he tried, but he kept seeing his time with Lissa ending one of two ways. Either she'd believe him and run away screaming like the smart woman she was, or she wouldn't believe he could love her and she'd walk out of his life.

He pulled into the open parking space next to her house but didn't look at her. "I've been thinking about giving Evelyn the answer she wants and going back full-time."

"Really?" She sounded so excited for him that he did a double take. "I've seen you in action," she said with a wealth of pride in her smile. "You'll always be the guy who jumps in and gives his all."

"That's how you see me?"

"That's how you *are*. The PFD will be thrilled to have you back, Carson." She hopped out of the truck and started up to the house.

Dumbfounded, he followed her and paused at the top of the porch. "I panicked when we were under fire on your roof."

"Please. You didn't even start to panic until we were out of immediate danger." She stepped up to him and ran her hands over his shoulders, leaned in. "And even then, I'd call it a flashback, not panic. When you go back, you'll be amazing. Trust me. You're one of the strongest people I know."

"You've made me stronger." Good grief. He searched for a better explanation, better words for the feelings churning in his gut.

"Same goes," she said, linking her hand with his. "Without your help, I think Noelle's murder might have swallowed me whole."

"Lissa, are we friends, stuck in a situation, or headed toward something more serious here?"

A smile bloomed on her face, lighting her eyes. "We're friends with a whole lot more going for us in any circumstance."

Only another declaration of love would have been a better answer. He almost couldn't believe how fortune had smiled on him, bringing her into his life. Lissa had become as essential as air and water. He needed her and wanted to be needed in turn. He felt it when they were together, and he could be happy with that. For now.

"You've been cooped up all day," Lissa said. "Why don't you wait here in the fresh air? I just want to check out the progress upstairs."

He shook his head. "We're more than friends and we're sticking together."

She tossed him a sassy grin over her shoulder as she unlocked the door. "Best news I've had all day."

She entered the code on the new electronic lock and opened the door, but when they stepped inside, he realized the trap was sprung.

Lissa stared at the man sitting on the landing, gun leveled at her head. He'd shed the doctor's coat, but there was nothing benign about his khakis, the white button-down and the pale blue striped tie, loose at his collar.

"Get out of my house."

"As soon as you give me my product. I know Noelle stashed it here. It's the only logical place."

Lissa willed Carson to run, to call for help, but he remained at her back, the barely leashed energy coming off of him in waves. She understood how it felt.

"Both of you come on in. Lock the door. This shouldn't take long."

"Let her go," Carson countered, "and I'll help you tear this place apart."

"No deal." Hammond's laugh was a sick, deep cackle. "She knows Noelle better than you or I. Come in. Now."

Lissa wanted to throw a tantrum as Carson closed the door and locked them in with Hammond. The patrol car was out there, but they had no way to signal for help. Damn it. She started up the stairs, one part of her all too aware of moving closer to danger, while her brain fitted the last piece of Noelle's puzzle into place.

"What did you have on her?" she asked as she reached the landing, Hammond backing up a few steps ahead of her. "She never would've done anything illegal without coercion."

"She came to me," he said with a slick smile. "Wanted in on the action."

Lissa knew better, from both Werner's lack of evidence and her own heart. "I don't believe you," she said as they reached her apartment.

Her gaze slid to the security panel. If it was fully operational, maybe she or Carson could hit the emergency button.

Hammond pushed at it with the gun. "Disconnected," he said. "You won't get out of here alive if you don't help me."

"There's no reason to add two more murders to your list," Carson said, standing close behind her.

"Why not? Without you two, I'm a free man. Free to start fresh somewhere else."

"You're alone," Lissa commented, a little surprised he didn't have the thugs around for backup. Two against one put the odds in their favor. With a distraction, they could overtake him and see justice for Noelle and Sarah at last.

"Start searching," Hammond ordered. "Try to double-cross me and I'll shoot your boyfriend."

Lissa shook her head. "Noelle didn't leave anything here. Your partner already searched."

"Really?" His lip curled in a snarl. "Then why did you stop by?"

"To see how the repairs were going." She saw the kitchen. "You jerk!"

He'd torn it apart, and the new laminate wood planks were peeled back as if he'd been looking for a floor safe. Her palms itched to take action, to fight, though it wouldn't be smart right here and now. She felt so helpless. "What are you thinking?"

"I want what belongs to me." He advanced, his breath hot in her face. "I want what your friend stashed here."

As he closed in on her, Carson jumped him from behind. The men wrestled for control of the gun. Dipping his shoulder low, Hammond got leverage. He shoved Carson back and fired the gun. Lissa screamed as Carson pinwheeled into the stairwell. Even with the silencer, the sound was horrible, compounded by the groaning down below. "Start searching or he dies now."

"Are you okay?" she called to him.

"Fine," came his reply.

She could tell he was gritting his teeth with some pain, and though she couldn't see him from her angle, she knew he hadn't tumbled too far. Hammond couldn't watch both of them, and she took advantage of it. Noelle had spent many hours here alone as well as with Lissa. She just had to stop and think where her friend might actually have hidden something she wanted only Lissa to see.

As she searched the kitchen cabinets, under the new couch and in the bookcase behind the chair she'd refinished, she heard Carson questioning Hammond. "Detective Werner is onto you," he said. "Lissa gave him a rock-solid ID when she saw you at the hospital."

"I know it. Shut up!" Hammond roared.

Carson didn't shut up at all. He kept peppering Hammond with questions, getting the timeline, she realized. Fitting together when and how Hammond had recruited Noelle. She listened with one ear as Carson got Hammond to brag about the details of his perfect drug-skimming operation and reveal the pieces they hadn't yet figured out. Sounded like Noelle had caught Hammond red-handed last year and forced him to let her in on it, until she turned on him and trapped him.

Now Lissa and Carson had to figure out how to finish the work their friends had started.

"Can I get some water?" Carson asked, his voice tight with pain.

"You won't live long enough to enjoy it," Hammond said. "Find anything yet?" he hollered at Lissa.

She planted her hands on her hips. "What am I looking for?"

"She robbed me." Hammond took a step closer, caught himself and halted, keeping Carson in view. "You remember how I tortured her? Doctors have skills," he said with a deadly sneer. "I kept her alive for hours. I even let you, her precious friend, go, and she still didn't give me all of it."

"All of it?" Lissa queried.

He motioned with the gun. "Check the bathroom. I swear that bitch made a drop out of the ladies' room at the hospital."

What did you do, Noelle? Lissa wondered as she searched behind the toilet, inside the tank, around the vanity cabinet. Carson continued to pester Hammond with questions, but she couldn't quite hear it all.

She almost missed the little red tab back in the corner on the floor of the vanity, inside the cabinet door. At first glance it looked like a ribbon snagged in the seam of the cabinetry. It took some effort to tug it up, and when she did, she saw an envelope with Sarah's name on it in Noelle's writing. At the sound of footsteps, she shoved the envelope into her back pocket and hid the find behind cleaning products and clutter.

"Well?" Hammond demanded.

"Clean." She wiped her dusty hands on her jeans. "There's a safe in my room she might have used."

He raised the gun. "And you're just now remembering this?"

She shrugged. "You said *bathroom*, I searched the bathroom."

He slapped her hard enough to have her seeing stars. He raised his hand again and she ducked, throwing herself toward his gun hand. They wrestled for control in the tiny space, bouncing between vanity and door. The gun fired again, the bullet speeding into the shower tile. She kicked and scratched and finally heard the weapon fall. She shouted for Carson to get help as it spun like a flattened black top across the bathroom floor.

Hammond swore, his face mottled with rage as he took her down. His hands clamped hard around her neck, and he squeezed with the strength of a madman. She fought, clawing at his face and bucking her hips, throwing knees, to no avail. Her vision hazed. Her lungs burned as her body struggled for oxygen. She heard something slam, felt the floor shake under her, and then Carson was there. His arms, his voice. She wanted to reach up, but her arms were too heavy. She was sure he was merely a hopeful hallucination.

The sirens had to be her imagination, she thought, another symptom of the ringing in her ears. The pressure in her chest was too much, and her head lolled back on her neck as she gave in.

Carson had dialed 911 when Hammond shoved him down the stairs and left the phone line open as he'd questioned Hammond. Every time the bastard looked away, he'd crept a little closer. At the sound of the fight and Lissa's shout, he shot to his feet and stormed into the bathroom. No way in hell was he waiting for backup.

He crowded into the tiny space to find Hammond strangling Lissa. He plowed his boot into the man's ribs and tossed him into the bathtub. Cradling Lissa in his arms, he carried her as fast as he could move downstairs and outside.

An ambulance had pulled to a stop behind the fire truck, and policemen were circling the house. He told them where he'd left Hammond.

No way the bastard would get away this time.

"Lissa," Carson crooned. He set her gently on the cool grass of the front yard. "Come on now." She hadn't been shot, wasn't nearly as bad off as she'd been last week, but the angry red handprints on her throat would take time to fade and her breathing was shallow. "Come on, sweetheart." His fingers cruised up and down her neck, checking for serious damage. "Come on back to me."

Why was it taking so long for her to come around? "Lane, move aside. Tell us what happened."

"I've got this," he snapped at the paramedics behind him. "Give me the oxygen."

"It's our job."

He whirled on Yardley, lip curled. "She's *my* responsibility. Hand over the tank."

Carson placed the mask over her nose and mouth, willing it to push air into her lungs. Was there damage to her throat? He played it over and over in his head. If he'd been two seconds faster, she wouldn't have blacked out. "Come on, Lissa. I can't go through this again."

He swallowed back a rush of tears, past and present getting twisted in his head. He wouldn't lose her. Would *not* let it happen.

Her hand lifted to his cheek and he caught it, held it close. "That's it. Breathe a little more. How bad does it hurt?"

"Carson." She held his gaze. "You're okay."

The mask muffled her words, but he understood her. "You, too."

Her eyebrows came together in an inquiry as she looked past him. "Werner just bolted upstairs to take Hammond into custody." He helped her sit up so she could watch. "Keep breathing another minute or two. Your distraction gave me an opening."

She pushed the oxygen mask aside and threw her arms around his neck, kissing him.

Carson cradled her in his lap, until they were both steadier.

"We can take you both in, just to make sure," Yardley suggested.

"Yes, please," Lissa said as Carson refused. They looked at each other and laughed.

"He shot you," she said. She repeated the news to the paramedics.

"Not really." Carson wiggled his steel-toed work boot so she could see the damage. "Hope he was a better doctor than he was a marksman, at least some of the time."

"Me, too."

"Ready to get out of here?"

"Almost." He stood up and helped her, waiting until he was convinced she wouldn't collapse. "Noelle did hide something in the bathroom. Under the vanity base. We should give it to Werner."

Carson stood there, stunned into silence as she pulled an envelope out of her back pocket. He saw Sarah's name, read through the papers along with her over her shoulder. "Noelle and Sarah were working together to stop Hammond."

The locations of Noelle's stashes were listed, as well as dates and times of Hammond's operation. On the last page they read a personal note for Lissa. Carson held her as she read her friend's final message. The note was an apology for any trouble or grief and assured Lissa she'd never once gone to the dark side of the prescription-drug scam.

"There's more," Lissa exclaimed. "She hid the money she'd been siphoning out of the operation in the access stairs to the roof."

"We'll take Werner back to that once Hammond is out of here."

"Right. No wonder Hammond was so furious," Lissa murmured. "We were both lucky enough to count two of the best people in the world as our friends."

He walked her closer to the detective's car, his knees quaking over the close call.

"If I'd lost you…" he began.

"Same goes." She turned in to his arms for another hard hug.

Relief and gratitude coursed through him in waves as they addressed concerned friends and neighbors and the various legalities. He wanted to whisk her away and hoist her onto his shoulders to celebrate her bravery.

"You were amazing," he whispered at her ear. "My hero."

"You got the open line to bring in the cavalry," she countered. "You're the hero."

"You knew?"

She grinned. "I figured you were at least recording him. Thank goodness. I wasn't sure how to keep stalling. Do we still need to worry about his crew?"

"Without him pushing to find the stolen money and drugs, they're likely to scatter like rats."

"Thank you for everything, Carson."

"Is that a precursor to 'see ya later, pal'?"

"No." She looked up at him, and he wanted five more minutes with Hammond for those marks on her neck. "Unless you want it to be."

"Friends," he reminded her. "Your words."

"I think I said we were more."

"I'd like more, with you." He added a kiss to the words whispered in her hair and tried to hold back all the things he longed to say to her. Instead he drew her close in another gentle hug. They were both alive and well. The words he yearned to say were probably best left until they were alone.

Lissa sighed into him as emergency teams wrapped things up and moved off. "Daniel never got the full tour of the house," she said, rubbing his back.

"That's okay," Carson replied. "I saw him chatting with the landlady. He's probably working up a bid to deal with the next round of repairs."

"Oh, that would be good for everyone." She gave him a small smile. "I liked those new floors."

"What was left looked good," he agreed. "Maybe I should offer to reinstall them," he offered quietly.

She slipped an arm around his waist. "I'm not sure I can live here again, even when it's done. Too many emotional ghosts."

With that opening, he decided to dive in headfirst. He drew her around to face him, linking his hands at the small of her back. "Then you'll just have to move in with me."

"Carson."

He wasn't sure what label to put on the emotion swirling in her eyes. "What? It would be nice to have someone to trade off breakfast duties."

His joke made her smile but left him feeling flat. They both deserved for him to do this right. "You made me promise to ask you a nosy, personal question when your memory returned."

"I remember," she said, rolling her eyes.

"You ready?" She nodded. "Did you mean it when you told your parents you loved me?"

She held his gaze, and he knew *he* stopped breathing while he waited for her reply. "Yes."

"Then I have another, even more personal question for you."

She arched her eyebrows.

He reached into the pocket of his jeans and pulled out a small velvet pouch. He opened the tie, and a square-cut diamond in a white gold setting fell into his palm. "My grandmother's ring," he explained. He'd pulled it out of the safe in his bedroom while she was in the shower yesterday, determined to have this conversation and to be prepared if it went his way. "For history and promises that last a lifetime. For a lifetime that leaves a legacy."

His heart pounded as he saw the love, the joy shining in her gorgeous eyes. "Marry me, Lissa. We'll sink all the roots you want, as deep as they can go, right here."

"Oh, Carson." Her fingers trembled, but he steadied her, sliding the ring into place on her finger. "How can you be so sure, so soon?"

"I love you." He kissed her, a gentle touch of lips full of promises. "The time isn't relevant. You are. You reminded me what trust and hope are all about. I'm sure of loving you, and I'm sure my life will be amazing with you in it."

"I love you so much." She pushed her hands into his hair and brought his face down for another kiss. "So much."

He laughed along with her, his heart overflowing with happiness he'd been afraid to hope for. He'd rescued her, but she'd saved him body and soul.

As the wind moved through the trees, he thought he heard Sarah's wild laughter.

* * * * *

Don't miss the first book in the
ESCAPE CLUB HEROES *series*

SAFE IN HIS SIGHT

*And watch for firefighter Daniel Jennings's story,
available from Harlequin Romantic Suspense
in November 2017!*

ROMANTIC suspense

Available June 6, 2017

#1947 KILLER COWBOY
Cowboys of Holiday Ranch • by Carla Cassidy

When a serial killer sets his sights on ranch owner Cassie Peterson, it's up to Chief of Police Dillon Bowie to keep her safe...and keep his own heart from getting broken!

#1948 COLD CASE COLTON
The Coltons of Shadow Creek • by Addison Fox

Claudia Colton never thought returning to Shadow Creek would unlock the secrets of her past, but when PI Hawk Huntley shows up on her doorstep, he brings more than answers. Danger—and love—is hot on his heels!

#1949 ESCORTED BY THE RANGER
by C.J. Miller

Supermodel Marissa Walker's best frenemy is found murdered backstage, and everyone is convinced Marissa did it. When the attacker targets her as well, Jack Larson, a former army ranger, is called in to protect her. But as the attraction sizzles between them, the killer is trying to get closer than they ever imagined...

#1950 SILENT RESCUE
by Melinda Di Lorenzo

Detective Brooks Small is on forced vacation in Quebec. He's cold, miserable and wants to go home. Until he spots a frightened woman held at gunpoint. Soon, he's convincing the woman—Maryse LePrieur—to let him help her save her kidnapped daughter. It doesn't take long for the attraction he feels to ignite, and the rescue mission quickly becomes personal.

———————

SPECIAL EXCERPT FROM

◆ HARLEQUIN®
™

ROMANTIC suspense

*When PI Hawk Huntley shows up on Claudia Colton's
doorstep, he brings more than answers to her past.
Danger—and love—follow them to Shadow Creek!*

Read on for a sneak preview of
COLD CASE COLTON *by Addison Fox,*
the next thrilling installment of
THE COLTONS OF SHADOW CREEK.

Tears she hadn't even realized were so close to the surface
spilled over with little prompting.

"Hey. Hey there." Hawk was gentle as he reached out,
his hands resting on her shoulders. "What's wrong?"

"It's just that—" Her breath caught and she hiccuped
around another thick layer of tears. "It's Cody. Something
could have happened to him. I mean, I understood it. But
until I saw him before and realized—"

The large, gentle hands that gripped her shoulders
tugged, pulling her close so that she was flush against his
chest. Before she could check the impulse, she wrapped
her arms around his waist as he pulled her close.

"It's going to be okay." The words were whispered
against her head, a promise she tried desperately to cling
to through her tears.

"But what if it isn't? She's—" Another tearful hiccup
gripped her. "My mother's still out there. My family is
still at risk."

Her fears raced faster than she could keep up with them.
The questions that whispered late at night through her
mind, wondering where her mother was since escaping

from prison. The continued fears that Ben wasn't done with her, determined to wend his way to Shadow Creek to come after her. And now the possible news about her own birth.

When had it all gone so wrong?

And would any of them ever be free from the diabolical influences of Livia Colton?

The tears that had pushed her into Hawk's arms faded as the rush of adrenaline and emotion worked its way through her system. In its place was the haunting realization of just how good it felt to stand in the circle of Hawk's arms and lean on him. She was a tall woman, and she'd always had a figure her mother had kindly—and not so kindly, pending her mood—dubbed big-boned.

How humbling, then, to realize he still had several inches on her and his big, strong arms were more than long enough to wrap around her soundly.

She felt protected.

Safe.

And for the moment, she was fighting an increasing attraction to a man she had no business wanting. Aside from the fact they didn't know each other, Hawk had plenty of baggage of his own and a life he likely wanted to get back to. His visit to Shadow Creek had a purpose.

A goal.

And once he reached that goal, he'd leave Shadow Creek and all its depravity and deceit in his dust.

Don't miss
COLD CASE COLTON
by Addison Fox, available June 2017 wherever
Harlequin® Romantic Suspense books
and ebooks are sold.

www.Harlequin.com

Get 2 Free Books,
Plus 2 Free Gifts—
just for trying the Reader Service!